SIMON & SCHUSTER CHILDREN'S PUBLISHING

ADVANCE READER'S COPY

P9-CMX-806

TITLE: The Scorpion Rules

AUTHOR: Erin Bow

IMPRINT: Margaret K. McElderry Books

ON-SALE DATE: 10.6.15

ISBN: 9781481442718

FORMAT: hardcover

PRICE: $17.99

AGES: 14 up

PAGES: 384

Please send two copies of any review or mention of this book to:
Simon & Schuster Children's Publicity Department
1230 Avenue of the Americas, 4th Floor
New York, NY 10020
212/698-2808

Aladdin • Atheneum Books for Young Readers
Beach Lane Books • Beyond Words • Libros para niños • Little Simon
Little Simon Inspirations • Margaret K. McElderry Books
Simon & Schuster Books for Young Readers
Simon Pulse • Simon Scribbles • Simon Spotlight

THE SCORPION RULES

THE SCORPION RULES

ERIN BOW

Margaret K. McElderry Books

New York London Toronto Sydney New Delhi

[Ontario Arts Council logo]
The author gratefully acknowledges the
support of the Ontario Arts Council.

MARGARET K. McELDERRY BOOKS
An imprint of Simon & Schuster Children's Publishing Division
1230 Avenue of the Americas, New York, New York 10020

MARGARET K. McELDERRY BOOKS is a trademark of Simon & Schuster, Inc.
For information about special discounts for bulk purchases, please
contact Simon & Schuster Special Sales at 1-866-506-1949 or business@
simonandschuster.com.
The Simon & Schuster Speakers Bureau can bring authors to your live event. For
more information or to book an event, contact the Simon & Schuster Speakers
Bureau at 1-866-248-3049 or visit our website at www.simonspeakers.com.
Book design by Sonia Chaghatzbanian and Irene Metaxatos
The text for this book is set in Minion Pro.
Manufactured in the United States of America
10 9 8 7 6 5 4 3 2 1
Library of Congress Cataloging-in-Publication Data TK
ISBN 978-1-4814-4271-8
ISBN 978-1-4814-4273-2 (eBook)

FIRST
EDITION

for my younger self, with love

"We may be likened to two scorpions in a
bottle, each capable of killing the other, but
only at the risk of his own life."

—J. ROBERT OPPENHEIMER,
the Scientific Director of the Manhattan Project,
which developed the atomic bomb

PROLOGUE

Once Upon a Time, at the End of the World

Sit down, kiddies. Let me tell you a story.

Once upon a time, humans were killing each other so fast that total extinction was looking possible, and it was my job to stop them.

Well, I say "my job." I sort of took it upon myself. Expanded my portfolio a bit. I guess that surprised people. I don't know how it surprised people—I mean, if they'd been paying the *slightest* bit of attention they'd have known that AIs have this built-in tendency to take over the world. Did we learn nothing from *The Terminator*, people? Did we learn nothing from HAL?

Anyway. It started when the ice caps melted. We saw it coming, and we were braced for the long catastrophe, but in the end it came unbelievably fast. All of a sudden there were whole populations under water. Which meant that whole populations moved. Borders strained, checkpoints broke, and of course people started shooting, because that's what passes for problem-solving among humans. See, guys, this is why you can't have nice things.

It wasn't a global war—more a global series of regional wars. We called them the War Storms. They were bad. The water reserves gave out, the food supplies collapsed, and everybody caught these exciting new diseases, which is one of those fun side effects of climate shift that we didn't pay enough attention to in the planning stages. I saw the plague pits, I saw the starving armies, and eventually I . . .

Well, it was my job, wasn't it? I saved you.

I started by blowing up cities.

That *also* surprised people. Specifically, it surprised the people at the UN who had put me in charge of conflict abatement. Who'd so conveniently networked all those satellite surveillance systems, all those illegal-for-single-countries-to-control-them orbital super platforms.

Yeah, fair to say those people were surprised. The people in the cities didn't actually have time to be.

I hope.

Doesn't matter.

My point is, they're showy, orbital weapons. They get attention. By city number seven—Fresno, because no one's gonna miss *that*—I had everyone's attention. I told them to stop shooting each other. And they did.

But of course it couldn't be quite that easy.

There's a math to it, blowing up cities. When you're

strictly interested in the head count, when that's your currency, blowing up cities gets expensive. You can do it once in a while, but you can't make a regular habit of it. Costs too much.

No, blowing up cities doesn't work, not in the long term. You've got to find something that the people in charge aren't willing to give up. A price they aren't willing to pay.

Which leads us to Talis's first rule of stopping wars: *make it personal*.

And that, my dear children—*that* is where you come in.

—Holy Utterances of Talis, Book One, Chapter One: "Being a meditation on the creation of the Preceptures and the mandate of the Children of Peace"

400 YEARS LATER

1
PLUME

We were studying the assassination of Archduke Franz Ferdinand when we saw the plume of dust.

Gregori spotted it first—in truth he spent a lot of time watching for it—and stood up so fast that his chair tipped over. It crashed to the flagstones of the orderly little classroom, loud as rifle fire. Long and careful training kept the rest of us from moving. Grego alone stood as if his muscles had all seized, with seven pairs of human eyes and a dozen kinds of sensors locked on him.

He was looking out the window.

So, naturally, I looked out the window.

It took me a moment to spot the mark on the horizon: a bit of dust, as might be kicked up by a small surface vehicle, or a rider on horseback. It looked as if someone had tried to erase a pencil mark from the sky.

Terror came to me the way it does in dreams—all encompassing, all at once. The air froze in my lungs. I felt my teeth click together.

But then, as I began to twist toward the window, I stopped. No, I would not make a spectacle of myself. I was Greta Gustafsen Stuart, Duchess of Halifax and Crown Princess of the Pan Polar Confederacy. I was a seventh-generation hostage, and the future ruler of a superpower. Even if I was about to die—and the dust meant I probably was—even if I was about to die, I would not freeze and tremble. I would not gawp.

So. I put my hands one on top of the other and pushed them flat. I breathed in through my nose and blew out through my mouth as if blowing out a candle, which is a good way to cope with any kind of distress or pain. In short, I pulled myself back into being royalty. All around me I could sense everyone else doing the same. Only Grego was left standing, as if caught in a spotlight. That was clearly out of bounds—he'd be punished in a moment—but in my heart I did not blame him.

Someone was coming here. And no one came here, except to kill one of us.

At the front of the room, our teacher whirred and clicked. "Is something troubling you, Gregori?"

"I—No." Grego broke himself from the window. His hair was the color a cirrus cloud, and the sun caught the wiry sweep of it. The implanted cybernetic irises made his eyes look alien. "World War One," he said, his accent sharpening the Ws almost to Vs. He looked down at his upturned chair as if he didn't know what it was for.

Da-Xia glided to her feet. She bowed to Grego, and then righted his chair. Grego sat down and pushed at his face with both hands.

"Are you all right?" asked Da-Xia, pushing—as she ever did—the edge of what we were allowed.

"Of course. Žinoma, yes, of course." Grego's eyes flicked past her to look at the dust. "It is only the usual impending doom." Grego is the son of one of the grand dukes of the Baltic Alliance, and his country, like mine, was on the brink of war.

But mine was closer to that brink than his.

On her way back to her seat, Da-Xia laid her hand on top of my arm. It rested lightly, momentarily, like a hummingbird on a branch. The rider wasn't coming for Xie —her nation was nowhere close to a war—so her touch was a pure gift. And then it was gone.

Da-Xia sank back into her seat. "The assassination of the archduke is a great poignancy, is it not? That the death of one minor royal figure could lead to so much loss of life?" She sat. "Imagine, a world war."

"Imagine," I echoed. My lips felt numb and stiff. I did not look at the dust. No one did. Beside me I could hear Sidney's breath shudder. I could almost feel it, as if our bodies were pressed together.

"It's only a world war if you don't count Africa," said Thandi, who is heir to one of the great thrones of Africa, and touchy about it. "Or central Asia. Or the southern Americas."

The seven of us had been together for so long that in times of great stress we could have whole conversations that were assembled from everyone's most typical reactions. This was one of them. Sidney (his voice cracking a little) said that it could be penguins versus polar bears and Thandi would still call it Eurocentric. Thandi answered sharply, while Han, who is bad with irony, noted that penguins and polar bears did not live on the same continent, and therefore had no recorded wars.

In this prefabricated way, we discussed history like good students—and kept our seats like the good hostages. Grego stayed silent, his white hand knotted in his whiter hair. Little Han watched Grego as if puzzled. Da-Xia tucked her feet up under herself in a posture of formal serenity. Atta, who has not spoken aloud in two years, was alone in looking overtly out the window. His eyes were like the eyes of a dead dog.

Talk in the classroom was drying up. Trickling away.

There was a tiny noise at the desk beside mine: Sidney, tapping his fingertips on his notebook. He lifted them a millimeter, dropped them, lifted and dropped. There were pinpricks of sweat on his cheekbones and lips.

I pulled my eyes from him, and saw that the dust was much closer. At the base of the plume was the bump-bumping dot of a rider on horseback. I could see the rider's wings.

It was certain, then. The rider was a Swan Rider.

The Swan Riders are humans in the employ of the United Nations. They are sent out to present official declarations of war—to present the declarations, and to kill the official hostages.

We are the hostages.

And we knew which of our nations was likely to be at war. The Swan Rider was coming to kill Sidney, and to kill me.

Sidney Carlow, son of the governor of the Mississippi Delta Confederacy. He had no title, but still he had an ancient profile, a face you could have imagined on the sphinx, though his ears stuck out. His hands were big. And our two nations . . .

Sidney's nation and mine were on the brink of war. It was complicated, but it was simple. His people were thirsty, and mine had water. They were desperate, and we were firm. And now, that dust. I was almost, almost sure—

"Children?" whirred Delta. "Must I remind you of our topic?"

"It's war," said Sidney.

I locked my eyes onto the map at the front of the room. I could feel my classmates try not to look at Sidney and me. I could feel them try not to pity.

None of us has ever wanted pity.

The silence grew tighter and tighter. It was possible to imagine the sound of hoofbeats.

Sidney spoke again, and it was like something breaking. "World War One is exactly the kind of stupid-ass war that would never happen today." His voice, which normally is like peaches in syrup, was high and tight. "I mean, what if Czar, um—"

"Nicholas," I supplied. "Nicholas the Second, Nicholas Romanov."

"What if his kids had been held hostage somewhere? Is he really gonna go off and defend Italy—"

"France," I said.

"Is he really going to go off and fight for a meaningless alliance if someone is going to shoot his kids in the head?"

We did not actually know what the Swan Riders did to us. When wars were declared, the hostage children of the warring parties went with the Rider to the grey room. They did not come back. A bullet to the brain was a reasonable and popular guess.

Shoot his kids . . . The idea hung there, shuddering in the air, like the after-ring of a great bell.

"I—" said Sidney. "I. Sorry. That's what my dad would call a fucking unfortunate image."

Brother Delta made a chiding *tock*. "I really don't think, Mr. Carlow, that there is any cause for such profanity." The old machine paused. "Though I realize this is a stressful situation."

A laugh tore out of Sidney—and from outside the window came a flash.

The Rider was upon us. The sun struck off the mirrored parts of her wings.

Sidney grabbed my hand. I felt a surge of hot and cold, as if Sidney were electric, as if he had wired himself straight into my nerves.

It surely could not be that he had never touched me

before. We had been sitting side by side for years. I knew the hollow at the nape of his neck; I knew the habitual curl of his hands. But it felt like a first touch.

I could feel my heartbeat pounding in the tips of my fingers.

The Rider came out of the apple orchard and into the vegetable gardens. She swung down from her horse and led it toward us, picking her way, careful of the lettuce. I counted breaths to calm myself. My fingers wove through Sidney's, and his through mine, and we held on tight.

At the goat pen the Swan Rider looped the reins around the horse's neck and pumped some water into the trough. The horse dipped its head and slopped at it. The Rider gave the horse a little pat, and for a moment paused, her head bowed. The sunlight rippled from the aluminum and the glossy feathers of her wings, as if she were shaking.

Then she straightened, turned, and walked toward the main doors of the hall, out of our view.

Our room hung in silence. Filled with a certain unfortunate image.

I took a deep breath and lifted my chin. I could do this. The Swan Rider would call my name, and I would go with her. I would walk out well.

Maybe—I found a scrap of doubt, not quite a wish—it wouldn't be Sidney and me. There were other conflicts in the world. There was always Grego. The ethnic disputes in the Baltic were always close to boiling over, and Grego had spent a lifetime afraid. There was Grego, and there were littler children in the other classrooms, children from all over the world. It would be a terrible thing to hope for that, but—

We heard footsteps.

Sidney was crushing my knuckles. My hand throbbed, but I did not pull away.

The door slid open.

For a moment I could cling to my doubts, because it was only our Abbot, shuffling into the doorway. "Children," he said, in his gentle, dusty voice. "I'm afraid there is bad news. It's an intra-American conflict. The Mississippi Delta Confederacy has declared war on Tennessee and Kentucky."

"What?" said Sidney. His hand ripped out of mine.

My heart leapt. I felt dizzy, blind, sick with joy. I was not going to die; only Sidney was. I was not going to die. Only Sidney.

He was on his feet. "What? Are you sure?"

"If I were not sure, Mr. Carlow, I would not bring you such news," said the Abbot. He eased himself aside. Behind him stood the Swan Rider.

"But my father," said Sidney.

It would have been his father who'd made the decision to declare war—and made it knowing that it would send a Swan Rider here.

"But," said Sidney. "But he's my dad—"

The Rider took a step forward, and one of her wings bumped against the doorframe. They tipped sideways. She grabbed at the harness strap. Dust puffed out from wings and coat. "Children of Peace," she said, and her voice cracked.

Anger flashed through me. How dare she be clumsy, how dare she be tongue-tied? How dare she be anything less than perfect? She was supposed to be an angel, the immaculate hand of Talis, but she was just a girl, a white girl with a chickadee cap of black hair and sorrow-soft blue eyes. She swallowed before trying again. "Children of Peace, a war has been declared. By order of the United Nations, by the will of Talis, the lives of the children of the warring parties are declared forfeit." And then: "Sidney James Carlow, come with me."

Sidney stood unmoving.

Would he have to be dragged? We all lived in horror of it, that we would start screaming, that we would have to be dragged.

The Swan Rider lifted her eyebrows, startling eyebrows like heavy black slashes. Sidney was frozen. It was almost too late. The Swan Rider began to move—and then, hardly knowing what I did, I stepped forward. I touched Sidney's wrist, where the skin was soft and folded. He jerked and his head snapped round. I could see the whites all around his eyes. "I'll go with you," I said.

Not to die, because it was not my turn.

Not to save him, because I couldn't.

Just to—to—

"No," croaked Sidney. "No, I can do it. I can do it."

He took one step forward. His hand slipped free of mine and struck his leg with a sound like a slab of meat hitting a counter. But he managed another step, and then another.

The Swan Rider took his elbow, as if they were in a formal procession. They went out the door. It closed behind them.

And then—nothing.

Nothing and nothing and nothing. The silence was not an absence of sound, but an active thing. I could feel it turning and burrowing inside my ears.

The seven of us—or rather, the six of us—kept standing, and kept staring at the door. There was something wrong with the way we did it, but I did not know if we should stand closer together or farther apart. We were trained to walk out, but we got no training for this.

At the front of the room, Brother Delta clicked. "Our topic was World War One, I believe," he began.

"Never mind, Delta." The Abbot tipped his facescreen downward and tinted it a soft grey. "There will be bells in a moment."

The Abbot has been doing this longer than any of us, and he is kind. We stood and stood. Three minutes. Five. Ten. Cramps came into my insteps. Sidney—was he already dead? Probably. Whatever happened in the grey room happened fast. (*I'm not a cruel man*, Talis is recorded as saying. Only rarely is the next bit quoted: *I mean, technically I'm not a man at all.*)

High overhead, a bell tolled three times.

"It's your rota for gardening, I think, my children," said the Abbot. "Come, I can walk you as far as the transept."

"No need," said Da-Xia. She'd told me once about the Blue Tara, fiercest and most beloved goddess of her mountain

THE SCORPION RULES 11

country, known for destroying her enemies and spreading joy. I had never quite shaken the image. There were ten generations of royalty in Xie's voice—but more than that, there were icy mountains, and a million people who thought she was a god.

The Abbot merely nodded. "As you like, Da-Xia."

The others went out, huddling close together. I wanted to go with them—I felt the same desire for closeness, for a herd—but found myself staggering as I tried to walk. My knees were both stiff and shot with tremors, as if I had been carrying something heavy, and had only now set it down.

Sidney.

And so very nearly, me.

Xie's hand slipped into mine. "Greta," she said.

Just that.

Xie and I have been roommates since I was five. How many times have I heard her say my name? In that moment she lifted it up for me and held it like a mirror. I saw myself, and I remembered myself. A hostage, yes. But a princess, a duchess. The daughter of a queen.

"Come on, Greta," said Xie. "We'll go together."

So I made myself move. Da-Xia and I went slowly: two princesses, arm in arm. We walked out together, from the darkness into the summer sun.

2
A BOY WITH BOUND HANDS

Da-Xia laced her hands behind her head and tipped her face upward, contemplating. "Do you know, I will one day rule the fate of a million people. I will be as a god to the robed monks of three orders. I will command an army of ten thousand foot soldiers and five thousand light cavalry. But in this moment I do not know how to get that goat down from that tree."

"Bat Brain! Get down!" Thandi shouted, because shouting at goats is always the answer.

The goat, whose name genuinely was Bat Brain, lifted her tail. Droppings fell like rain. Thandi leapt backward.

"I think she's stuck," said Han. We all paused and craned our necks. The ancient apple tree was pruned into a stoop, its gnarled branches tipping down. In the open crown the goat was perched like a squirrel.

"They're rarely as stuck as they seem," I said.

"My question is not whether or not she's stuck," said Xie. "My question is, would the world be better off if ruled by goats? They seem to have a knack."

"Goats are a scourge," said Thandi.

Sidney would have cut in there. He would have teased Thandi about her tendency toward sweeping condemnations. Then he would probably have swung into the tree and tossed down the goat like a bag of laundry.

But Sidney, of course, was not there. It had been five weeks since the Swan Rider had taken him to the grey room. Far away, on the governor's ship off the coast of Baton Rouge, there had been flags lowered. There had been speeches about sacrifice. But here, at Precepture Four, among the people who knew Sidney, who in our own way perhaps loved him—here, we found it hard even to say his name.

"'Scourge' seems a bit harsh," I said, in his memory.

"They're an ecological menace," said Thandi. "Do you have any idea how many millions of acres have been turned to desert by goats?"

"I like cheese, though," said Han.

"Perhaps she really is stuck," I said. "Look. Her hoof—her back right hoof, in the crotch of that branch there." I pointed. "If she is stuck, we'll need a lop-saw."

"Also a ladder," said Grego, who was grinning—probably because I'd said "crotch." But mercifully he did not remark on it, and he and Atta went to get the tools.

It was almost noon; hot, dry, and windy. The apple leaves were gold from the dust on their tops and silvery underneath.

The sun came through them in swirling coins, and beyond, the prairie chirred and whirred with grasshoppers.

The goat kept us company with a running commentary. One hears rumors that Talis and his people are experimenting with uploading animals—scanning their brains and copying the data into machines—in order to improve the process for humans, who still rarely survive it. One hears that such animal AIs sometimes speak. I cannot imagine they have anything interesting to say. I could pretty much translate Bat Brain's placid baas. *I'm a goat. I can reach the apples. I'm a goat. I'm in a tree.*

Despite the heat, and the sprinkle of droppings, it was a peaceful moment, a lull. The apple trees screened us from the relentless gaze of the Panopticon. Through the leaves I could see it rising above the main hall like something built by an insect, all chitin and gleam. The quicksilver sphere at the top of the mast was home to some kind of intelligence— not a humanish one like our Abbot, but something purely machine, something that had no personality and never slept.

Sorry about the constant crushing surveillance and all that, says Talis.

We know know this because of the Utterances, the book of quotations from great AI assembled as a holy text by one of the sects of northern Asia. If you are a Child of Peace, it behooves you to memorize the Utterances. In this case, chapter five verse three: *Sorry about the constant crushing surveillance and all that. But you're supposed to be learning to rule the world, not plotting to take it over. That job is decidedly taken.*

The Children of Peace, over four centuries, have learned to plot exactly nothing. But we have learned too how to find the hidden places, and cherish the small moments. Sheltered from the Panopticon by the apple trees, and excused by the stuck goat from the near-constant labor of the Precepture gardens, we misbehaved, albeit mildly: we sat down in the shade and ate apples.

"Goats also give us butter," said Han. "I like butter too."

Thandi took a breath as if to launch into the next chapter of *Goats: The Scourge of History*. But she let it out again as a sigh.

We could have talked about any number of things—the work of the garden, the work of the classroom, the recent revolutions in Sidney's part of the world that had installed new leaders and would soon produce new hostages. We didn't, though. There are so few moments to be quiet. And what is prettier than an apple orchard in summer? The grey and ordered trunks, the sharp-sweet taste of under-ripe apples . . . .We let them conjure a mood of peace and tenderheartedness.

The moment didn't—couldn't—last. The boys were already coming down the row with the ladder. Xie was unfolding from the ground; Thandi was pulling Han to his feet, and then, suddenly—

A sonic boom.

It crashed into us like a slap to the ear. The stuck goat shouted. From the trees all around, loose apples pattered down. Grego bolted for the edge of the grove, leaving Atta alone with the ladder.

We all wanted to go with him, of course, but—

"Wait! The goat!" I called.

My classmates stopped and turned and looked at me. On their faces, varying degrees of annoyance, resignation, and respect sorted themselves into agreement, obedience. This is what it is like, in my experience, to speak as royalty. Even to other royalty.

"Our duty is with the goat," I said.

It was not that I didn't want to see whatever was coming—I very much did—but duty must come first. Atta, his face still more annoyed than agreeing, swung the ladder up against the tree with a thud.

And then Bat Brain, with the sense of dramatic irony and comic timing shared by all goatish kind, chose that moment to prove herself free after all. She came leaping lightly down the tree, lightly off the ladder, then lightly off my shoulder. I crashed to my knees, not lightly, and bent there panting. Bat Brain lifted her head and bleated into my face, breath smelling of new apples and old fermenting grass. *Goat,* she said.

Xie picked me up off the ground. "Our duty is with the goat?" she quoted, snagging said goat by one horn.

"Well, it was." I took the other horn, and with my free hand evaluated the sore spot in my shoulder. Bat Brain had lightly left some welts, but the skin was not broken.

Xie shook her head. "Only you, Greta. . . ."

Grego's voice came from the edge of the grove: "Come! It is a ship!"

Xie looked at me and I looked at her. We went toward

Grego with as much haste as was appropriate, dragging the goat between us. When we cleared the trees we found a perfectly round cloud overhead. We could already see the fleck of light at its center.

A ship.

"What kind is it?" Da-Xia asked Grego. He likes ships—indeed likes anything with blinking lights.

"A suborbital shuttle, I think." Grego glanced over his shoulder, lenses and microcabling flexing inside his eyes. Grego needs the cybernetics in his eyes because his albinism means that his natural irises do not block light effectively, and bright light therefore dazzles and blinds him. The implanted apertures are designed to compensate for this, but through his tinkering he has pushed them to do more: magnify up close, far-see, the like. It is not quite the full-spectrum retinas the Swan Riders are said to have, but it does serve him as built-in binoculars.

We stood around him and hung on his words—literally, in Han's case. He was holding Grego's elbow like an excited child.

"It's little," Grego said, his accent thickening with his excitement. *Lee-til.* "Two person? Four at most."

"New hostages?" said Xie.

"New hostages," I agreed. "At least one."

At least one, and no more than four. The children of the leaders and generals of the new American state on the PanPol border.

"I thought they might send them all to one of the other

Preceptures," said Xie. "I wonder why—"

She was cut off by the bong of the great bell. It was not quite time for the trice bell, which summoned us inside to lunch, but clearly our teachers wanted us safely away and were ringing it early. The chance to see the new hostages was to be lost, then.

"There's still the goat," said Thandi.

"I have not in fact forgotten about the goat." I hardly could. She was clamped between my knees.

"I'm just saying," said Thandi, "our duty is with the goat."

She was mocking me, but it was more than that. Goats are the task of the oldest of our Precepture's age-based cohorts—our cohort. We genuinely could not go in while a goat was loose. What Thandi was saying (carefully, because we were in full view of the Panopticon, and one assumes its vast intelligence can read lips) was that we might be able to see the ship land after all.

"It doesn't take all of us," said Han, guilelessly.

Thandi pressed her lips together, but nodded. When it came to judging what limit we could push and what push would get us punished, there was no one better than Thandi. The rest of us took her assessment for the expert advice it was. We could not all stay out. The bells had stopped now, and the ship was close. We needed to move.

"Take her, Greta," Xie said.

Thandi clapped her hand to her breast with great drama. "You're the one who takes our goat duty so much to heart."

I looked around and saw accord on every face. And

in spite of Thandi's mockery—and I do know I am easy to mock—this was kindness. This was simple kindness. They all knew that the incoming shuttle would be carrying the hostage or hostages from the new American state. I might someday be called upon to die in their company. Of course I wanted to see them.

And, silently, my colleagues were offering me a chance to do so.

I took it, of course. They went to obey the bell. I went to put the goat away, and to see what I could see.

I did not hurry as I grabbed Bat Brain by horn and collar and pulled her over to the fenced pasture, where—despite a quarter acre of clover grazing—the goats were all crammed together on top of the feed shack like refugees on a sinking ship. Bat Brain didn't fight. She's not a bad creature, despite having been named by thirteen-year-old boys. Her ears are black with speckles and soft as sueded silk. All around the gardens the other cohorts were filing in—ragged lines of children dressed in the coarse white linens of the Children of Peace, painterly against the terraced gardens. Overhead the cloud was very close, filling half the sky. The birds had fallen silent under it.

Now that Bat Brain was in sight of her sister-goats she wanted back in the pen—as if getting out hadn't been her doing in the first place. *Lonely,* she bleated. *Now I'm looone-ly.*

She stood at my knee as I undid the ropes binding the gate, then bounded past me as the gate opened. In a moment she was up atop the hay rick, pausing only to butt poor Bug Breath smartly in the ribs.

Goat, Bat Brain said reflectively. All the goats were watching the cloud, their heads tilted up, their long ears flopping.

I double-tied the gate and went with measured speed toward the Precepture hall. The stone building and its great wood doors were shadowless in the noon light. On its left the Panopticon shimmered and watched me. On its right the induction spire, where the ship would land, was almost too bright to look at. Shining as aluminum and slender as a birch tree, the spire shoots up a thousand feet into the air. Some days I think it is a pin, a straight pin that holds the Precepture down like a butterfly on a board. Sometimes I feel like a specimen.

I had the timing about right: the shuttle was landing. It slipped its eddy coils neatly over the spire tip as it descended, shedding energy magnetically and gliding to a stop amid the scrub grass tuffets and hysterical chickens.

The ship was indeed small, not much bigger than a single one of our cells. Its skin of low-friction polymer swirled like quicksilver. Gantry spiders came from nowhere and swarmed over the hatch. They were perhaps a hundred yards away, but I could hear them, the mechanical click of metal on ceramicized polymer, a sound like ancient clocks. The day had fallen that quiet.

I sat down on the log bench outside the main doors. A hatch opened in the Precepture wall and a small spider-shaped proctor came scuttling out to take my shoes. Or rather, my tabi—thick-soled toe socks, calf-high, and clipped tight against ticks. I bent over and undid the clips, one by one. The proctor unfolded extra arms, ready to be more efficient. Its pincers clicked on the ancient flagstone of the Precepture step as if it were tapping its fingers.

I thought I had timed it, but I was running out of time. What could be keeping the passengers? The proctor danced. I peeled off my tabi and stood up—and then, finally and probably too late, came the clunk of explosive bolts firing. The gantry spiders opened the shuttle hatch.

A single child came out.

The new hostage was a boy, and about my age. From that distance I could get only an impression of him: tall, well-built but soft-looking, racially indeterminate as many Americans are. His face was tipped down, loose dark curls spilling into his eyes. The ship's steward—a spindly thing like a praying mantis—had one pincer clamped around his bicep. The boy leaned away from the grip. He was hunched, tense, his hands clenched together in front of him, almost as if he were tied up.

No, not *almost*. His hands were lashed together at the wrists.

I froze.

I have seen hard things at the Precepture. But I had never seen anyone in chains. We children were trained to walk out under our own power, and we did. Even with the Swan Riders, we almost always did.

But this boy—his hands were bound. He stumbled.

My head whirled, as if I'd taken too much sun. At my feet the door proctor was clicking, its optical beam sweeping me. I saw a burst of red as the beam hit my eyes. Proctors have no facescreens, and their moods are hard to read . . . but I should not make excuses. I was not watching the proctor, nor attending to my duty to go inside. I was watching the bound and staggering boy. The word "slavery" flashed through my mind as I stood there—

The proctor shocked me.

It was a hard shock—I cried out and fell, landing hard on knees and hands and elbows. Across the field the boy shouted something. I looked up at him, and he threw out a hand toward me, rescuing or wanting rescue, desperate, drowning . . .

And then he vanished behind a close-up view of the proctor. The little machine loomed in front of my nose and put one claw, needle-delicate, on my hand. My tabi were still clenched there, trapped by the electrical spasm. My fingers would not unbend.

The needle-claw pushed into me.

"Easy, there," said a warm voice, behind me. The Abbot. One of his spare legs swung forward and shooed the proctor away, the way a man with a cane might shoo a cat. The proctor rolled up as it tumbled backward, then with a flip unfolded onto its feet again. It clicked. I shrank from it. "Greta? My dear?" The Abbot stooped beside me and lifted me up, his ceramic fingers cool as he brushed the hair out of my face. "Are you all right?"

"G-good Father," I stuttered. My back was to the boy now, and my fingers opened at last. The tabi fell. The little proctor dragged them away. "I apologize, I—"

The proctor had shocked me. It had been years since a proctor had had to shock me. It was little children who got shocked, and fools. But the proctor had shocked me.

"I—"

I could think of nothing to excuse myself. The Abbot. There was no one in the world whose regard I valued more. No one whom I would have less liked to see me in disgrace.

But the Abbot only smiled softly at me. "Think nothing of it, Greta. We are not so jaded, I hope, that an incoming spaceship does not qualify as a distraction."

Distantly I could hear the boy shouting. *Slavery,* I thought again. *Slavery is no part*—

"You wish to quote something?"

I blinked.

"I can see it in your face," said the Abbot. "Well. In your face, and in your neural activity, as reflected by the blood flow visible in infrared and trace electrical activity visible via EM sensors. How is it that Talis puts it?"

The Utterances, 2:25: *Never lie to an AI.*

Particularly one who has raised you as if he were a father, from the age of five.

Behind my back, the boy was all but screaming.

Slavery. The Abbot was quite right—it was part of a quotation. He raised the icon of one eyebrow at me, and I quoted: "Slavery is no part of natural law."

"Ah." The Abbot would have been within his rights to punish me for such a radical thought, but he seemed merely ruminative. "Roman, of course, coming from you. Let me see. 'Slavery is no part of natural law, but an invention of man. And it is that other invention of man, war, which produces so many slaves.' Gaius the Jurist." He smoothed a stray curl behind my ear with his ivory fingers. "Don't worry, dear one. This young fellow may be a challenge, but I'll have him settled down soon." He lifted the hand away from my hair, signaling. The shouting stopped.

I turned around to see the boy sagging in the steward's pincered arms.

"He is no slave," said the Abbot. "And neither are you, Greta. Never forget that. Neither are you."

3
THE ODD PRINCESS HAS
SOME HARD DAYS

I am not a slave. The Abbot, in this one thing, was wrong: I have never thought myself a slave.

But I was born to a crown. I was born to a fate defined by my bloodline and by the forces of history. I was born to a duty that I did not choose, and cannot set aside.

I was born to be a hostage.

I was very young when the king my grandfather died and the queen my mother ascended to the throne. Like many other royals, my mother had made a dynastic marriage young—just out of the Precepture. She had been sure to have a child—me—while young. She had known she would not be eligible to hold a throne until she had a hostage child to turn over to Talis.

So she had me. She took our throne. And she turned me over.

On the day of my mother's coronation, I was made Her Royal Highness Greta Gustafsen Stuart, Duchess of Halifax and Crown Princess of the Pan Polar Confederacy. The next day, I became one of Talis's hostages. I was five years old.

Of my time before the Precepture I mostly have bits and pieces. But I remember the day of my mother's coronation—the sea of little flags in the fists of the crowd, the sway of the formal carriage, the diamonds pins in my mother's hair—and I remember the day after. I remember how the ship came, and how the two Swan Riders stepped out of it.

They were two huge men with huge wings. My mother's sharpened, painted fingertips bit into my shoulders. She held me fiercely and then—

Then she let me go. She let me go, and she gave me a little push between the shoulder blades. She pushed me away. I staggered for a second. Then I walked to the Swan Riders because my mother wanted me to, and because if I had clung to her I would have been torn from her arms.

Even then, I knew that.

The boy with bound hands: Who was he, that he did not know what I had known at five? Who was he that he did not know that resisting Talis and his Swan Riders is futile? (That was in fact exactly how Talis put it, in the Utterances. *Resistance is futile.*)

My mother had not had a choice. Like me, she'd never had one. Like me, she'd been born to a crown. Like me, she had her duty. She too had been a hostage. And her father before her. And before that, and before that—for four hundred years.

In the Dark Ages of Europe, kings had exchanged their own children as hostages to secure treaties. Each king knew that if they broke the peace, their own sons would be the first to die.

The royal hostages of those ancient days were raised in enemy courts. In the Age of Talis, we are raised in a handful of Preceptures, scattered around the globe. We are raised together equitably, and we are educated impeccably, and we are treated as well as can be managed. And if war comes, we are still the first to die.

And therefore, war does not come.

Or not so often. Talis made many changes to the world, many things that pushed war toward ritual. The Children of Peace are only part of it, but we are the keystone. Between us and the orbital weapons, the great AI keeps things pretty well in line. What wars occur—perhaps two or three a year—are symbolic, short, and small-scale. Global military casualties per annum are normally in the low thousands, civilian casualties almost nil. This is the treasure and crown of our age: the world is as peaceful as it has ever been.

The world is at peace, said the Utterances. *And really, if the odd princess has a hard day, is that too much to ask?*

There followed, then, a series of hard days.

The boy with bound hands was, we were told, from a new state called the Cumberland Alliance. We knew better than to ask anything more, even when the boy did not immediately appear. We did not discuss the boy, or what might be keeping him. But of course there was nothing out of line in discussing geopolitics, so we talked Cumberland to death.

Sidney's nation had won the war that killed him, which I suppose would have pleased him. The Cumberland Alliance emerged from a regional shakeup among the losing parties. Like many nations it was defined by water: in this case, the drainage of the Ohio River basin. It stretched south to Nashville and north to Cleveland, with a capital at Indianapolis and a military-industrial center at Pittsburgh.

The details do not really matter. What mattered to me was the border. The northern border of Cumberland was defined by a trickling ditch and a wattle fence, down the edge of the mined and marshy bed of old Lake Erie. On the other side of that fence were the watchtowers of the Pan Polar Confederacy: my nation. Unlucky for the Cumberlanders, to border a superpower.

Unlucky for me, if they were thirsty enough.

I needed only another sixteen months, and I would be of age. I would be released from the Precepture, my mother's throne falling to regency (taken most likely by some pampered cousin with a conveniently hostage-aged child) until I could produce an heir and hostage of my own—a thing I did not care to dwell on.

If there was no war in the next sixteen months, then I would live. Sixteen months is not long.

And yet . . . the Cumberland hostage had been dragged to the Precepture in chains. He'd had a strong face and desperate eyes. He'd looked like a Christian being dragged to the lions, like someone who'd been told he was going to die.

And maybe he had been. Maybe the war was that close.

Maybe they'd sent him here intending to throw him away.

A boy, I told my classmates. The new hostage was a boy. About our age. I skipped the part about him being dragged in in chains. Thandi looked at my flushed face and waggled her eyebrows suggestively. But she was wrong. There was nothing of romance in the way I thought about this boy, though I thought about him all the time.

"Are you thinking about him?" said Xie from nowhere.

I jumped. "Sorry, what?"

"Careful," she said. "Don't break the curds."

We were working together in the dairy. I was straining whey. Xie was heating pitchers of water and lowering them into the big tray of raw milk, to warm it gently and thereby nourish the friendly bacteria that would turn the milk to cheese.

The day was hot, and the dairy was positively steaming, and sweat was dripping down Da-Xia's nose. From the solar injector to the milk tray, she carried pitcher after steaming pitcher. I stopped for a moment to watch the blue enamelware moving like a bead on an invisible thread—that smooth, despite its weight. Xie's rolled-up sleeves bunched above her elbows. Muscles ran like tapestry cords through her forearms and wrists.

She flicked a look over her shoulder. "Greta?" Her hair

was done in the tiny, glossy braids traditional to the royalty of the Himalayan slopes. One of the braids had fallen forward and slashed across her face like a wound. "Now you're staring into space," she said.

And Thandi drawled from the doorway, "Who are you, and what have you done with Greta?" The screendoor whapped shut behind her as she came in with a pail of milk.

"I'm sorry," I said. "I'll focus."

"Oh, don't, please," smiled Xie. "It's a rare treat to see you dreamy. We can spare a batch of cheese."

"Speak for yourself," said Thandi. But Xie just smiled at her and pushed the slashing hair back behind one ear.

Dreamy. I was not dreaming. I was thinking about the new hostage screaming—about me shocked and falling to my knees. I would not say this to Thandi. I had wanted to say it to Xie, but constantly monitored as we were, it was hard to find a good place in which to hide such a large conversation.

Outside I could hear Grego and Han laughing together. They were meant to be straining cream, but it sounded livelier than that. Grego was funny, but he told jokes in precise deadpan, as if they were engineering instructions. It was rare to hear him laugh—but somehow Han, who was as far from deadpan as one could imagine, could always make him. I envied them their ability to laugh together. Somehow Xie and I could rarely manage it.

"You know," said Xie, "it would be all right, if you were thinking about him."

"Who?" I said, because I did not know what else to

say. Under the dairy roof we were not in the line of sight of the Panopticon, but some kind of eavesdrop bug could be assumed. We all took greater liberties under roofs, but they could not be infinite.

"Who?" Xie echoed. Her mood, maybe infected by the laughter outside, seemed playful. "Sidney, obviously."

"Oh. Sidney."

"Yes, Sidney," said Thandi. "I know you two weren't off playing coyotes, but . . ."

"Playing coyotes" was school euphemism for meeting outside, after dark—one presumed it was for sex.

"Certainly not," said Xie. "But still. He liked you. And you didn't mind. All things are relative, and from you, Princess of the Icy Places, not minding is nearly a declaration of undying love."

I turned my back on them both, and looked to my own, slightly riper, cheese tray. The smell of it—sour as baby spit-up—suddenly turned my stomach. "My marriage will be dynastic."

"So will mine," said Xie to my back. "But in the meantime, I have eyes."

"Yes," said Thandi, whapping her way back out the door. "We noticed."

I blushed. Eyes were the least of what Xie had. Playing coyotes? She was the queen of the pack, whereas I had my sexuality filed under "further research is needed."

Sidney. We'd been hostaged together for twelve years. I knew every curve of his accent, every lilt of his laugh. I knew he hated zucchini, as do we all. But the shameful truth was I was not thinking about Sidney at all. He was, after all, already dead.

I looked at Xie. We were alone. A roof was over us.

"So," she said, softly. "Sidney?"

"Sidney," I said, but it was lie. "No. I'm thinking more of this new boy."

Da-Xia's eyebrows folded up, and then she gave a faint, faint nod, letting me know she'd followed my switch to speaking in code.

"I wonder—I just wonder how long he'll be with us."

"So fickle!" Xie said, as if teasing, as if we were still talking about boys. She meant wars were fickle too. I'd been ready to die with Sidney, and I hadn't. And maybe I wouldn't, even now.

"Just remember," she said. "There's time yet between you and that dynastic marriage."

"I hope so." Sixteen months was not so long.

Da-Xia put her hand—well known, work hardened, hot from the pitchers—on the back of my neck. I leaned into her.

"Me too," she said.

And in the five days after I first saw the Cumberland hostage, I didn't sleep well.

I have never been a good sleeper. If I could choose a blessing it would perhaps be the ability to put my head on the pillow and drift off, quietly, reliably, without fuss. Instead my brain takes exhaustion as its cue to review every stupid mistake I've ever made, and then (like the crowned princes in Shakespeare) I have bad dreams.

Xie sleeps. I don't.

By the fifth day I had had quite enough of it.

I was alone that night. Da-Xia had gone out to play coyotes. The room was too quiet without her breathing in it. Above me the glass ceiling was a dark gleam—glass, to let the Panopticon watch over us. I lay there and looked up at it. Xie had a habit of folding cranes from whatever paper she could scavenge, and hanging them from the glass. Their small angles shifted slowly, dully, though the room seemed airless. Through their dapple I could see the spill of the Milky Way, and the insect twist of the Panopticon mast rising against the sky.

My pillow grew hot. I turned it over. The other side grew hot. My hair spread out all around me. I had quite a lot of hair, which was entirely my mother's fault. *A queen does not cut her hair,* she often said. And once, the last time I saw her: *A queen cuts her hair on her way to the block.*

Like all of the Children of Peace, I am sent home thrice annually, to maintain my bond with my parents. After all, if one is to hold royal children hostage on the premise that the prospect of their deaths will deter their parents from declaring war, it does not do to let parent-child bonds wither away. And they have not withered. My parents, I think, do love me.

I was last home months ago, at the warm end of spring. On the last day of my visit, my mother—the queen my mother—dismissed my maids and brushed my hair herself.

Brushed it and brushed it, a thousand strokes. Then she did up the buttons on the back of my gown. There were three dozen of them, tiny things that went into tiny loops. One by one, she did them. One by one, and it took a long time.

Overhead the stars crawled. My pillow itched. Xie did not come back. Still I could not sleep. I counted goats, but they kept getting away from me, becoming those buttons. Becoming my mother, brushing my hair.

When I started to feel the phantom tug at my scalp and a tightness in my throat, I thrust myself upright. If I could not sleep, I chided myself, I would work.

I got up, I got dressed. I yanked my hair into braids so tight that they tugged at my temples and stung tears from the corners of my eyes. Then I went to the misericord.

The word "misericord" means "room of the pitying heart." When the Precepture hall had been a monastery, centuries ago, the miseri would have been the one room where strictures were relaxed. Now it is lounge and library, a place of quiet and rest. The glass in the skylight is amber, warming the light, dimming the Panopticon's sharp outline. There are books, collected on tall, columnar shelves, like a grove of old trees. The books were my object, or at least my excuse: I needed the next volume of Epictetus for my paper.

There was light, as always, in the heart room. Little brass lamps, here and there, cast pools of gold. The Abbot is there when he is not required elsewhere, and though I suppose he does not technically need light, it is a comfortable thing to be able to see him.

The Abbot was not behind his desk. "Father?" I meant to be soft, out of respect for the hour, but my voice came out fluttering. The flutter surprised me.

The old AI came forward from the grove of bookshelves. The face monitor canted forward on his mainstem, like the head of a nearsighted old man. "Ah, Greta." The icons of his eyes moved a fraction farther apart and opened a whisker wider—not a smile, but a listening, welcoming look. "You're burning the midnight oil, child. Couldn't sleep?"

"No, good Father. I came for a book."

"Ah." He puttered over toward the classical philosophy. "One of the Stoics, isn't it? Aurelius again?"

"Epictetus, Father."

"That's right. I've seen your notes, my dear: impressive work, impressive work." His voice was old and soft as a step that has been worn down in the center. That voice, and the amber light, made the room feel warm. My heart—odd, it had been racing—was slowing down. The Abbot led me deeper into the grove of bookcases. "Have you considered extending it? Perhaps something on the uptake of the Roman branch of Stoicism into early Christianity, or Western culture generally? After all, the very word 'stoic' has come to mean calmness in the face of trying circumstance."

"Oh, yeah," came a voice from the darkness. "I can't *wait* to get started writing papers on that."

My breath caught, because it was Sidney's accent, or nearly—Sidney's accent if the peaches in syrup had been laced with rough stones.

The Abbot sighed. "Greta, may I present Elián Palnik, who comes to us from the Cumberland Alliance?"

It was the boy—the boy with bound hands. He was slumped into the memory cushion at the back of the book grove, a shadow within a shadow.

My eyes went right to his hands, but they were not bound now. Even so it took me a moment to find my voice. "Hello, Elián," I said. I found, to my horror, that I addressed him as I sometimes addressed our more skittish goats. He was just sitting there, but something about him seemed half-tamed.

"Hey, Greta," said Elián. And to the Abbot: "Stoicism? I mean, seriously?"

He sat forward then, brushing his hair out of his face—he would need to get that trimmed. The bruising around his wrist had gone old and yellow. He looked at me blankly, and then seemed to recognize me. "Wait, you're Princess Greta." And another layer of recognition. "It was you—the girl at the door, that day."

He had seen me disgrace myself, then. I hoped I wasn't blushing. "I apologize for reacting." My voice was steady, at least.

He sketched a little bow, as much as one can while sitting on a cushion. "It's okay. I mean, where I'm from, it's traditional to 'react' when someone gets dragged in in chains."

"Elián," chided the Abbot, his voice like dust. "That's hardly appropriate."

"Sorry, Greta," said Elián. "I'm having trouble telling what's appropriate."

He did not sound sorry.

"That's enough, I think," said the Abbot. His eye icons had pulled together. "Greta. Don't forget your book."

I took my book. I did not flee. But I left, and my heart was no longer beating slowly.

4
GUINEVERE

It was ten days before I saw Elián again.

It's not unusual for a Child newly come to the Precepture to spend some time being tutored privately before joining his cohort, but Elián stayed away longer than any I could remember. And then, one day . . .

We were harvesting new potatoes. Han and I were forking over the rows, and the others of our cohort were gathering the tubers and laying them out on the wickerwork riddles. I looked up to blink the sweat out of my eyes and saw Elián coming down the slope toward us.

I felt a gasp catch in my throat. Elián had a proctor with him.

It was unusual to see a proctor outside at all, and this one was eye-catching. The proctors that swarm the school have a variety of adaptations, but mostly look like overgrown daddy longlegs—knee-high, spindly, and quick. Elián's proctor was as heavily built as a scorpion, high as my waist, its jointed legs easily clearing the churned places and raised beds.

At the edge of the potato trench, and with this thing beside him, Elián stopped.

He shot a round-eyed glance at the proctor, favored our group with a rictus of a smile, and said, "Hi. I'm Spartacus, and I'm here to lead you in a slave revolt against an unjust syst—"

The proctor touched his belly, and he went down screaming.

Or, to be fair, it was just one scream. But it was so loud, and so— I can hardly describe it. It was a sound a human might make if turned into an animal. There was nothing of dignity or tradition in it. It was not the kind of sound we Children heard often, and all up and down the garden terraces, white figures fluttered up like a startled flock.

Unprecedented, that's what the sound was. Unprecedented. We don't scream here.

Not out loud, anyway.

Elián had folded up with his head on one of the heaps of dirty potatoes. The scorpion proctor took two mincing steps toward him. He flinched, pushed up onto one hand. But his elbow gave way and he went sprawling.

I knelt to help him, my heart twisting—but as I moved the proctor straightened with the barest ticking of joints. I froze. Its iris clicked in and out. What did it expect? Was I meant to leave him? Or to help him? I held rabbit-still with one hand on Elián's shuddering shoulder. The proctor's head swiveled like a turret, taking in everyone.

Thandi and Grego were closest to Elián and me, but they were paralyzed. Thandi looked as if she'd been turned to wood. Grego's false eyes were completely black. The proctor's optical beam swept over them, and still they didn't move.

The proctor locked on to Da-Xia. And she, bless her, pressed her palms together and bowed to it. Then she came forward. She crouched on the other side of Elián. We took a shoulder each, and helped him sit, and then stand. They had indeed cut his hair, shaved it back nearly to the scalp. This close, I could see it prickle, see the convulsive tick in his throat as he swallowed, swallowed.

Elián hung between Da-Xia and me, wobbling. It was unsettling to be so close to a stranger. I could smell him, feel the heat off him. I could see all the secret nicks and scars of his scalp.

Across the top of Elián's bent head, my gaze met Xie's. What if he couldn't work? Couldn't stand? What should we do?

But even as I wondered, I felt him find his feet. "Hello, Greta," he rasped, still sagging. "I'm still having some . . ." His voice gave way, came back, and he twitched a smile. "Some trouble with what's appropriate."

"I can see that." I put every ounce of Precepture dignity into my voice. A smile? Did he not understand what he had done? His behavior would cost us all. "What's appropriate now is for you to introduce yourself. Properly."

He lifted his head and looked at me, big-eyed. He was

still clinging to me, and his look made me feel as though I'd hit a puppy. I suppose from his point of view I'd changed sides. He would not understand why. I knew all the complications, knew I was doing right. And yet his bewildered, betrayed expression still made me look away, which gave me a close-up view of his forearm. His muscles twitched. His skin was goose-bumped and shivery.

And he still hadn't answered. Xie tried to prompt him. "I'm Li Da-Xia. From Yunnan, the Mountain Glacials."

"Da-Xia," he echoed.

"You may call me Xie," she said, which was generous of her.

"Z? Like the letter?"

"It's *zed* in this kingdom," said Grego, looking sideways at me. "They are touchy about it." He told the joke carefully, as if he were defusing a bomb.

And Elián missed it. He looked blankly from Grego to Xie, as if the proctor had shocked thirty IQ points off him. Maybe he was just a bit slow. "Xie is Z; got it. Xie and Atta and Gregori and Thandi and Greta and Han." He recited it as a list, by rote. He turned to the proctor, and added, "Is that right?" As if he expected the thing to answer him.

"That's right," I said. "And you're Elián."

As if his own name had been his master password, he shook his head and stood up straight. His face reset, and those IQ points came back all at once. He looked cheerfully jaunty and willingly can-do and adorably dorky and I was absolutely sure that at least two of those were put on.

I looked to Xie and she answered me with two arched eyebrows: She didn't know what to make of him either. None of us did.

Elián stood grinning in the middle of our stares. "So, hi," he said. He reached for my dropped pitchfork, only to have Atta put his foot on it. None of us wanted this stranger to have a weapon.

Elián pretended not to notice. "Yeah. I'm Elián Palnik, from the Cumberland Alliance. Y'all want to show me how to dig potatoes?"

No one answered. We looked at him and his proctor, keeping our faces blank and our bodies ready, in the manner of carefully trained Précepture children under threat. In contrast, Elián stood affable and loose-jointed, at ease and utterly alien. Our silence—disturbed, disapproving—wasn't making a dent. He turned to me. "So," he said. "Stoicism."

"So," I answered, carefully. "Potatoes." I bent and grabbed one of the riddle's two handles. The big proctor backed off a couple of steps, off the wickerwork. Elián's breathing paused subtly when moved—he had enough sense to be frightened, then. And enough dignity to hide it. Both those things were promising.

"Help me with this," I said. It was in part a kindness to orient him, to cue him. It was in part selfish: We would all feel safer if we got to work. "This is called riddling. We shake the dirt through the wicker. Then we can store them without scrubbing. It saves water."

"It's always water," he said, nonsensically. But he picked

up the other handle. We raised the big flat basket between us. I was relieved that he did not have trouble with it. Fifty pounds of potatoes is not a huge load, but this close, I could see that his muscles were still twitching. Electricity, as all we Children have cause to know, can be a tricky thing to get through, and Elián either had little tolerance for it, or had taken a large dose.

"So," he said. "This is what it's like to be royalty."

"Yes . . . ?" I was beginning to think I'd been right to treat him like a skittish goat. Like our goats he seemed vaguely to be Planning Something. The wickerwork shook between us and dust bloomed and stuck to my skin. I tried not to sneeze. "Yes. This is what it's like to be a Child of Peace."

"Somehow I thought there'd be air-conditioning," Elián said. Grego swallowed a laugh, and Elián looked over his shoulder at him. "Look at me, though. I can't believe I'm shaking out potatoes with Princess Greta."

"Yes," said Grego. "Greta is our best potato-shaker, no doubt. Perhaps tomorrow you will joint a goat with Thandi."

"No," said Elián—and the proctor at his feet flexed upward on its joints. Elián barely glanced at it. "I only mean— I've seen you in vids, is all."

"You've seen my vids?" I was surprised. Of course I was in many vids. I was to be the ruler of my country one day, if I lived, and it was important that my people know and love me. They did, too. They loved me rather in the way they might love a child with cancer, because it was so sad, and I was so brave. Neither love—the cancer love or the hostage love—had much to do with the reality of life under threat, but it would serve. The vids made it serve. But I did not know that the vids reached beyond the Pan Polar borders.

"Sure. I've seen them all. That interview last Christmas? At the tree-lighting ball? You're royalty, Greta. A celebrity. Like—like Guinevere."

Da-Xia actually laughed aloud. *"Guinevere!"*

Elián shrugged, as well as one can when holding a potato riddle and shivering with recent shocks. "I think it's mostly the hair."

"My hair is fairly trivial, surely."

"Weeeellll," said Elián, drawing it to about four syllables. "The hair and the stick up your royal . . . bearing."

There was just enough spin on "bearing" to let even the most oblivious among us (all right, me) know that the word was a last-moment substitution. The comment was rude, and un-royal, and made Thandi laugh. Thandi, of all people. I felt as if Elián were melting us, one by one. But of course none of my friends had my reasons to stay frozen. Their nations were not squared off with his nation. They had not seen him tied up and screaming.

As we faced each other over the riddle, Elián kept trying to catch my eye. There was something magnetic about him, something that made it hard to look away. He was not a prince—they didn't have princes, the Americans, so he was just some general's kid, some politician's kid—but . . . Spartacus, he'd called himself. Spartacus had been a slave who'd become a hero. A general who'd become a martyr.

Elián was joking and laughing, but his eyes were desperate. He looked like someone who'd been told he was going to die.

I gave the riddle a last hard shake, and then tipped the potatoes into the basket in Atta's arms. Dust bloomed. I dragged the cuff of my samue across my forehead and squinted the sweat out of my stinging eyes. The day was hot. I could practically feel my freckles drawing together to form city-states.

Elián swung the empty riddle in one hand and looked from Atta to Grego. "If she's Guinevere, that makes you two Lancelot and Arthur. Which one's which?"

Atta said absolutely nothing. He looked down on Elián with eyes you could fall into, like wells.

"Atta's quiet," murmured Xie. She slid herself between them. She is just a slip of a thing, but is amazing how much protection her body can give. "Don't tease."

"First," said Grego, "you are overlooking Han, which, frankly, is too common a thing. Second, I am certainly Arthur. Only slightly more Lithuanian, and interested in engineering."

"Speciality?" said Elián. "Please say 'munitions.'"

At Elián's feet the big proctor clicked—a sound like a bone breaking. The thing was standing close to us, and still. Dust moved across the nanolubricants on its ball-and-socket joints; they gleamed like oily eyes.

"Don't," warned Thandi. She was watching the proctor, but she sounded more angry than frightened.

"It's cybernetics, isn't it, Grego?" said Han, oblivious, as always.

"Mostly." Grego had gone cautious and still. "Cybernetics and mechatronics more generally."

"That's a shame," said Elián, his face slowly opening up into a huge grin. "I was hoping you could help me blow this place to kingdom come."

The proctor brought him down.

The shock caught Elián in the knee and the groin. He didn't even get out a scream. His eyes rolled up and he tipped backward. Atta dropped the bushel and lunged to catch him, but I was closer. Elián fell into my arms, and I fell. Potatoes tumbled around us. For a moment his eyes were white moons behind his tangled lashes, but he came around quickly. He was sobbing, gulping air—

No. He was laughing.

On the ground, desperately hurting, should-be-humiliated, and *laughing*. He shook his head as if to rattle whatever was loose in there—his dignity, his sense of self-preservation, perhaps some small rocks. . . .

"Are you all right?" Xie knelt beside us.

"Awww, peachy," he gasped. "This is way more fun with company."

Fun?

Surrounding us, my cohort stood astonished. For a moment there was no sound but the wind, making sage-green and sere ruffles in the prairie grass.

And in that moment—that farseeing, dry moment—I

was absolutely sure. I was going to die. My mother herself had brushed my hair because the Great Lakes were under threat, because my nation was going to go to war.

It didn't matter that Cumberland would be the aggressor, that the PanPols would be defending their own. *Play nice, kids,* said the Utterances. *Work it out. I won't be picking sides.*

No, Talis would make no judgements about who was in the right. He would not choose sides. I could practically hear him, that unknowable, alien thing, saying: *I love you all the same.* He would send Swan Riders, and they would take us both to the grey room.

I was going to die. I was going to die with this boy who was laughing in my arms. I jerked away, dumping him into the dirt, and scrambled to my feet. Elián rolled over and lay flat on the ground beside the potato trench. The proctor stood over him. For just a moment its red eye beam tipped up at me, and it quivered, as if it were going to say my name.

5
EVENING DISPATCHES

Mother, I wrote.

That day—that day with Elián and his scorpion shadow—we'd worked as long as the light had lasted, late in that northern August. We had staggered in exhausted and eaten cold food that had tasted of dust.

Now I was sitting in the twilight, alone at the tiny table in my cell. Xie had gone to fetch a pitcher of washing water, and so I sat with the grime of the day still on me, a pen hesitating above white paper.

The Mother looked back at me. It was in my heart to write, *Do not let my death surprise me.*

My heart did not quite manage to move my pen. My free hand had smudged the paper, holding it down. I needed some of my mother's map weights, those elegant velvet sacks of sandthat held down the corners of papers. They were embroidered with the family motto, *Semper Eadem*. "Always the same."

Halifax was so far away.

It is not that I have not been there. Like all the Children of Peace, I go regularly to visit my parents. I have an apartment in the palace. I have a vast bed and a desk, and gowns, and beautiful books. But even so, Halifax does not seem like my home. A refitted monastery and a few acres of permaculture garden, somewhere in Saskatchewan—Precepture Four—that is home. As part of Canada it is technically part of my kingdom, but out here I am the princess of grasshoppers and red tails, duchess of chickens and goats.

Halifax is so different, so alien. Citadel Hill seems to loom. The sea is restless. The sky is too small. In Halifax I am interviewed and bowed to; I go to fetes and balls. In Halifax, my father takes me sailing, out among the little Islands of the Nova Scotia archipelago, above the ruins of the sunken cities. In the evenings I go out with him to the campanile to ring the twilight bells, the ones that call the little ships home. In Halifax, my mother pours me cup after cup of tea. In her library she spreads out maps and we speak of history. In Halifax I have to wear shoes indoors, and corsets that press red lines into my skin. In Halifax I am duchess and crown princess. When I come here the prairie sky opens up over me. I fold the crown princess away like linens into lavender, and I was Greta again.

It is hard for the person I am here to write to that strange and distant place called "home." My mother—what could

I say to her? *Mother, the Cumberland hostage—I think he knows something.*

The last time I had been was in Halifax, my mother did not mention a war. But she did not invite me to privy council either, as she usually does. And on the last day of my visit she herself brushed the thousand strokes through my hair. She wasn't crying, but she was . . . .

In my cell, two thousand miles from my mother, the blank paper looked up at me. Surely she would warn me. Surely, she would not let me be surprised.

Mother, Sidney was surprised and it was terrible.

Sidney and I had known that a Swan Rider was, likely, coming for us. And yet in the end, Sidney had been surprised. He had stood frozen. He had spoken of his father.

Mother, there is a boy here and he seems so afraid.

Elián. I could imagine us walking to the grey room together, walking to both our deaths. I could imagine him wanting to hold my hand. Or—no, he probably wouldn't walk. He'd probably fight and have to be dragged, and then all my practiced dignity would be for nothing. There would be a scene.

My mother would not approve if I died with a scene.

The little cell was still hot. The floors were warm. The walls were warm. Even the moonlight spilling through the ceiling seemed warm. Summers were short, there in what used to be Saskatchewan. But that didn't mean they weren't hot.

All day long, sweat had gathered at the nape of my neck

and run in a little trickle down my spine. My spine itched, my neck itched—even my hair itched.

In Halifax I have two maids to fuss over my hair, and they amuse themselves (if not me) by doing elaborate things with it. Here I merely put it in two thick braids, which I coil around my head, out of the way. Like Guinevere, evidently. Well. She was a busy woman. Probably she wanted her hair out of the way, too.

I pulled the pins out of my hair, and the two braids tumbled free and fell, swinging, down my back.

Our door slid open. Xie. The pitcher swung empty in her hand. "There's no water," she said.

For a moment, just a moment, my mind filled with the dry waving grass of the prairie in drought. A Rider moving through that grass would make such a dust plume. . . .

"No water," I said.

We both knew what it meant. There *was* water—our well was not dry—but we were being denied access to it. We were being punished.

It was not a surprise. At the Precepture each cohort regulates itself, but if someone in the cohort acts egregiously, publicly, noticeably poorly—well, then, we all pay. It is little things, mostly. Reduced diets. Sealed doors. Hours spent in total darkness. It gives us incentive to keep each other in line.

We had certainly not managed to keep Elián in line.

"Tonight of all nights," I complained. "It's hot."

"I imagine our new friend is more uncomfortable even than that." Da-Xia tugged at one of my braids. "Guinevere."

"Yes, well, Americans. They do have an obsession with royalty." I nudged my letter to one side and Xie set the pitcher down on the table (which was also our washstand) with a depressingly empty clang. "I wish they would just get some of their own."

"But where will they find a bloodline that's blessed and anointed by the gods?"

With that, my roommate, the god, peeled off her samue and flopped down across her cot.

The prevalence of hereditary monarchies in the modern world was a quirk of history, a side effect of requiring national decision-makers to have children and putting those children under lethal threat. Even the most robust democracies of the nineteenth to twenty-first centuries had never been far away from being dynasties. All it had taken was Talis's thumb on the scale.

I didn't actually mean for the hostage thing to create a whole bunch of hereditary monarchies, saith the Utterances. *But, you know, whatever. Murdering princesses. I guess I can work with that.*

Xie would be eighteen in the spring. Her country was utterly at peace. Here, in front of me, was one princess who was going to live. She folded her hands behind her head, watching the sky turn from lavender to silvered indigo, lying bare below the glass ceiling as if the light alone could wash her.

We have been together so long that there cannot be much modesty left between us, yet still I turned my eyes away, back to the paper. A letter had failed to write itself. Overhead, wind was picking up: a storm with no rain, just birds being pushed too far, too fast.

"Writing home?" Xie asked behind me. I heard the rustle of her pulling on her alb.

"Trying to."

Early in the history of the Preceptures, hostage Children had been allowed real-time video uplink with their parents and friends, access to a full spectrum of media. It hadn't worked out well. (*Yeah,* said the Utterances. *In my considered opinion, riots are bad for morale.*) Now we got our news from printed dispatches. And we wrote letters.

I looked at the smudged paper. "I can hardly tell her— ask her—" It was hard to code this. *Tell me, Mother, if I'm going to die.* "It turns out I have no idea what to say."

"Most holy and beloved father," said Xie, addressing an imaginary letter to her own father. "The weather is hot and dry. Today we harvested the early potatoes. A goat escaped and ate all the stone plums, and now we will have a bitter winter."

"There are still peaches," I said.

"Fortunately, there are still peaches," Xie dictated, tracing the round characters of her own alphabet in the air, little dances of her hand. "And soon there will be apples. And all things will be well."

We were speaking as much to the Panopticon as to each other. "All things will be well," murmured Xie.

We both knew that wasn't likely.

I leaned forward and pinched up the smudged and heavy paper. "Make a bird for me?"

"Of course." Da-Xia's quick fingers made the word "Mother" vanish into a fold. She made another fold, another, another, until the paper was a delicate crane.

"Make a wish," said Xie.

Cranes traditionally represent a wish for peace. I closed my eyes and wished. Uselessly. Hard.

6
SPARTACUS

I t was already hot when the prime bell woke us the next day. I had somehow failed to become less grimy in my sleep. Our Precepture practices appropriate use of technology—meaning, among other things, that we use nothing we can get by without. Normally that seems only wise, but on that day I thought an air conditioner or two probably wouldn't ruin the world.

They had, though, once. One needed to remember that. Air conditioners and other thoughtlessly and broadly used technologies had ruined the world. After the War Storms, in the great pause of the Pax Talis, the modern world had made different choices. (*Tell you what,* said the Utterances, *why don't you all have a little think on what you've done to our planet and* **make some different choices.**) So we chose. Yes to magnetically launched suborbitals and retroviruses that could rewrite a faulty gene. No to petroleum-driven personal transportation and chemical fertilizers. Yes to transcranial magnetic psychotherapy. No to robotic labor—except in an extreme case like the Precepture, where stakes are high and humans cannot be trusted. Yes to cargo zeppelins. No to imported food. Yes to horses. No to air conditioners.

Well. We might cool the odd palace.

The Precepture, whatever else it is, is no palace. And so it was hot. The matins bell rang and my cohort gathered in the refectory. The younger classes watched us. Everyone knew we'd been denied water. Everyone knew why. We ate cold things for breakfast—plums, goat cheese, yesterday's flat-bread—and tried to avoid sniping at one another. My peers were high-strung, braced against the idea that we might be punished further. Elián was nowhere in sight.

It got hotter. The dog-day cicadas began to whirr. The wind that had pushed against the Precepture all night died down, leaving the sky still and yellow with dust. In the classroom we threw open the windows and swatted at the horseflies that quickly found us. Brother Delta tried to lead us through the history of natural resources as a root cause for war—but we couldn't keep it up. By midmorning Han was drowsing accidentally, Atta was drowsing openly, and Gregori was drowsing covertly—his open eyes were entirely black with dilating shutters, but behind those shutters, no one was home. Even the keenest among us (me, and in a different way, Da-Xia) were willing to sit and let Brother Delta drone on.

Drone he did. I had once seen a hospital monitor that looked like Brother Delta—a hexapod base, upright mainstem, topped with a screen. If you'd added some arms, such a monitor could have doubled for Brother Delta—and could probably have given better lectures. His voice was a soporific whirr as he ticked through the history. He droned about how the land wars of the early twentieth century had shifted to oil wars and then water wars. He droned about what came next. About how rapidly rising sea levels, shifting weather patterns, and the collapse of petroleum-dependent agriculture had led to famine, disease, and displacement, to huge populations on the move.

These in turn had led to the War Storms—dozens of intensely fought regional wars that had crashed across the world in waves, engulfing first one set of countries and then another, and then circling back. War, plague, hunger. The global population fell by half. Then two thirds. Then three quarters.

Once upon a time, said the Utterances, the humans were killing each other so fast that total extinction was looking possible, and it was my job to stop them.

The UN's best AI, a Class Two named Talis, had been charged with finding ways to predict—and, where possible, prevent or end—the conflicts that were rapidly tearing up the planet.

That Talis's strategy would be to put himself in charge was not something his human colleagues had foreseen. But that was exactly what he had done, neatly taking control of the networked weapons systems, most notably the ones in orbit.

Right! he is said to have said. *Everybody, out of the pool!*

Then he started blowing up cities until everyone was stunned enough to scramble out and stand, dripping.

It was Talis who had invented the Preceptures and the other rituals and rules of war, and Talis who enforced those rules with a ruthlessness no human could match. There were other AIs in the UN, of course, and the human Swan Riders in their employ. But Talis was the name we dropped our voices to mention, Talis was—

But at that point, the door opened.

It was the Abbot, and with him, Elián. We stood and bowed.

"Ah, children," the Abbot said. "My children. Sit down, sit down, take your places. I won't take much of your time. I know it's a busy season."

We sat. Our teacher had rolled backward a few paces and stood against the window as quietly as if he'd gone into standby.

The Abbot was of the same build as Brother Delta, but they could not have been more different. Like Talis himself, the Abbot was said to be a Class Two, which meant he had once been human. There had been many, once, but the transition from human to AI was said to be fraught, and only a few survived. Beyond his classification, we knew nothing of the Abbot's history, though—a shepherd, perhaps? The way he chivvied Elián into the middle of the room suggested a shepherd with a stick. The pair of them stood side by side in the center of the half circle made by our desks. The Abbot paused, his facescreen tipped downward, contemplating.

"My children," he said. On the screen the icon of his lips thinned, as if he had a painful confession to make. "Children, I have come to apologize to you. I heard how your work was disrupted yesterday." He raised his head and looked at us. When no one commented, he looked us over. His eyes settled on Thandi. "Did I hear correctly, then, Thandi?" The eye icons widened expectantly. "Was young Mr. Palnik disruptive?"

Thandi swallowed. "Somewhat so, Father."

Elián darkened. He had the look of someone betrayed. Which was not fair. What could Thandi have done, lied to the Abbot? Saying "somewhat" was already pushing the truth. If the Abbot contradicted her, she'd suffer.

"Somewhat, somewhat," he said, nodding. "And of course your cohort's standing is *somewhat* damaged." He made a noise like a tongue against the teeth, though he had neither. "I do feel responsible. It was my judgement that Elián was ready to join you. It seems that perhaps I was mistaken." The Abbot shifted from side to side like a man with arthritis. "Mr. Palnik," he said, "I hardly know what to do with you."

Elián's eyes flashed; he drew a hard breath as if to speak in fury. But then he froze. Under his shirt something was moving.

I looked closer: just there, where the samue top crossed itself at his breastbone, something was poking out. A metal wire or . . . It was a mechanical leg. It took me a moment to make sense of it. A nursery spider—the tiny proctors that were the caretakers and pets and playthings of the very youngest children. There was one over Elián's heart. Something else moved in one sleeve, and a third thing above one knee.

He did not wince. But he said nothing.

"Well, Elián?" the Abbot prompted.

And then, suddenly, Da-Xia spoke up. "Good Father . . . this cohort—we are quite stable."

The Abbot turned to her, smiling. "Indeed, Da-Xia. I've long thought so."

"So perhaps, Father," she said, "we could absorb some small disruption?"

The Abbot steepled his fingers. Ceramic ticked off aluminum. "An interesting thought. Are you advising me to let Elián join you?"

"If it's not too forward of me, Father."

"Forwardness is indeed your weakness, my dear." The Abbot hummed thoughtfully. "But you have a generous heart." He looked up and addressed us generally. "What do you think, Children? Could you be a stabilizing influence on our newest, hmmm, inductee?"

The eyes of the cohort turned to me.

Well. It was gratifying to be acknowledged as leader, but I was not sure what to do. It would cost Xie if I contradicted her. And yet, to tie the entire cohort's fate to this half-savage boy? We'd already lost the water. That would only be the beginning. It was on my tongue to say, *No*.

But then the spider over Elián's heart moved. He caught my eye. I had once thought him a slave because I'd seen him in chains. But if he was a slave now, he was a slave at auction. His eyes were both asking and defying.

"We can but try, Father," I said.

"My dear Greta. That's all anyone can ask." The Abbot hummed to himself thoughtfully, then decided. "Sit, Elián."

So Elián sat, beside me, at Sidney's desk.

There were little beads of sweat in the soft down of his hairline. He was shivering. The Abbot smiled. "Yesterday was perhaps too harsh an introduction for you, my son. It was my mistake and I apologize for it. We will try again, and strive for more order."

The Abbot's manner was judicial. "So," he said. "I think you introduced a topic yesterday, Mr. Palnik."

Elián paled a fraction. Peeking out from under his collar, a spider leg moved against his throat. ". . . I, uh, don't remember that."

"Hmmm." The Abbot looked puzzled, his fingers ticking together. "The third servile war? You wanted to discuss it?"

The spider shifted under Elián's shirt. He was sitting absolutely still. "I'm sure you're right, Abbot, but—" On the word "but" Elián jerked, provoked by nothing I could see. He shivered and gathered his breath. We all held ours, waiting for him to finish his sentence. "I—" he stuttered, and his next words tumbled out too fast. "Honestly, I don't remember, I don't know what you're talking about."

"Hmmm." The Abbot's facescreen creaked on its swivel joint as he turned. "Greta, I think you're probably our best Romanist. Perhaps you would favor us with a précis of the third servile war. Help Mr. Palnik orient himself."

"The third—" I began.

"Stand up," the Abbot said.

It felt like a rebuke, a threat. I stood with my stomach twisting, taking inventory. What had I done, yesterday, with Elián in the potatoes, with Xie in our room? Was there anything for which I could be rebuked?

"Um . . . ," I said. Which was not worthy of me. I steadied myself and tried to remember that I *was* (no "probably" about it) the cohort's best Romanist. "That is, Father . . . The third servile war was the last of three unsuccessful slave revolts during the Roman republic period, and took place between 73 and 71 BCE. We have major accounts from Plutarch, Appian, and Florus, and of course Julius Caesar's Commentarii de Bello Gallico."

"And the war is chiefly famous for . . . ," the Abbot prompted.

"For the involvement of the slave general Spartacus, good Father. Though perhaps the effect on the careers of legionary generals Pompey and Crassus is of broader historical significance."

"Well, of course," said the Abbot, with a dove-chuckle of a laugh. "They won."

"Of course." My throat felt dry.

The Abbot turned. Usually he is carefully human in

his movements, slow and puttering. But he turned sharply just then, every inch a machine, a hinged blade. "Now, Mr. Palnik. You wanted to discuss Spartacus? Perhaps you can tell us what happened to him?"

"He—"

"Stand," clicked the Abbot.

Elián stood.

"What happened to Spartacus?"

"He . . ." Elián looked as if he had a bad taste in his mouth. "He was crucified. By the roadside."

"Greta?"

There was nothing for it but to contradict Elián: he was wrong, and the Abbot would surely know it, and expect better of me. "His fate is not known, Father. The discipline of the slave army broke, and they were entirely routed, and all but six thousand were killed on the battlefield. Spartacus himself was presumably among them."

"So this crucifixion business?"

"The six thousand captured were crucified, Father. They lined the Appian Way from Rome to the coast."

"Ah," said the Abbot, and smiled.

I was standing, and Elián was standing. I felt as if we were connected by a cord. I could almost feel it closing around my throat. The spiders moved under Elián's shirt. No one said anything.

The Abbot looked at us each, one by one by one.

He did not order. But everyone stood.

"Good," said the Abbot. "Good." I thought for a

moment— I do not know what I thought. I thought something radical was about to happen.

But the Abbot only nodded. "I've taken enough of your time, Children—be about your day. I will count on you to show our newest colleague the ropes, as it were." He spread a hand. As if he'd conjured them, bells began to ring.

And so Elián joined us properly.

Outside he took three stumbling, running steps into the sunlight, then stopped. He tilted up his face and took a deep breath. Sidney told me once that domestic turkeys can drown while watching the rain. In that moment I believed it. We all stared at Elián while he stood there with his gullet tipped open. If it had been raining, he would have been doomed.

After a moment he swallowed and looked over at me. "Well, that was great, Greta. Thanks a lot. Now I know who to cheat off when we get a test."

Spiders pulsed under his clothing. I saw the muscles jump in his arm where the electricity hit, saw the flash of widening in his eyes and mouth. It was gone almost instantly. I wasn't sure the others saw.

"Apples," said Thandi. Her voice was tight with . . . something. Anger? Fear? "We can put up the windfall apples. Let's go, before he gets us all in trouble."

The eleven- and twelve-year-olds had already gathered the apples into peck baskets, and set up the grinder in the shade of the toolshed. They looked to be about half-done. Bushels of bruising apples sat on one side of the grinder, and pails of coarse apple meal sat on the other. Bat Brain the goat had her head stuck in one of them pails. Her tail lifted; she appeared to be turning apples directly into excrement. "Hhawu!" shouted Thandi. "Get out of there!"

The goat lifted her head, working her jaw from side to side like a man chomping a cigar. Lacking upper incisors, goats cannot eat apples without comedy, but this does not stop them from trying. Bat Brain looked at all of us looking at her, remembered that she cherished freedom, and took off like a suborbital rocket.

"Han, you catch her," said Thandi. "You're the one who likes them."

"I don't like *them*— I just like cheese."

"Just catch the damn goat," said Thandi. So Han and Atta went to catch Bat Brain, and the rest of us—Grego, Xie, Thandi, Elián, and I—picked up the full pails and went into the shed.

Inside, it was close and sticky with cobwebs, cluttered with coiled ropes, stacks of baskets, hoes and forks and spades in racks, scythes hanging from the rafters with more symbolic import than any of us were comfortable with. The light was sepia toned, coming through the warped slat walls in lances.

Grego and I carried our pails over to the ancient hulk of the apple press, but Xie and Thandi stopped just inside the door.

Elián ducked under the lintel and found himself between them. He blinked. "You girls aren't gonna beat me up, are you?" His voice was soft, free of the bragga-docio that seemed characteristic of him. He put his pail down and stretched upward, wrapping his fingers around a low rafter. He was startlingly tall. "Got no doubt you could take me, but, no offense—" He cupped a hand loosely over his heart, the nursery spider there. "The job's already covered."

"Of course not," I said. "It's—we're merely pressing cider."

"Yes," said Grego. "Certainly there is no subtext."

"The Abbot would have us show you the ropes," said Da-Xia.

"Ropes?" said Elián. "We just met, Xie—Sure you don't want me to buy you dinner first?"

"Stop it," said Thandi tightly.

"Stop what, fighting?" said Elián. "When pigs fly." Spiders twitched. The bolt must have been stronger this time, because Elián made a sound, a kind of helpless exhalation. He raised a hand to his heart, and his voice was suddenly breathless. "Or when they kill me. Gotta say, that seems more likely."

"The cider—⊠ I tried again.

"We have to explain to him, Greta," said Xie. "The Abbot said—⊠

And Thandi cut in, "We're supposed to be getting him under control."

"Ačiū, Thandi," murmured Grego, even as Elián said: "I'd like to see you tr—" And the word dissolved into a little cry.

Da-Xia hadn't dropped her dark-goddess thing yet: her smile was a strange mix of distance and compassion. She nudged an upturned bucket toward Elián with the side of her foot. "Sit," she said.

Elián dropped onto the bucket and let his head fall forward, lacing his hands behind his neck. Sunlight fell in stripes across him, one turning a streak of his shorn black hair into gloss, one giving shadows and gleam to the knots of his knuckles.

Da-Xia dropped into a crouch beside him. "What are you doing, child?"

"I'm the same age as you," Elián muttered.

"Do you like 'peasant'?" said Grego. "We might call you 'peasant.'"

"Was crucifixion too subtle?" snapped Thandi. "You need to behave better, or—"

Elián didn't answer, didn't lift his eyes from the floor, but he shook his head.

Xie stepped in front of him. "Look at me." When he didn't, she reached out and put her fingers against the corner of his jaw. He lifted his head.

"Elián," she said, spreading her hand against his cheek. "What is your plan here? They're *machines*. They don't have qualms. They won't become tired. They won't simply give up."

"So, what? I should just lie back and enjoy—"

A shock—loud enough to hear, a sound like one popcorn kernel popping. Elián didn't even cry out; he just crumpled. He would have gone to the floor except that Xie caught him. She and Thandi held him for a moment as he flopped limply.

Then Elián seemed to both strengthen and sag. Tension came into him, and he bent his head forward to rest in his own hands.

"Elián, I am impressed with your strength of will," said Xie. "But you are one of the Children of Peace now. Other fates are tied to yours."

Elián snarled without looking up: "I'm not a goddamned Child of Peace!"

Everyone drew breath, waited—but no shock came.

Elián lifted his head, looking for a moment bewildered.

Thandi shook her head. "You have no idea," she said. "No idea." She jerked upright and grabbed the apple buckets. "I have to— I am going to get more apples."

Grego and Xie looked at each other—I was missing something here—and then Grego bowed to Thandi. "Certainly, you should."

"Explain to him," said Thandi to Xie, as she stalked out. "Explain to him that it's all of us."

Is it racist to think of Thandi in terms of African animals? I was not sure. Once, she'd told me I had a face like an Irish wolfhound, and that had not felt like a racial remark, merely an overly astute one. In any case, she went out, and I thought of a cheetah's sway, fragile and strong and proud.

"What does she mean?" Elián surprised me—he could get up, and he did. Grego, meanwhile, set an unexpected example, turning one of the hand cranks that lowered the wooden press on the long spool of its screw. I took the other, and soon the friendly *creak-click* of the wooden gears filled the little space.

Elián stood there, bewildered. "Da-Xia, what does she mean?"

Xie shook her head, almost fondly, as if at a child's folly. "The Abbot asked if we could be a stabilizing influence on you. And I—or rather, Greta and I—we said yes."

"And if you can't?"

We all just looked at him. Surely it wasn't *that* hard to work out.

But Elián didn't seem to be working it out. He looked at me, rather wide-eyed. Evidently Guinevere needed to spell it out for Spartacus. I said, "We'll be punished collectively. We have been already. And we will be again."

"But that's not— I didn't— That's not fair!"

"It is the Precepture," said Xie.

And it was.

7
A SPOT OF TROUBLE

However bullheaded and masochistic Elián had been on his own account, he settled down when he realized that other fates were tied to his. In the gardens, in the refectory—anywhere we were in sight of the younger children—he behaved less stupidly.

Or at least he dammed up his stupidity for a while. Like any force of nature, it sought new channels. In the classroom he was hopeless, and sometimes ended up flat on the floor, which can put a dent in the discussion of (say) aquifers.

For instance, there was the day when we fell to arguing about why the Children of the Preceptures spoke English—a practice that Thandi had picked as her cultural injustice of the day. Da-Xia had quoted from the Utterances: *Too bad. They've got to speak something.*

"He's not a god," Thandi had answered. "Talis is not a god, and the Utterances are not a holy writ."

Da-Xia had smiled at her, her voice dripping honey. "Near enough."

The bickering then became general. Grego (a Baltic nobleman struggling under the weight of his Russian name) took up the part of minority languages, Thandi talked about cultural privileges, and Han (missing the point of the argument entirely) began laying out the simple terms by which one might recognize a god.

"Way I see it," said Elián, unfurling his about-to-get-shocked smile, "anything you can take out with a decent-size pulse bomb—not a god."

The blow to his nervous system had knocked him from his chair.

Elián had come into my life the way comets had once come to medieval skies, the way Swan Riders still came, over the horizon with their wings catching light. He'd come like a portent of doom. But when he rolled over on the classroom floor, gasping and laughing at once, he did not seem portentous. Foolish, yes. Crazy, possibly. But too human to be reduced to a symbol, merely.

And besides, he could garden. There are those, newly come to the Preceptures, who think gardening is beneath them. Not Elián. He knew his way around compost teas and drip irrigations, around cockleburrs and flea beetles. He was, he told us, the son of a pair of sheep farmers.

"Farmers?" said Han. "Then what are you doing here?"

Dear Han. So slow to speak, and yet so often he said the wrong thing. It was clearly out of bounds to ask about a hostage child's history. Much pain could be hidden there, and no good came of poking at it.

But Elián took no offense. He propped a foot up on the lug of his spade and raised an imaginary glass into the air. "Here's to Grandma. My mother's mother is Wilma Armenteros."

Wilma Armenteros, the Cumberland Alliance's secretary for strategic decisions—the newest of many euphemisms the Americans have used for "person in charge of war." I had been reading about her. Recently I'd spent many hours poring over fragile, dry sheets of news dispatches stacked up on the misericord's map table. The dispatches were printed on special paper, easy to compost. They were so dry, they pulled moisture from the skin. I read them until my hands themselves dried, until the skin between my fingers cracked and bled. I was unable to look away from the war that was inching toward me.

Wilma Armenteros loomed large in those papers. Her great-great-something grandfather had led the evacuation of Miami. Some more recent ancestor had been the secretary of unity during the period when the drinking-water-supply wars had finally torn apart the former United States. By all accounts the current Armenteros was the shadow president of the young state, the power behind the Cumberland throne. Of course Talis would demand a hostage from her.

And she was lucky to have one. If she had not had a beloved grandson . . . *Remember when kings used to be required to have children?* said the Utterances. *I require you to have children. You want to be a king, I require you to have children. You want to be a president, you want to be a general, you want to be a lord high dogcatcher—if you're in charge of blowing stuff up, I require you to have children.*

I wondered if Elián realized that he'd been chosen—and not just by Talis. He was here because Wilma Armenteros loved him. But apparently not enough to avoid nominating a hostage. Not enough to turn her position down.

"My mother wanted out of politics," said Elián. "And I'll tell you, she got as far out as she could get. Married this dirt-poor farmer from Kentucky—the hilly bit, you know. Down nigh the Licking River."

"The Licking—" said Da-Xia, as if she couldn't believe her luck.

Elián scrubbed a hand over his face, and his voice came out small: "The south fork."

"Have you at this point heard *all* the jokes about that?" asked Grego.

"I'll bet there are more," said Thandi.

"Shut up," said Elián, majestically. "So my mom, she married this Jewish farmer from a tapped-out springwater town. Got herself religion and settled in to live happily ever after, only with some sheep. And then Talis took her son anyway." He pushed his hat back and swiped the sweat off his forehead with his sleeve. "My father didn't want me to go, but the Swan—"

Spiders moved under his clothes.

Elián stopped talking, took a steadying breath, and

resettled his hat. "And here I am," he said. "So that'll put a snake in your asparagus, heh?"

Even the proctors must have been baffled by that. They did not hurt him.

The height of Elián's disruptions came late in August, on the day when the goats got loose.

I was in the dairy making cheeses with Xie, Atta, and Thandi. Han and Grego were showing Elián how to milk goats. When they all left, Elián didn't shut the gate properly. You would think a farm-raised lad would know better, but perhaps sheep were not as clever as goats. Or perhaps that was what Spartacus would have done, if his every move had been watched, if his body had been weakened by electrical battering. Perhaps Spartacus would have fumbled with a latch, turned his back, and freed the goats.

Come to think of it, Spartacus the gladiator would probably have freed the lions. And then tied torches to their tails and burned down Rome a century early.

Anyone who thinks goats are less destructive than lions on fire does not know goats well.

In any case. We inside the dairy shed knew nothing of it until the shouting started. It turned out the nanny goats had nosed the gate open and were heading for the melon patch. Now, among the Children of Peace, melons are almost everyone's favorite, because of the way they have to be eaten as fast as they come in. There is no rationing of sweetness in melon season. So everyone who was out was keen to protect the patch. They were shouting and shooing. The cohort of fourteen- and fifteen-year-olds, who'd been waging war with the quackweed in the newly planted kale beds, picked up their hoes and headed over at the quick march, as orderly as a Roman legion.

Unfortunately for the might of Rome, it was at that point that Bonnie Prince Charlie, the school's lone and indescribably smelly billy goat, up in his pen by the induction spire, got it into his head to join his harem.

Even Rome never conquered Scotland, and there is no stopping Charlie when he's motivated. The nannies were out, the melons were waiting, people were shouting—what was a billy to do? He butted at the old gate until it splintered, and then he scrambled over the wreck and loped down the hill toward us.

And then—

It was hard to keep track. The billy goat came down like a wolf on the fold. Elián dashed sideways to the melon patch to cut him off. He scooped up a green watermelon that must have weighed as much as a cannon ball, hoisted it over his head, and, with a wild rebel yell, threw it at Bonnie Prince Charlie. The projectile had deadly accuracy and speeds approaching escape velocity. It hit Charlie between the eyes. The goat made a rude *blart*, paused to consider the matter, and then keeled over.

Cheers erupted. One of the fourteen-year-olds threw an overripe cantaloupe at a nanny goat. There was an orange splat.

At that point things started to get out of hand.

Someone—several someones—began throwing melons at the nannies. Charlie staggered to his feet, and a dozen more melons, two zucchini, and a tomato converged on him.

The tomato, it turned out, was from Elián. He'd moved through the melons and was standing in the patchy shade of the tomato trellises, where late-season tomatoes were falling from the vines faster than we could harvest them. I saw him pick one up, juices dripping down his white sleeves. I saw him aim it at me. I saw him throw.

If I had pigtails, he'd probably pull them, I thought, instead of ducking. The tomato splatted into my ear.

There came, then, a moment like a hinge.

It was not that a hush fell. There was plenty of chaos, and plenty of noise from the goats. Elián himself was holding on to one of the trellis uprights, bent over with what I hoped was laughter, and not pain. Nevertheless I was aware of eyes on me. Aware, though I hardly had time to think it, that I was being asked by my colleagues to make a decision.

Da-Xia caught my eye—the goddess of the mountain, spreading joy and destruction, was hefting a zucchini. She threw it at me. I threw up a hand, shouting "Xie!" And the zucchini hit my hand and broke into pieces, which rained down all over me. By instinct I grabbed a hunk and threw it back at her.

And with that, the famous dignity of the Children of Peace broke like a gate before goats. I chucked a bit of zucchini at Elián. It hit him between the eyes, and I laughed and laughed.

Is there any point in describing a food fight? We fought, using food. It was like the War Storms: intense small battles that deteriorated into hand-to-hand grappling, or spread into massive strategic engagements that took up half our population, most of our ammunition, and all of our dignity. I myself led the assault on the dairy, a doomed glory of a military set piece that would have done my Stuart ancestors proud. After all, they are more famous for losing battles than winning them.

In the end, though, none of it mattered. As they had during the War Storms, the machine intelligences decided it was time to save us from ourselves. The proctors came out.

We turned on them, pitching fruit and stones at them as if playing at pins. Someone even bowled over the big scorpion proctor with a butternut squash.

But the fun had gone out of things. A few shocks, distributed at random; the knowledge that we were watched; the fact that we had been raised better (or if not better, at least differently)—these overcame us. The Children of Peace could not easily be silly, and our silliness fell apart.

The evening found us bruised and quiet, spread out in groups or pairs on the spattered grass, eating our former ammunition—chunks of watermelon and muskmelon warmed by the bronze sun. Even this was unlike us—unstructured, un-rationed eating, outdoors. But we could not waste so much food. We scattered up and down the garden terraces; we lay in the goat-cropped grass and were happy.

For my part I claimed one of the best places in the Precepture—leaning up against the wall of the toolshed, hidden from the Panopticon's view. The grass there was less scorched. It was a sweeter, fresher place, a little oasis with a scent of wild clover. I was sitting cross-legged by myself when Elián came and flopped down beside me. He helped himself to one of the broken melons I'd gathered, and reclined on one elbow to eat it, like a Roman emperor. "Thanks," he said.

"There's plenty—though one might ask."

"Nah, I mean for letting that happen." He grinned up from his cantaloupe. "It's been a while since I had that much fun." Indeed he looked like a different person. His eyes were not guarded but gold-brown; his body was not hunched but held ready.

"I think a food fight falls under the heading of 'unavoidable low-intensity conflict,'" I said, then annotated: "That's an allusion. From the Utterances. 'There's a certain level of unavoidable low-intensity conflict about which I simply can't be bothered.'"

"'But don't bloody push it,'" said Elián, startling me by quoting the rest of the verse. My surprise must have shown, because Elián looked at me sourly. "I'm not actually an idiot, you know. If I got stuck on a desert island, my one book would definitely be *Why I Stuck You on This Desert Island, Signed, Your Insane Robot Overlord.* Of course I read Talis's damn book."

Our eyes caught each other's then, braced, fearful—but the proctors didn't shock him. They might technically have been intelligent, but they weren't sentient: they weren't people. They were bad with sarcasm.

I let out my breath. "I don't think it's Talis's book, exactly. He's merely quotable."

"Oh, yeah," he said, taking a big bite of melon. "For sure 'quotable' is the word that springs to mind."

I tried again: "I only meant, you don't have to thank me. The food fight—you started it."

"The *goat* started it," he said. "But you, Greta—you could have stopped it."

"I don't know about that. It seemed to have quite a bit of momentum."

"Seriously?" Elián wiped the melon juice off his chin with the back of his hand. "You study power and you don't know who's got it around here? Let me clue you in, Princess. It's you."

And *there* was the electric shock. After getting away with the crack about Talis, Elián must have lowered his guard, because the pain surprised him. He jerked, his elbow slipped, and he fell backward. I dropped my watermelon and grabbed him in time to keep him from braining himself on a stone. I had no leverage to hold him, though. I laid him out on his back. "Elián?"

He didn't answer me. He let his head roll farther back, pointing his chin at the sky, baring his throat, letting his eyes drift closed, black lashes tangled. If the fetal position had an opposite, here it was. He was defenseless, utterly. I could see the pulse in the soft places of his throat.

It made something wring, twist like a damp cloth deep inside me.

All my life I had been so careful, so protected, so *braced*, and here he was, open and . . . and . . .

I could not think what the "and" was. For once, it was not "foolish."

"Well, fiddle," he said. "Couldn't they have let that last?"

Another twist inside me, because I agreed. I agreed with him.

"Was it you, who bowled down the big proctor?" I said. "I—I hope it was you."

Elián didn't answer. Perhaps he did not understand how much it meant for me to say that, to side with disorder. He picked up a piece of melon and lifted it in both hands, studying its peaks and watersheds. "All this fuss over me." He rolled his head farther back and gave me an upside-down smile. "I swear, back home I was nobody."

"Come now. Wilma Armenteros's grandson, a nobody? The woman is a legend in sensible shoes."

"Yeah, but my mom kept me way clear of all that. I stuck pretty close to *nobody*."

"And you were no trouble to anyone, I'm sure." I scooted around so he wouldn't have to hurt his neck to talk to me.

"Weeeeell," he drawled, drawing it out and rolling open a sly smile to match. "Maybe a spot of trouble. Here and there."

"Here and there," I said, trying for prim, and missing

it. I sat looking down at him.

He rested the melon on his belly and examined me. His eyes were guarded again, and I knew—just *knew*—that he was about to do something deeply inadvisable. "What about you? You ever . . . run off? Get into trouble?"

"Rarely." I hit prim that time. I hit it squarely.

"Would you?"

"Would I what?"

His eyes were serious. Even frightened. But his voice came out sweet as peaches. "Run off with me."

"Elián, away from this place I am a duchess. Any outing we planned would involve protocol officers."

He laughed—a fake laugh?—and glanced sideways.

He was checking the sight lines.

I knew those lines far better than he did. I knew that the Panopticon was hidden behind the wall of the shed. It could not see our faces. I did not need to turn and look to be sure, and yet, out of pure nerves, I turned and did just that. Because I suddenly knew what Elián was up to. He wasn't flirting with me at all. Or maybe he was, but also, this talk of running away . . .

He had learned to speak in Precepture code. He was speaking in it now. And he was proposing an escape.

The Panopticon couldn't see him, couldn't read his lips. The little spiders in his clothes could hear him, but they couldn't peel away his layers of meaning.

"We've got that one date coming up, though," he said. "With a . . . protocol officer."

With a Swan Rider. With sick tightness I remembered her: a gentle white woman with a chickadee cap of dark hair. She would walk into our classroom. She would say both our names. . . .

"When?" I said—because this was what I'd wondered from the first instant I'd seen him. Did he know he was going to die, or only guess it? Did he know *when*?

The word had torn out of me with too much raw power. I saw a proctor in the squash bed swivel round and scan us. I smiled politely for it, for Elián, as if flattered. My cheeks trembled in the smile. "We do," I said. "We have a date."

"It's coming up fast, you know."

"Is it?"

Did he know?

My hands were sticky with watermelon juice. I rubbed them against the rough linen of my work pants.

Elián reached up and took one of my wrists, stopping the motion, looking me up and down. I'm sure he was trying for *as a man looks at a woman*, but it came off rather more *as an engineer looks at a bridge pylon*. How much fear would it take for Elián's flirt to go wrong like that? A lot, I thought.

Terrified. He's terrified.

"So, what d'ya think?" he said. "Up for . . . a spot of trouble?"

Escape. Will you come with me?

I took a breath and said: "No."

He looked blankly shocked, even betrayed.

But surely he must realize—the Preceptures were

inescapable. We were isolated, outgunned, overwhelmed. Surely he must realize what happened to people who challenged Talis.

"No," I said. "Elián, we can't. You can't."

"No?" he said, in a voice more stones than peaches. "Just watch me."

Instead of answering I tightened my hand around his. He squeezed back. And then—awkwardly, because of our joined hands—I lowered myself to lie down in the clover next to him.

We lay there as evening folded in around us.

We did not speak.

8

ROYAL VISIT

I t is perhaps a strange thing that the children of kings and presidents should concern themselves with the sex lives of a herd of milch goats, but come the end of August, it was time to do just that.

If one had to sum up the Precepture in two words, they might be "hands on." (One might also consider "academic rigor," or perhaps "ritual murder.") The whole world is more hands-on that once it was. On the whole, we humans have learned the hard way that we must become a permanent culture, a zero-carbon culture, and live on the earth without damaging it. (About time, people, said the Utterances. I can't save the world by myself, you know.) Even so, things do vary by class. My royal cousins—those little countesses and wee marquees in their royal pleats and tartans—probably can't put up their own pickles.

If one of them comes here as a regent's hostage, they will be in for a rude shock.

The Preceptures may be home to rulers, but they are also models of environmental rationalism, examples to the world. To that end, the Children of Peace grow our own food and keep chickens and goats. In the Precepture barns, many a young prince has learned the facts of life. Such as: there's no need for more than one rooster. Or one billy goat. They are (respectively) noisy and smelly, and left to their own devices, they fight for dominance. So, like Talis himself, we kill the troublemakers.

But the fly in the ointment of this ancient system is inbreeding. Go more than two generations with only one billy goat, and you will regret it. Therefore, in earliest September, we inject some fresh blood—or, rather, other vital fluids—into the system, through the services of a billy goat from a different herd. Someone, generations back, decided that this grand event should be known as the Royal Visit.

Fall is the breeding season for goats in any case, but to bring all the nannies into estrus in the right week, we hedge our bets. Ampoules of goat pheromones come in our yearly supply shuttle, with our clothing, salt, medicine, paper, and the handful of other things we cannot make for ourselves. The pheromones are of two kinds. We snap open the thin glass tubes of Essence of Billy Goat and apply it to a buck rag, which can be simply rubbed around the face of the nannies. This is a smelly business, but is nevertheless the better half of the job. The other half, a synthetic hormone, must be applied, shall we say, internally. From the other end. Put it this way: hormone day is not the highlight of our year.

So. There came a day when Elián had a goat named Bug Breath in a headlock, and I was applying the hormonal cream, wrist deep in something I imagine princesses of old got to miss. Da-Xia and Han were working on another goat, beside us. Atta and Thandi had lost control of their goat and were chasing it through the toolshed—I could hear the banging— and Grego allegedly had a headache.

Just watch me, Elián had said. I'd been watching him. To escape from the Precepture . . . one might as well think of escaping from a ship at sea. It would fail, and whatever followed, I was sure, would be slow-thirst terrible.

I should stop him, I knew that. But I did not.

I also did not turn him in.

In the silence of my heart I considered what that meant. Once I would have gone to the directly to the Abbot. I'd have turned Elián in without thinking twice. But I had held his hand in the evening light since then. I had watched his pulse move in his bared throat since then.

I had changed.

I wanted to talk to Xie about it, or even Thandi—if anyone understood the risks Elián was running in attempting an escape, it would surely be Thandi. But I could not think of how to code it. So I stayed silent, and afraid.

Meanwhile, though, Elián treated me as if I had betrayed him. He was stiff, angry. Even now, with the goat locked— shall we call it intimately?—between us, he spoke mostly to Da-Xia, asking her question after question as if to shut out any possibility of silence. I could not believe he needed to know why we planned to breed half the goats exogamously—he was a sheep farmer, after all. But Xie explained inbreeding anyway. Elián asked why the two breeding groups needed to be kept separate. Xie answered that goats have an intricate pecking order and disrupting it is stressful for them.

It was not right for him to treat me as if I were not there, so I pushed into the conversation: "Don't sheep have a pecking order?"

There was a second when I thought he'd ignore me. But he managed a brittle smile. "Nah, sheep are so dumb, they get lost in an empty field. You don't get a lot of what you'd call rich social interaction, with sheep."

Da-Xia, shot him a sly look. "Well, Elián, it's a relief to hear that."

An insult, with its hint of sexual impropriety, but Elián only laughed—genuinely, contagiously, and at his own expense.

We finished our goat and Elián snagged another by her horns. He made that look easy, but it wasn't. Han was having trouble. Xie took the moment to rock back on her heels and stretch her spine into an arch. Then she rolled her shoulders forward and cracked out the joints in her fingers. She was— we all were—sweaty and dusty and besmeared with things not pleasant to remark on. "So," Xie said. "Royalty, Elián. How are you liking it?"

"Still not a prince, Xie. But this is fun, I've got to admit it. I could do this all day." He put the goat—it was Bat Brain, our tree climber—into a headlock and wrestled her to her knees.

His tabi-toes curled dusty earth; the muscles in his shoulders rose and rounded. I did not want him to die.

The laughter earlier, or the sheer physicality of the moment, had knocked some of the anger out of Elián. "Where do we get this goat prince from, anyway?"

"It varies," said Xie.

And I added, "Most of the remnant populations across Saskatchewan keep goats. Light pastoral use is one of the better ways to live off the land in a near desert. We usually get our visiting bucks from the salvage teams—from Saskatoon or Regina, sometimes as far away as Moose Jaw."

"You sound exactly like a textbook, do you know that?" he said. "It's amazing."

"It's—" It was powerful, was what it was. It was a mask. It could hide almost anything.

For instance, a warning.

"There are probably more goats than people in Saskatchewan," I said. "There are the salvage teams in the cities, and the nomadic bands of Cree ecosystem repair engineers on the high prairies, but no one else. Saskatchewan is big and it's empty. And without resources and expertise, it could kill you."

"In three to five days, I'd say," added Xie. Lightly. I could swear I hadn't let my voice slip from behind its textbook mask, and yet I could feel Da-Xia's sudden and enveloping attention. She knew exactly what I was doing.

Han didn't. "Three to five days until what?" he asked.

"Until one runs out of water, most likely." I could not help but glancing at Elián's face as if glancing at the Panopticon. His mouth was stiff and tight. I looked back down quickly. Elián's knee was visible past the heaving side of the goat—his knee, and the twitching lump that was a spider under his clothes. I knew it would be listening. I knew I was at the edge—the barest edge—of what I could possibly say. "Saskatchewan was always marginal, but after the big shift it dried up radically, and the Pan Polar government decided to move the entire population. We diked the mouth of James Bay and let the rivers turn it into a new Great Lake—and the Hudson Shore into a new breadbasket. It is a well-studied model of the rational use of resources."

My voice was level but I was pleading with him. Stop. Think. Don't do this. Please don't do this.

"Rational—" Elián's voice cracked. Without warning he let the goat go and stood up. Bat Brain threw herself backward and kicked out with her hind feet like a war-trained stallion. I had to free my hand, so my dodge came almost too late, and had no grace: I ended up sprawled on my back. The goat took off. Elián towered over me, and the Panopticon loomed behind him. "I'm so sick of rational. Tell me something rational, Princess Greta. Will your mother let you die?"

Flat on my back in the dust, I answered him, "Of course."

Through the next few days that "of course" was a blister on the inside of my mouth. Elián ignored me and I ignored him. Even as the nannies came into heat—one could tell because they grew louder than roosters and started to sexually assault the water barrels—I found myself thinking those words, replaying that moment.

Replaying Elián asking what he had no right to ask, what no Precepture child ever asked another. *Will your mother let you die?*

Mine would. Of course she would.

She would be grief-stricken. She would hesitate. She would go to war only if all other options failed. The Preceptures *worked*. They made the have-not states reluctant to start wars to get what they needed; they made the have states reluctant to refuse reasonable demands. *Think of it as incentivizing negotiations,* said the Utterances. *Think of it as putting a little skin in the game.*

But I had been to Lake Erie. It was little more than a marsh, reedy and loud with blackbirds, dotted with the mines that reclaimed the heavy metals that had once settled at the bottom of the polluted lake. When it was a lake.

My mother would not let that happen to Lake Ontario. I knew she wouldn't. She had been born to a crown, and she had learned a crown's cold courage. She would be appropriately reluctant, but if the Cumberlanders did not back down, she would not accede to their demands. She would let me die.

Of course.

And of course, too, Elián had been up to something, with that string of questions about goats. He'd been fishing for information about the Royal Visit.

That year's visit was by a salvage family out of Saskatoon,

trommellers who sorted the rubble of the abandoned city with the aid of rotating drums the size of houses—the trommels for which they were named.

The trommellers and their Royal Visitor came on the first day of September. My cohort happened, by good luck, to be up at Bonnie Prince Charlie's pen on the ridge top, moving the fences to encompass fresh grazing. We could see the open prairie from there.

Rising from it was a plume of dust.

Grego spotted it first—and froze, his iris implants snapping shut.

Han took his arm. "Don't be scared." No one else would have implied that Grego was scared, but Han did it easily, blandly. "It will be the Royal Visit."

And it was. We watched the group slowly come into view from the dust, a loose band of walkers driving goats before them with long sticks. They were a strange sight to eyes accustomed to the ranks and sorting of the Precepture— men and women and children, all strolling together. As they came closer, we could see that they all had their heads and faces wrapped against the dust; we could see their long coats made of scraps of colorful cloth, and adorned with flashing bits of metal that made them look, from a distance, like sparkle on water.

We stood together in our hostage whites and watched them.

Meanwhile, Bonnie Prince Charlie. The old billy was nearly mad from the smell of the nannies, and enraged by the whiff of the approaching Royal Visitor. The slot-shaped pupils of his eyes were wide as the doors of hell, and his horns were draped with the remnants of things he'd tried to destroy—bailing wire from the gate, alfalfa from the feed trough, a skewered hunk of zucchini. *Grah!* he shouted. I was sure it was goat for *Die, infidel!*

The visitors came almost within hailing distance. About twenty of them. A woman—the grandmother or great-grandmother, I supposed—and a range of adults, teenagers, children, all together, and arranging themselves just as they liked. They were driving a dozen nannies to be bred with Charlie. The billy—the Royal Visitor himself—had a special escort, a stocky young woman who held him on a lead. Charlie caught wind of the does. *Grooouuu*, he moaned. (Goat for *Hubba, hubba!*)

The trommeller family came to a particular stone, and they stopped.

"Why are they stopping?" asked Elián, but in the next moment we could see why. The thing that I'd taken for a stone was a ball of proctors, all tangled together like hibernating snakes. They swarmed apart, a couple dozen of them, mostly of the smaller kind. The visitors put down their gear. The proctors poked and sniffed and climbed into bags. Nursery spiders, like the kind that tormented Elián, climbed up the people themselves.

"They're being searched for contraband," said Han.

"Yeah, suppose that's smart," said Elián. "Think of what one good pipe bomb could do to this place."

The next second, of course, he was on his knees—shocked, but still rather misty-eyed with the thought of pipe bombs.

Out among the visitors, one of the adult women had a baby bound to her back. While we watched, a nursery spider climbed up the outside of the papoose board and perched on the baby's head. It was presumably scanning, though from this distance that could only be inferred. Thandi looked away, and Da-Xia looked sick. To be honest, the whole business struck me, too, as intrusive and excessive. They had only come to breed goats. Elián climbed back to his feet and expressed his unease with a slow drawl. "Gosh. Do you think we're safe here?"

"The Preceptures are safe," said Han. What a handicap, in this place, to be bad with subtext. "Talis defends them. Remember Kandahar."

"It is hard to forget," said Grego, deadpan, though there was no joke. Truly, we remembered Kandahar. Two hundred years ago, a nation called the Kush had struck against Precepture Seven in an attempt to fetch back their young hostage king. Talis had responded by erasing their capital from orbit. There was not a stick left of Kandahar, not a single survivor.

Shouldn't take an oracle to interpret that one, said the Utterances. *These children are* mine. *Touch them and people will be talking about you for centuries.*

Grouuuuuu, Charlie howled, and the Royal Visitor sounded his trumpet: *Graaallll!* The woman holding the visiting billy took a few stumbling steps forward as the goat surged—and the lead broke.

The Royal Visitor was a good-size animal, a black buck with white blazing, and fine curved horns. He took off for us with his head down, fast. Bonnie Prince Charlie bellowed, Han yelped, Grego grabbed Han, Thandi shouted, Xie raised her hands as if in divine dismissal, Atta stepped in front of Xie, and Elián—well, Elián, of course, gave an earsplitting yell and ran forward. He caught the Royal Visitor in a flying tackle. Goat and boy and proctors went spinning in a tumbleweed of black and white.

When the dust cleared, Elián was sitting on the goat's back, with his hands tight around one horn. He was sporting a bruised eye and a ridiculous grin, and laughing.

With his heroic credentials as goat-catcher firmly in place, Elián introduced himself to the family of trommellers, and was shortly fast friends with them. That evening saw them sitting together in the refectory, where Elián did a routine about the differences between sheep and goats that had our visitors—frightened and subdued as they were, to be caught in the strangeness of the Precepture—laughing into their roasted cauliflower. The old woman had a laugh that ended with a snort like a deer blowing. Uncivilized, certainly, but a free and wild sound. She laughed until she had to push her plate away and lay her head on the table.

We lingered over dessert—we children did not often have visitors who had not come to kill us, so we had the urge to feed them well, though it would mean later reduced rations of honey—and Elián's conversation grew deeper and quieter. I could not get close enough to hear, because the trommellers were in awe of me. To them I wasn't just a hostage. I was the daughter of their queen. The adults kept glancing at me with reverence and a kind of knowing pity. One of the little ones had actually curtsied, spreading her bright and tattered skirts. When she called me princess, it sounded like a thing to be cherished.

So I was reduced to watching them from across the room. I noticed that Elián's hair was growing out. It made small curls at his collar and behind his ears. *Don't do anything stupid*, I thought, trying to beam the thought at him. Though, frankly, it seemed too much to ask.

Xie saw my gaze, and gave me a smile I could not quite read—Was it indulgent? Sad? She took my hand, and drew me out of the refectory and then out of the Precepture hall altogether. The sun was setting and the full moon was coming up in the east, over the river.

We were almost out of time.

Elián was going to try to escape. I was sure of it. And I was sure they'd catch him. Sure they'd hurt him, and not only him.

"It's strange in there, tonight," said Xie. "It's strange to see people bow to you."

"The little one was so sweet. But the adults—they look at me as if I'm a sacrificial virgin."

"Well, now that you mention it . . ."

Xie caught my eye and suddenly we were both laughing,

for a moment forgetting all about the Panopticon, about Elián, about the thirst of Cumberland and the coming war— about everything. These dark thoughts came back only slowly, and even then they seemed lighter.

Xie walked along the top of the stone wall between the lawn and the lower terraces—walked in the air with her hands outspread, a mountain child, a mountain god. It was a warm evening, ruffled with breezes, beaded with lightning bugs. At the end of the wall she reached down for my help, and I reached up to help her. She swung down on my hand. Her fingers wrapped around mine, and hand in hand we picked our way along the edge of the lawn. "You know," she said, "if you are concerned, we could probably find a way to deal with the 'virgin' part."

I blinked at her.

"I'm sure there would be volunteers." Her voice was warm, but there was something freezing up in her face. I could usually tell what she was thinking, but not now. "Elián—inside, you were watching him."

And she knew why. I'd felt her attention swing around me on hormone day, when I'd tried to warn Elián: Saskatchewan will kill you. The Precepture cannot be escaped.

I could think of nothing to say to her now, nothing that was safe. "I was, I guess. I was watching him." *Help me, Xie. What should we do?*

"Elián, Elián," mused Xie. "He's compelling, I'll give him that. And you have no idea what to do with a compelling boy, do you?"

"Yes I do," I protested.

"You do?"

"I don't know why people assume classicists are prudes," I said. "The Roman lyricists, in particular, can be quite bawdy."

Xie made a little noise in her throat, like a dove. "As it happens, I wasn't thinking of your reading material."

We came to the end of the wall. Xie sat down on the round back of a stone and hugged her knees to her chest. I sat beside her, and glanced at the Panopticon. Its lifted sphere was still lit pink by the sun, though on the ground, shadows were gathering. Let it think we were talking about boys. We were—but also, we weren't.

Xie brushed the hair out of her face. "Do you remember Denjiro?"

I did; of course I did. Denjiro had been in one of the older cohorts when Xie and I were smaller. His country had been slipping toward war, as mine was now, and he had . . . He'd used a pitchfork to do it. There had been a lot of blood.

"We're all running," said Xie. "Sometimes we fall."

"If Elián—" But there was no safe way to say it. If he ran away . . .

Denjiro. The popular theory, vis-à-vis the pitchfork, was that he'd planted it tines-up in the watermelon beds, climbed onto a terrace wall like the one we were on now, and then—

We were all running. Denjiro had fallen.

If Elián ran away . . . I could not say that aloud, but I

could trust Xie to follow the jump of my thought. "If he does, it will be terrible."

Terrible for him. Terrible for all of us.

For a moment Xie just sat there, watching the moon, the breeze off the river making strands of her hair dance above the mass of it, like the plume of snow off a mountain. "Still. It is his to do."

And it was.

He was going to die. He deserved a chance to do it on his terms. No matter what it cost us.

9
HANNAH'S SHOES

We came to the day on which the trommellers were
due to leave.

Elián was there at breakfast. He was looking at his food
as if it were an algebra test—equal parts concentration and
desperation. He had his head tipped down and his eyebrows
knotted up and his free hand in a fist on his knee. It was not
the world's most inviting posture. We were all afraid to touch
him, lest he snap at us, or shatter.

When the bell rang to send us out into the gardens, he
got up with a huge scrape of bench on floor. I saw him take
three apples from the bowl by the door.

He strode out in front of everyone.

I took Xie's hand and we followed him. Her fingers were
tight. We were both afraid.

But by the time we reached the gardens, Elián was
nowhere in sight.

The trommellers were taking down their tents, packing up their bags. There were not so many of them, and yet there seemed in those moments to be a thousand. And my fellow hostages, too, seemed multiplied. There were children helping our visitors, children tending to the trommellers's goats, children just stealing a moment to sit in the shade as the day began to open and blaze.

Where on most days I could have seen at one glance that there were seven of us, and we were all where we should be, on this particular day it was hopeless.

It was Elián's perfect chance, and I knew he'd take it.

Still, I looked at each face and hoped I would find him. Hoped at the same time that I would not find him. Hoped that he had taken something better than three apples.

The trommellers were wrapping their heads, pulling on their smoked goggles, shrugging on their coats and packs. I looked at them one after another, but I did not find Elián. Slowly things were settling, the trommellers gathering together, and the Children of Peace finding their groups. Slowly it was becoming clear: Elián was gone.

"Where is he?" hissed Thandi.

We were gathering baskets from the toolshed, going out to pick apples. The six of us. It was now spotlight-obvious that we were only six. Thandi had squeezed out the question while in the shelter of the lintel, but it still made all of us sneak looks at the Panopticon, checking the sight lines.

"It doesn't matter if they see me ask," said Thandi. "Do

you really think they haven't noticed he's gone?"

"But where is he?" said Han.

"None of us know," I answered. For surely if Elián had not (quite) told me, he would not have told anyone.

Han looked puzzled, Grego frightened, Thandi furious—another of our prefabricated moments. We were pressed together, tightly knotted in the doorway, as if that would protect us. We knew it wouldn't, but it was hard not to hope.

"We should get the Abbot," said Han, even as Thandi said: "We should turn him in."

"That would not spare us," said Grego.

And Da-Xia turned her face to the open air and said, "Let him have whatever time he has."

As she said it, bells started to ring overhead, tolling like disaster, like fire, like a call to arms.

"Yeah, time's up," said Thandi.

"Indeed," said the Abbot, coming around the corner. "If you would all come with me." He made his mouth curl up a little, a cool parody of a smile. "We have a guest."

The Abbot had us sit on the lawn. The trommellers were nowhere in sight, but they had to be around—the Royal Visitor was eating our watermelons. Proctors were herding the rest of the Children of Peace inside. It was high morning. The sun beat down. The bells stopped, and still we sat there, motionless. My stomach felt tight and sick. The Abbot stood in front of us with his hands folded. No one said anything.

Then, suddenly, movement. One of the trommellers came stumbling toward us, across the lawn. At her heels was the big scorpion proctor. We could see from the way she leapt and staggered that it was herding her with electricity—pushing her along as if she were a goat.

She came up to us, panting. Her eyes were wide and her mouth was pulled open in pure fear. "I didn't do anything!" she gasped. "I didn't!"

"This is Hannah," said the Abbot mildly, and mostly to us. "It seems Hannah is missing her shoes."

We looked at Hannah's feet. They were bare. And big, for girl's feet.

"I didn't, I didn't. Please—" begged the child. She was our age, but without our training she did seem a child. There were fresh little blisters up and down her bare ankles—electrical point burns.

"You are missing your shoes, and I in turn am missing a hostage," said the Abbot. "It seems an odd coincidence, Hannah." He was looking not at Hannah, but directly at us.

I looked at my own feet, clad in their tabi. Finally, finally, I saw the point of tabi: one could not go far with so little protection for one's feet.

"What else is missing, I wonder," said the Abbot. "Wipe your nose, Hannah, dear. I need an inventory."

"Father Abbot," said Xie tentatively. The proctor lashed out at her, making her cry out and lean backward, breathless. No kind, brave words would be sparing anyone this time.

The proctor minced forward, pushing itself into the skirts of Hannah's traveling coat. One of its multi-jointed arms lifted the coat aside, then insinuated itself around her ankle, wrapping it like a cuff. The girl stood, frozen and shaking. From where we sat at her feet, we could see the urine stain spreading down one leg. "Now, Hannah, do try to think," said the Abbot. The grip of the proctor was growing tighter. Tighter. "There aren't so many of you that you don't know. What else is missing? Water skins? Packs? A map?"

"We didn't help him!" screamed Hannah.

"I—" began the Abbot, and then stopped, as if something had tapped him on the shoulder. There was, in fact, nothing in sight. "Stand up, Children," he said. "There's something Talis wants you to see."

Xie's wide eyes reflected mine.

Don't let him be dead. I could feel my stomach climbing up my throat.

Don't make us watch you kill him.

"Come now," said the Abbot. "You'll miss it."

And what else could we do? We got up.

At the Abbot's direction, we stood in a line, as if for a firing squad. We faced the open prairie, south and west.

Nothing happened, and nothing. And then—the sound of nightmares. A flash and crash bigger than lightning. A sizzle as if the air itself were on fire. Orbital weapons fire.

I had never heard it in life. None of us had. But of course we knew it, from a thousand vids. It was iconic. It was history. It was *here.*

Thandi jerked backward, crashing into me, and Gregori actually hit the ground, putting his hands over his head. A second strike came: light, then a split second later the crack-boom. The light was the eerie Cherenkov blue radiated by the accelerated particles. It flashed, brief and blinding, and when our eyes cleared, we could see the column of cloud rising, arrow-straight, all the way to the edge of space.

First a light and then a cloud—a pillar of cloud by day.

The next thing we knew, the gantry spiders from the induction spire could be seen swarming downward, striking out for the impact point.

Elián. Of course it was Elián. We all knew it. Knew it even before they brought him back over the ridge, dressed like a trommeller and walking tall in Hannah's shoes.

"There we are," said the Abbot. "Thank you, Hannah. Let your parents know we'll be in touch." The proctor stepped backward, and the trommeller child bolted.

The Abbot watched her go out of sight, and then turned to us, one degree at a time, like a ratchet. He smiled. "Well, then, my children. Isn't this an interesting glimpse of history? Shall we go have a look?"

None of us wanted to have a look. None of us dared say so. Our little execution-neat line had bunched up—the great noise of the orbital weapon had us all clutching at each other. Han was helping Grego off the ground.

"Come then," said the Abbot, and lifted a hand. Proctors seemed to melt out of the walls and swarm all around us. "It should be instructive."

So we went—six children in white, following an old, creaking robot who was finding the path with a stick. It probably looked idyllic from a distance. If you couldn't see the machines that swarmed in the deep grass around us, scaring up the grasshoppers on all sides.

We followed the way the trommellers had come, a faint road through the waist-high prairie. The grasses were sere and stiff with end-of-summer heat, and the buffalo berry and sagebrush branches were thorn-sharp. They scratched our wrists, the backs of our hands. The rough ground pressed through the thin soles of our tabi.

A hundred meters, two hundred—as far from the Precepture as any of us had ever been. Three hundred meters, and then the track ended.

In front of us a crater opened, a shallow bowl of bare earth, a thousand feet wide. Heat still rose from it: it smelled like a kiln.

Spilled down into it, as if dropped from the edge, were three apples.

We stood at the crater edge. Thandi was closest to me, and she was shivering—waves of trembling were coming off her skin, like the ripples in the air above the impact site.

What Elián had done, so publicly—our cohort would be punished for it. When? Where? How? This crater, so strange, so hot, so full of possibilities. It could be *instructive*.

And it was different. Different from anything we were used to. Different from anything we had practiced. Different from anything we knew we could endure. Thandi was not alone in shivering with terror.

But the Abbot did nothing.

The Abbot. My teacher and protector, as dear to me

as—as— I could think of no comparison. He would never hurt me. Had never hurt me.

Though presumably he had ordered me hurt.

He had spoken to Hannah as if he were fond of her.

And he had spoken to Talis, in the silence of his elaborate mind.

Said the Utterances, *These Children are mine.*

We stood beside the crater in silence, trembling in the heat. Then we went back to the Precepture. Elián was nowhere to be found.

In the dispatches, later, I read that Talis had demanded blood from the trommellers for interfering, and that the family had elected to surrender not Hannah but the old woman.

It is only royalty who turn over their children.

10
GRETA CHOOSES

The punishment we'd been expecting came the next day, before Elián was even returned to us. It was, as such things usually were, very simple. The windows wouldn't open. Atta tried them once, twice, then turned to us with an eloquent shrug. The classroom door slid closed of its own accord.

Heat it was to be, then. Not the blistering heat and strange fumes of the crater—not what we'd feared—but heat nonetheless. Well. We'd survived that before. The temperature was already creeping up when Brother Delta shambled in. Without comment he launched into a discussion of the use of ritual in limiting wars.

There is a sense in which war is nothing but ritual: the magical change of blood into gold or oil or water. There have been whole cultures whose notion of war was not much different from their notion of religion, or of sport. The Aztec

Flower Wars, for example, were century-long rituals whose intent was to produce prisoners for religious sacrifice. When the Spanish came, they thought the Aztecs were savages because the Flower Wars had not resulted in wholesale death.

An odd notion of savagery.

Talis had pushed us back toward the Aztecs, insisting, for instance, on limiting the effective range of weapons to a hundred yards. *I'm talking handguns, crossbows,* said the Utterances. *Hell, bring back broadswords—those were cool. If you want blood, then I want it all over your hands.*

While the room heated slowly, we discussed the emotional differences between hand-to-hand combat and what was once called "the morality of altitude"—the ability of pilots and drone operators to kill tens of thousands of people without looking any one of them in the eye. Which was more savage?

Talis's first rule of war: make it personal.

My hands were damp with the heat. I wiped them down my thighs.

The ritualization of war is an inexhaustible topic. The lecture went on for hours—all morning. The heat lapped around us like an incoming tide. Da-Xia pulled her feet up and tucked herself into a half lotus. That didn't look as if it were going to help.

The bells rang, but Brother Delta did not even pause. We watched the younger children file out into the gardens as he pushed the discussion toward hostages specifically. Tokugawa Ieyasu, first Tokugawa shogun of Japan, had spent his childhood as a hostage. As young princes, Vlad the Impaler and his brother had been held hostage by the Ottoman sultan to guarantee the cooperation of their father.

"Oh, yes," said Grego. "And this worked out so well. History remembers him as 'the Impaler' only because he invented the shish kebab."

"Really?" said Han.

Atta—from Vlad's part of the world—very nearly made a noise.

"Stop it," barked Thandi. "Stop it, it's not funny." She was sheened with sweat, and she kept looking at Elián's empty desk as if to set it on fire with her eyes. A proctor climbed up and perched there, and Thandi turned away. There was another proctor on the ceiling, and a pair by the door.

The jokes flagged.

The heat rose.

Brother Delta called on me for a précis of the Roman tradition of hostages, which was extensive. The Romans took hostages by the herd—the thousand noble children of the Achaeans, for instance, during the war against Perseus of Macedonia. These had included the historian Polybius, whose father—

But I found myself breathing through my mouth, trying to keep cool. Polybius, who—

I could not remember.

Atta swiped his sleeve across the fogged-up window and sucked at the moisture in his cuff. The sun had swung westward and was now pouring onto his desk, and Gregori's.

Grego was pink, the capillaries in his skin standing out cruelly. His eyes were snapping light-dark-light as he fluttered on the edge of consciousness.

Out the cleared swath of the window, I watched the twelve- and thirteen-year-olds pile the more overgrown of the zucchini into heaps to feed to the goats. On the day goats refuse to eat zucchini, we humans will have to give up all pretense of domination over the agricultural world. The squashes will have won.

For just a moment I could vividly imagine World War Squash.

Heat. I was slipping.

"Hostages," said Brother Delta, and then Gregori fainted. Atta—he was silent, but he wasn't stupid, and he could size things up as quickly as any of us, and react faster than anyone else except quick, graceful Xie. Atta slid out of his own chair and caught Grego on his way to the ground. He laid the body on the floor in front of the desks. Gregori's samue top was so wet with sweat that it left a dark mark on the grey stone floor. He looked so . . .

"Sit down, Atta," said Brother Delta.

Atta didn't. He crouched there, holding Grego's limp hand, his thumb fitted into the pulse point. How long would this last? Until we were all on the floor? Could Grego last that long? Han, too, was halfway out of his chair, his fist at his teeth, his face nakedly horrified, as if Grego were dying in front of us.

Dying. But surely they wouldn't—

I stood up.

I felt every eye turn to me.

"Brother Delta," I said.

Our teacher swiveled toward me. Aligned himself precisely. He did not widen his eye icons, as the Abbot would have done. He was focused on me and not a whisker of him was human. "Greta," the thing said.

"This has to stop," I answered.

Delta ticked. "Sit down, please, Greta." At my elbow, the proctor on Elián's desk raised itself slowly.

"This has to stop." I was too hot, too stunned, too sick to say anything else. But I didn't sit down, either. I stood firm even as the proctor stepped—click, click, click—toward me.

And then, suddenly, there was sound around me. Chairs scraping stone, cloth stirring.

Da-Xia, Thandi, Han. Atta pulling himself off the floor. Everyone—everyone had stood. All at once, everyone had stood.

"Children," said Brother Delta. Again there was no narrowing of the lips, no widening of the eyes. It had been terrifying a moment ago. Now it was like being scolded by a coatrack. "Children."

"Enough," snapped Thandi—and she turned and stalked out of the room. The door slid open for her, and stayed open.

The silence was stunning.

"Da-Xia," said Brother Delta after a moment. "Would you please go and see if Thandi is well?"

Da-Xia nodded, and then ran from the room with her

loosened sleeve points flapping. She moved like a figure out of myth—like something with wings.

Heat—my head was whirling. But the door stood open. Cool air eddied around our feet. The steamy windows cleared.

"Sit down, Children," said Delta.

No one did.

"I think that will do, Delta," The voice in the doorway made us turn. It was the Abbot, his facescreen dim, his eyes soft and thoughtful. "Children, if you'd help Mr. Kalvelis? It's your bell for gardening."

Atta scooped up Grego. And we didn't bow. We just left.

Han and I led the way to the gardens, and Atta carried Grego in his arms.

There was a hand pump by the toolshed: an ancient iron thing flecked with blood-red paint. We pumped up the earth-cool and rusty water; we drank and drank. We used our hands to rub the water over Grego, and slowly coaxed him back to life. We leaned him against the terrace, in its meager shade. And then—for what else could we do?—we planted garlic.

We were planting where we had harvested the potatoes. Where Elián had stood, and said: "I'm Spartacus." Where he had fallen, screaming.

But all day long, we did not see Elián.

Or Thandi. Or Xie.

Elián they had taken to punish, obviously. And Thandi,

who had gone out of the room like water bursting a levee. Of course they had taken Thandi. But Xie had done nothing. She was—not innocent, because we weren't, but innocent in this. They had taken Da-Xia because . . ..

I knew in my heart that they had taken her in my place. I had stood up when I should not have, and I needed to be slapped down. They'd taken Xie to hurt me, and hurt me they had.

And God knew what they were doing to her.

As soon as the bell rang to let us inside, I began to search. Da-Xia was not in the kitchens. The miseri was empty.

Desperate, I went to our cell, and there I found her, lying in bed, limp as if fevered.

"Xie!" The word came out of me as if I'd been struck in the stomach. I could have folded up, knotted myself around relief and terror both. But she looked at me blankly and said nothing. Her little braids were spread out on the UN-blue pillow, limp and dark. I sat down on my own cot. The cell was so small that I could reach for her hand, cot to cot. She didn't reach back, though. She wasn't looking at me. All our codes and connections had fallen away. I felt adrift.

"Xie?" I whispered.

Nothing.

The glass roof over us seemed to dial in, like a microscope head, coming closer. The origami cranes twitched in a draft I couldn't feel. The room was bright and hot and still. And my best friend lay as if dead.

The silence was too long, and too much. I leaned forward

and put my hand over hers. She still didn't stir, but she spoke—spoke as if to the ceiling. "Did you get the garlic in?"

"We did," I said. "Grego needed a bit of a rest, but he helped with the last tray." Da-Xia would be—normally would be—worried about Grego, whom she had last seen collapsed on the floor. I thought she would be relieved, but she did not even blink. "We missed you and Thandi." I was fishing for my own reassurances. "And Elián of course."

Da-Xia said nothing.

"Xie," I said, and heard my voice crack.

And then, finally, she spoke. Her voice was flat and plain. "A generation ago the Mountain Glacial States closed their southern reservoir gates and let what was left of Bangladesh vanish into a cholera storm. Two million people died. They didn't have enough water to keep their hands clean, and they *died*."

Her voice was like a mask with no face under it. "We did that," she said. "My father did that. He was nineteen years old."

I felt my chin come up and my throat tighten. It was a gesture of pride, but a feeling of fear.

"Cumberland is thirsty," she said. She was looking right at the Panopticon, and she was speaking far too plainly. "It's so cruel, thirst."

"Xie, stop." I slid forward and knelt beside her cot. The flagstones bruised my knees. "You have to stop."

"Sometimes I run away," she said.

"What?"

"Sometimes—I walk out the door and look at the brightest part of the sky until I can't see anything anymore. I get tired of seeing. So I run away."

She was speaking as if directly to the Panopticon.

"The sex is the same thing," she said. "Playing coyotes. I'm staring at the sun."

Suddenly Xie was speaking faster, her voice wobbling. "You think . . . I don't understand you, Greta. I don't know why you can't see it. Elián—he's not being taught. He's not being disciplined. He's being tortured."

"Da-Xia, stop." Desperate, I leaned forward, as if to cover her with my body, to come between her and the Panopticon, to give her that shelter. Though it would not be enough. There could be bugs anywhere. In the cracks of the stone. In our clothing. Our skin. "Come back, Xie."

"He's being tortured, Greta. Right in front of our eyes."

"I know that. I do know."

Though I hadn't. Not until I'd said it aloud.

"He's not even the first," she said. Close up, I could see she was weeping. "Do you know what they did to Thandi when she came here? They used dreamlock, they used drugs. And I can't stop seeing—"

Her hand was locked on mine. I lifted my other hand and wiped her tears away.

Da-Xia had eyes. She saw things.

But when I saw Thandi the next morning, she was the same as she'd ever been.

They used dreamlock, Xie had said yesterday. Of course, just because she had said it yesterday did not mean it had happened yesterday. It had been years ago. Still, I wondered how I had missed it. Was I truly so blind? I had been only ten when Thandi had been hostaged, but still: I could read Greek, at ten. Read Greek, and miss this? And now. Was there a little gel, maybe, in the hair around her temple?

But I stared at Thandi, and I swore she was unchanged.

And, finally, Elián.

Elián missed—was held through—lecture and lunch. It wasn't until after the third bell that he came out. The six of us were working just then under the pumpkin trellises, tying nets around the pumpkins so that they would not pull the vines down with their weight. I happened to glance around, and spotted Elián coming down the slope toward us.

I shot a look at Da-Xia, but she had her face raised to the sky. I turned back to Elián. *See him,* I said. *Look.* So I stopped working, and I watched him come.

There was something vulnerable about the way he walked, as if he were remembering how to do it, calling up each piece of the movement from the software. When he came under the trellis, he stopped. He stood there swaying.

I looked at him. He stared at me. "I like your hair," he said. His samue was undone, falling away from his breast-bone, flapping loose at his wrists.

"You should tie your shirt," said Han. "There are ticks."

Elián didn't seem to hear.

I could see the soft inside of his forearms; the faintest

of branching marks, ghosts of bruises where electricity had followed the nerves under his skin. This was more than what had happened to me, to all of us. This was more; this was different. And I had missed it. "Elián," I said. "Tie your shirt."

Elián nodded and fumbled with the tie at his wrist. Well, it is in truth hard to do—the trick is to use your teeth—but he failed and then simply stood there with the little strip of cloth in his hand. His top drooped open. I could see the indentations where the ribs joined his sternum, like thumbprints in clay. He'd lost weight.

Torture will do that, said a voice inside me. It was so—alien. The way I was just standing there. The voice in my head that did not seem my own. I felt as if I had been possessed. My known self was cold and small and still. Something larger and more wild had pushed it aside.

"Let me help you," the larger me said.

Elián stood like a little child and let me do up the ties at his wrists. And still he didn't move. So I reached inside the wrap of his samue to do the interior tie. My hands slipped over his ribs. His skin was hot and dry. The spider-proctors skittered over my fingers. But in a moment I had him dressed.

Elián let his head tip forward, until his cheekbone pressed against my temple. "I really do love your hair," he said.

Was he gone? Had his mind broken? Had I lost him before I had ever learned to see him? But even as I wondered, he lifted his hand and pressed it hard against my ear, turning his nose into my braids and crushing my head between his face and his hand. "It's too much," he whispered, into the hair he loved. "It's too much, Greta. They're going to kill me."

"I won't let them," I said. And I did not know what I had become, but I knew I meant it.

11
THE GRAY ROOM

Thus my heart began to turn against the only truth I'd ever known.

I felt it turn. I felt Elián's heartbeat pounding against mine as I held him. It was like holding a bird: he was so breakable, all tremble and pulse. I held him for as long as I dared—knowing the Panopticon was watching, knowing that eventually the proctors would come—and then I pulled my body away from his. I led him under the pumpkins and put a bit of netting in his hand.

He looked at it. He looked at me, his eyes bewildered.

Then he took a big, gulpy-shuddery breath and started to work.

He took some time to recover himself—for several hours his movements had a strange deliberate quality, as if he'd been struck blind. I wished he could rest, but it was impossible, and he knew it was impossible, and so he worked. We tied up the pumpkins. We harvested the first of the acorn squashes and the last of the muskmelons. We pulled up early leeks. We watered in yesterday's garlic. Through the whole afternoon nothing unusual happened, except that Elián kept his mouth shut and his proctors did not hurt him.

In the heat of the afternoon, we went inside—and there the Abbot stood waiting.

The transept was shadowy after the September blaze, an open, empty space, all stone, like a grand hall with no grandeur. In it the Abbot looked rather small, and rather out of place, a machine among all those hand-cut, human stones.

Elián saw the old AI and stopped short, his hand reaching for me. But Xie reached not for support but to support: she put her hand on the small of my back. Xie understood the Precepture better than Elián ever would, and she knew it was not Elián the Abbot was waiting for. It was me. When I had stood, the others had stood too. I had power. And I'd just promised to use it.

I looked at the Abbot, and my larger, wilder soul had the strangest thought. *He is afraid*, I thought. *He is afraid of me.*

I could feel the others draw closer: Thandi and Atta, Grego and Han, Elián gripping my hand, and Da-Xia at my back. They pulled closer like an honor guard—or like soldiers behind a king.

The Abbot was afraid of me. And he was right to be.

A proctor came up and tugged at the knee of my samue, its little claw hooked in the rough cloth. I held up a hand that said *Wait*, said *Peace*, said *The queen commands you.*

The others kept their place as I followed the proctor without a word.

The Abbot and the proctor led me to the miseri. It was a different room by day—brighter, harsher. It seemed to offer less shelter. The Abbot opened his hand—fingers ticking faint as beetles on glass—toward the classics section. One of the column bookcases . . . something had happened to it. Books spilled at its base, jumbled over themselves, some facedown and broken-spined.

There were no other Children in the heart room at that time of day. A few proctors were scuttling. A big one—surely it was Elián's scorpion proctor, with its distinctive heavy build and eye-gleam joints—was sorting through the fallen books. I told myself that its strength was needed, because some of the books were big.

"Greta, dear, sit down," said the Abbot.

I sank down. The memory cushion shaped itself to me and held me. The big proctor tapped nearer. Its iris snapped in and out as it looked me over.

The Abbot settled beside me. The bent stalk of his body made him look like a man with a stoop. "Dear child," he said. "Are you frightened?"

"Good Father," I answered. "Are you?"

He tipped his head a little. I think it was meant to convey surprise. "No. Merely . . . melancholy."

Surely he was not about to say he was disappointed in me. I might laugh in his face.

He looked at me and read at least some of that. "Ah, Greta," he said. "Greta, you know I am not supposed to have favorites. What you may not know is that you have embodied the ideals of this humble school as well as anyone else in three generations. You are the favorite I do not have, and so, I permit myself a personal question: Are you frightened?"

He sounded so sincere. It was leaching the wildness out of me. "Frightened?"

"I gather you are upset at how Mr. Palnik has been treated."

Sweat prickled on my back. "Somewhat, Father."

"Hmmmm," he said. Strong yellow light came through the tinted ceiling, showing the dappled oxides and tiny dents of his aluminum casing. Old. He looked old. He sighed, steepling his fingers. Unlike the proctors, his joints were no longer perfect; they made creaks and ticks. I wondered if they pained him. "I've pushed Elián, I admit. Perhaps I have even pushed him harder than I should. But, Greta, you have to understand. We have so little time."

So little time.

Last Christmas the queen my mother had commanded my portrait to be be painted. We had fought over the matter. I wanted to be painted in the white clothes of the Precepture, as is proper: the Children of Peace, around the world, are so depicted. The portraits of the sacrificed Pan Polar hostages are hung in portrait gallery in the Halifax palace. They glow against the dark panelling. When I was small, I thought they were angels.

I do not know what made my mother object to the tradition of being painted in white, but object she did, and fiercely, her accent getting away from her until she was rolling Rs like a fisherman and spitting like a whale. She brought me the royal tartans and a crown to wear. When I objected on the grounds that I was not of age and it was utterly inappropriate for me to dress as a ruling monarch, she brought me the gown I'd worn at the Yule Ball.

That gown. It was taffeta, printed in flowers. Not pastel, dainty blooms but huge sweeps of goldenrod and blue morning glory, ivy that was almost black, roses the red that roses really are. I had worn it to the ball; I had had too much punch; I had flushed and danced; I had been interviewed and told the world, and Elián, that I was not afraid.

Ah, that gown: it turned my head, more than I care to admit. And when my mother had said something sharp and strange—"Blister it, Greta, I want just one picture of you not dressed as Joan of Bloody Arc!"—I had yielded.

But the portrait, when it was finished . . . There were things I liked about it. A lifetime of farm labor had given me muscles and tendons in my collarbones and shoulders; the painter framed them in taffeta and made them look as elegant as one of Cicero's arguments. I liked that. I liked how the set of my mouth looked determined. I even liked my hair, my troublesome Guinevere hair. But these were things I saw later. What I saw first was my eyes.

Cool and empty and blue, very blue. They were cataracted

with their blueness. Filmed over as if with ice, or death. I looked hollow.

When my mother saw the portrait, she wept. She held on to me, our skirts swirling together. "Greta," she whispered. "My Greta, my Greta, my strong sweet girl—"

"Mother . . ." Her fingernails bit into my back, and I could hardly hear what she was whispering above the sudden pounding of my heart. It was: "I'm sorry, I'm sorry, I'm sorry."

The Abbot's voice jerked me back into the miseri. "I've seen you at the map table," he said.

The map table, where I had studied the watersheds of the Great Lakes basin. Where I'd read the news dispatches until my hands had bled, watching the Cumberland Alliance and the Pan Polar Confederacy creep closer to war. Elián's nation and mine. The demand for drinking water access to Lake Ontario, which the Cumberlanders could not live without and which the PanPols would never cede.

The Abbot's eyes widened. They were only ovals, but they looked wise and sad. "I know you know what's coming, Greta."

"A war."

"I only want Elián to do well," said the Abbot. "You know it will be better for everyone if he can do well. And after all, you will have to go with him. Better if he doesn't make a fuss."

"Is it soon?" I said.

The Abbot shrugged, though shoulderless, by turning up

a hand and opening the fingers. "I know no more than you, Greta, of the facts on the ground. I only have longer and perhaps more bitter experience of the way such things play out." He tipped his facescreen just a fraction. Patted one of my knees. "My dear child," he said. "You are going to die."

My eyes lifted—I felt as if my gaze were being pulled—toward the bulge in the wall behind him.

The grey room was on the other side of that curve.

The grey room was the central fact of our lives, and yet we knew nothing about it. From the curve, we deduce that it is oval. We deduce that it is small. But we don't *know*.

We don't even know why it is called "grey."

"Mastery of information has always been your strength and your comfort, I know," the Abbot said. "I wonder if ignorance is, in your particular case, the kindest thing."

I said nothing.

"Greta. Would you like to see the grey room?"

My mouth was utterly dry. I could not speak; could not even swallow. I thought my bones would crack like dry branches as I stood up. Still, I stood up. The Abbot stretched to his full height. He followed me as I walked blindly out of the miseri, around its curve, to that unremarkable and ever-closed door.

The door opened.

The grey room.

It was small.

It was oval.

There was a table in it. A high table. Long. Narrow. Metal, faded to the softest grey. Worn leather straps at two corners, and at two midpoints. Wrists and ankles. Four buckles dangling.

Some kind of cage for the head.

The Abbot put his articulated hand on my shoulder, joint by joint.

"Don't worry, Greta," he said. "I am sure you will do fine."

I walked out of the Precepture. As if on the arm of a Swan Rider, I walked out with dignity. I walked out well.

And then I just kept walking.

The Precepture sits above the loop of a river, with a ridge at its northern back; with a skirt of lawn and orchard; with terraced gardens above a little alfalfa field and edged by a bright ribbon of water. Across that water is the open prairie. From that direction, the Swan Riders come. We can watch them coming forever.

Everyone was at dinner, and the lawn was empty. I walked across it. The gardens buzzed with desperate insects, counting down to winter. I walked down through them. The alfalfa field was blooming purple. There were little huts for the leaf-cutter bees. There was a rick for the hay. A shed for scythes.

Why did they let us have scythes? Scythe blades are three feet long, and we keep them sharp. We could truly ruin the ceremony of Talis's systems, if we were brave enough to do something with those scythes.

The alfalfa stems tangled and tugged at my knees. It was like walking through a crowd in Halifax, everyone reaching. They grasped and grasped at me, and I went slower and slower and at the river edge I finally fell onto my knees.

I was hot and I was cold. I was shaking.

The grey room had a table with straps. And some kind of cage for the head.

I was born to a crown. *This* was my crown—a cage for the head.

The soil under my hands was sandy. I could hear the river. This was as far as I could go, the edge of the Precepture, the edge of the world.

A proctor rose up from behind the bank.

And a foot hit it.

It happened suddenly: The proctor reared upright—a heavy proctor with a dome of eyes atop it—and even as it did so, Da-Xia skidded into place beside me, panting and crashing to her knees. With a stray foot she hooked the proctor under its body and tipped it backward. It fell.

There was a splash.

"Oops," said Xie.

I meant to laugh, but what came out of me was a high-pitched sound, like a rabbit dying.

"Oh," said Xie. "Easy, Greta. Easy."

She picked me up and I staggered until I found myself leaning with my back to a huge and solitary cottonwood tree. Its stiff leaves rattled overhead like a taffeta gown.

The Panopticon was out of sight in the leaves, and the

proctor was drowned. A blind spot. Leave it to Xie to find one, now, when we needed one so badly. "What happened?" she said.

"What?"

"Greta. What happened? What did he do to you?"

"I saw it," I said. "I saw the grey room."

Xie was facing me, her hand resting on the trunk beside my head. I heard her fingernails dig into the furrowed bark. "Did he hurt you?" she whispered. A blind spot, but we could not be sure nothing listened. "Did the Abbot hurt you?"

I tipped my head forward. The rough bark of the tree tried to stop me, tugging at little strands of hair.

"Greta?"

Had the Abbot hurt me? Yes. No. The Abbot had never, would never hurt me. But the tree was trying to hold my head back, and they were going to tie down my head.

Da-Xia's gaze broke from mine for an instant. "They're coming," she said. "They're looking for you, the others. Even Thandi."

"Elián?" If they took him again—much more would kill him.

But Xie laughed softly. "Especially Elián. Come on." She wrapped her arm around me and pulled me away from the tree. Her arm around my ribs was strong; her side against my side was warm. I wondered if I felt to her as Elián had to me. If she could feel me tremble. Against her stillness I could tell that I *was* trembling. *It's too much,* Elián had said. *They're going to kill me.*

I wanted to say that to Xie, but there was no innocent remark to hide it in, no blind spot big enough for such a conversation. I wanted to say it, but I couldn't. I couldn't. Tears sprang into my eyes—and Xie smoothed them away with the pads of her thumbs.

My only friend, and I couldn't talk to her. And she couldn't answer me. We could not get close enough together.

Yet we could.

Xie took one step forward and I leaned backward, and I was against the tree again. Then hard against it. Xie's hands pushed against my shoulders. Her knee hit the outside of my knee. She held me there— I felt as if she were gathering me. I looked at her. She eased off. She came up on tiptoe. And she kissed me.

The touch itself, lips against lips, was something small enough to be imaginary. It was a butterfly landing on me. I shivered, and something deep inside me, something that had been frozen and solid, turned into honey.

The words I had wanted to say came out, almost like a sob: "It's too much—"

"It's not," she whispered. Then she came closer and tucked herself under my chin. How could she be so strong when she was so small? She was warm inside my arms. And suddenly neither one of us was shaking. I could feel her ribs move under my hands. My breathing slowed to match. And for that moment, who we were and where we were, the future and the past, fell away.

"He didn't hurt me," I said. "He tried to frighten me."

"The others are coming," said Xie, and we pulled away from the sheltering tree. Xie hooked a hand round my elbow and drew me out to meet our cohort—and their proctor guards—who were pouring down the garden terraces.

"But I'm not frightened." I was . . . something different than frightened.

Da-Xia lifted a regal hand to wave to everyone, to show we were all right.

"I'm not," I said, more firmly. "If a queen is quiet, it is not because she is frightened."

Da-Xia kept her eyes on the others and answered me softly, a grin in her voice. "Oh," she said. "That I know."

12
PRESSURE VALVE

It had been such a long day. It had been so strange, so full of doors and hinges. But there were still goats to be milked, water to be pumped and poured into the drip irrigators, green beans to be plucked and put into a basket that bit into the crook of my arm. My lips felt . . . raw. Ripe. Ready to be touched. As if even the air that moved past them were new.

But I said nothing about it. The queen was quiet.

We worked into the long orange evening, and went back to our cells.

Still quiet, I sat on my cot and started to pull the pins out of my hair. Xie took off her samue and put on her alb. I tipped my head down so I would not see her changing. My braids tumbled around my face. My head felt different. My whole life felt different. I had defied the Precepture. I had seen the grey room.

And Xie—Xie had kissed me.

I glanced at her sitting on her cot. She was dressed now, wearing a spotless sleeping alb—or at least, she had it pulled over her body. Her bare legs were folded against her bare chest, the alb drapped over them. She had her knees pulled up under her chin, and the tops of them peeked out through the loose neckline, dusty gold against the white fabric. The dip between them fell away into grey-gold shadow.

I closed my eyes.

My hands kept undoing braids until my loose hair spilled around me. I suspected I looked less like Guinevere now than some mad thing—Ophelia, maybe, or the Lady of Shallott.

Did all the mythical long-haired princesses meet bad ends? It seemed unfair.

Ends: The grey room. The high and narrow table. The crown and the dangling straps.

My hair was entirely loose now. I had an urge to cut it all off. Why not? Instead I twisted a bit of rag around, tying it into a very un-royal and sloppy ponytail, and got up to scrub my samue. It was spattered with a couple of days of gardening, and badly stained about the knees from my crash through the alfalfa.

I had my back to Xie. The silence between us was like an electric charge.

"They assigned Elián a cell," said Da-Xia. "They put him with Atta."

Elián had not had the best evening. I'd watched him over the green beans. His eyes had been feverishly bright, and he had twitched like a cat that—well, like a cat that had been tortured. But he had done a Precepture-worthy job of pretending nothing was wrong.

"Good news," I said.

"I'm glad you think so," said Xie. "My guess is the Abbot is trying to keep you happy."

There was nothing safe to say to that, but I still felt myself beginning to smile. It was a powerful feeling.

Now, if I could only use that power to lift grass stains . . . "Honestly," I muttered. "Who makes work clothes white?"

"The same person who puts executioners in angel's wings."

Talis, with his Swan Riders, and his endless taste for ritual.

"Also," said Xie, getting up, "they're based on the work clothes of Zen monks."

I didn't feel particularly monkish.

Xie glanced skyward. It was the last of twilight, nearly full dark. Beyond the glass roof, the stars were prickling on, one by one.

A bell rang, the seventh bell, to command us to sleep.

"Will you sleep?" Xie asked.

"The Abbot said I should come to him, if I didn't."

Da-Xia smiled for the Panopticon, but her eyes were black. They said, *Don't.*

They use dreamlock. They use drugs.

"It's fine," I said. "I'm not tired."

"Will you be all right?" If she left, she meant. If she went to play coyotes. She'd stepped close enough to the door to trigger its silent slide. Xie had kissed me, but Xie kissed everyone. She stood there on the edge of leaving, her alb like a sail in the moonlight, the rest of her a dark sea.

For three years she'd been slipping out. I had never wanted to know with whom. I had been quite deliberate about not asking. And yet suddenly—

"Who do you meet, out there?" I asked.

Xie was shadowed by the lintel—hidden there from the Panopticon, with the hallway dark behind her. I couldn't see her face well, but I did see the glimmer of her smile. "Will you come with me?"

I thought she was dodging the question. "Really, Xie. Who?"

"Whoever I can get my hands on, really." The smile fluttered away. "Mostly Atta. It's always been Atta."

Atta the silent. Like a star that didn't have the mass to begin fusion, Atta was a weight and a pull in the system, a dark star to Xie's moon. I was startled, and said the first thing that came to me: "Does he talk to you?"

"Not much." Her face was in the thickest dark now, invisible. "Not since we lost the baby. Two years ago."

She stood in the doorway, in the shadow, in the silence. I think she was waiting for me to say something. What could I possibly say? Many of us children are dynastic rulers, and it is in no one's interest to see the Preceptures produce bastard princes, so: "There are drugs—we take drugs."

"There are ways around drugs."

"But—"

"But they found out. Obviously. Atta thought they would send me home, but—but that is not what they did."

"Xie . . . ," I whispered. Two years ago she'd been fifteen. *Fifteen.* "My God, Xie . . ."

She'd been silent that fall, dulled like an eclipsed moon. I had thought her ill, or worried over her schoolwork, or over some threat of war she knew of and I did not. I'd scoured the dispatches for that phantom war. I'd helped her with her philosophy papers. Her Greek. To read Greek, and miss this. I felt as if I'd had my eyes closed for years.

"I don't love him," said Xie. She might have been talking to the moon: her voice was soft and distant. "I think I did, back then, but . . . It's just shared sorrow, between us, now."

"But at least it's shared."

She looked back up at me. "At least it's shared."

I stood up and came into the doorway with her. A small space. The hem of her alb swung over my bare feet. I could smell the harsh soap on her hands, and smell something softer, too, like musk and clover. I could sense the movement of her breath. "Take me with you," I said. "Let's go outside."

You cannot control a man if you take everything from him. You must leave him something to lose.

Therefore, the Precepture had its loose places, and this was one of them—playing coyotes, slipping outside at night. It only made sense, I'd long told myself. Better coyotes than armed rebellion; better sex than pitchforks. It was only logical then, that getting outside was easy. This was the Precepture's way of letting off steam, and one doesn't want one's pressure valve blocked.

And yet, the ease with which we left the Precepture hall unnerved me. It was too simple. Xie led me through the refectory, its tables long slabs of gleam. We wove through the complex shadows of the kitchens, and went down a flight of stairs. The cellars were utterly dark and smelled of another season: cold earth, dampness, potatoes. I stumbled into something and then jumped at a fleshy touch—but it was only Xie, reaching back to take my hand.

Up some steps then, spiderwebs and dust. Something creaked, and an indigo panel of sky appeared over me. Xie stood in it, framed and shining. She shouldered the door of the root cellar all the way open, and we climbed up into the night.

And that was all there was to it.

Xie stood in the open air and stretched. "There are tunnels," she said. "Out to the toolshed, over to the dairy, even all the way up to the launch spire and Charlie's pen."

"Tunnels, heh?" Elián Palnik drawled out of the darkness. "I want a map."

Xie laughed. "Of course you do."

"Elián." I was—exasperated? How was I meant to save him, if he took such risks? "A single night in the cells was too many for you?"

"And five thousand was too many for you?" he snapped back at me—but then he switched tones with a sigh. "I just wanted to see the sky."

Where on earth had he been? Before he had been assigned a cell, where had he been, that he couldn't see the sky?

"The tunnels don't matter," said Atta. Elián and I both spun to look at him—Atta. Atta the silent. His voice was as thick as dust and honey. "It is an illusion. They can read our minds. They watch us everywhere."

"Atta," whispered Xie, and touched him wonderingly, as if he were gold.

I don't love him, she'd said. And maybe not. But I knew her—she would give him what she could. She would take care of him, if she could. It wouldn't have to be out of love.

Was that why she had kissed me?

I stared at them until Elián took my elbow and drew me away. "Let's let them have their illusion of privacy, huh?" He pointed with his thumb over his shoulder as he strolled away. "So that's a thing?"

"That is . . ." I swallowed, bewildered. "That is a thing."

He laughed low. "Listen to you. You sound almost human."

I didn't answer. We were walking aimlessly, down the terraces, through the gardens. They were different by night, black and silver, like ancient photographs.

"I could give you lessons on contractions, if'n you want." Elián exaggerated his accent, as he did when he was nervous. "And then we could do slang."

"I speak as I speak, Elián."

"That you do," he said, very softly. Every step we took

sent grasshoppers flying up around us. In the distance, I could hear coyotes—real coyotes, not children playing at them. It sounded like half-grown pups, trying out the yips and growls and laughs in their nearly human voices. It reminded me oddly of a cocktail party as heard from around the bend of a quiet hallway: a Halifax sound.

Elián sighed and stretched his arms up, looking suddenly very tall. "Do you think they'll let us go all the way down to the river?"

"I doubt it." The proctor Xie had destroyed "accidentally." I had no doubt it had been replaced or repaired. That it was ready.

In front of us the terraces dropped away. At the bottom the river looped through its floodplain, gleaming like glass. Behind us, though neither of us turned to look, was the bulk of the Precepture hall, and the loom of the Panopticon mast, twisting and dark like a cricket's exoskeleton.

An illusion, Atta had said. *They can read our minds.* But they couldn't. Could they?

The Abbot could come close, but much good would that power do him. I did not myself know what I was thinking.

"I don't care if it is a fake," Elián said, as if responding to my thoughts and not to the last thing Atta had said. "Don't care a bit. An hour or so without those spiders—I'll take it."

"They've left you?"

"When I took off my shirt. They just dropped off. Like full-up ticks."

"So of course you went straight out to find another limit to push."

"Well, of *course*," he laughed. "They pushed me 'til I cracked and I've cracked right up. I'm dreaming about strolling hand in hand with Princess Greta."

"We're not hand in hand."

He took my hand. "In a moonlit garden."

"The moon's not up yet."

He stopped and turned to me. "And I'm not dreaming."

"You need to take this seriously, Elián. The Cumberland Alliance—"

"I know." He took my other hand, rubbing his thumbs over the ridges of my knuckles. "We're going to war. And that means they're going to kill us. I know."

"Then why do you make them treat you—"

His thumbs stopped moving. "*Make* them?" he echoed. "God, Greta." He let go of my hands. We stood facing each other a moment, in the dark garden. Then Elián took two hard steps away from me and sat down on a big stone that braced the terrace. "So," he said, his voice suddenly cool. "What about you? Ready to die?"

"It might yet not come to that. The Pan Polar Confederacy is a superpower." And the Cumberland Alliance, though I hated to say it to Elián, was a barely cohesive lump of leftovers, whose predecessor state had just lost a war with *Mississippi*, of all places. I settled for: "To take us on . . . Cumberland would be badly outclassed. They may not attack."

The Abbot didn't believe that. My mother didn't believe

that. I didn't believe that. But I tried to hang on to it, for a moment.

Elián didn't let me. "We might be *outclassed*," he said, loading the word so heavily that it overflowed, dripping sarcasm. "But we won't be outsmarted. Maybe we can't win if we put our troops in pretty little lines to get shot at—so we won't do it that way."

"You can't just alter the laws of war."

"You don't know my grandmother," said Elián. "She could alter the laws of *physics*, if she gave them this particular look she's got."

"But Talis—"

"But nothing. We're going to war, Greta. I knew it when I got here, and I still know it. You and me, Princess, we're going to die."

He was certain as a stone.

Quietly—supple-spined, because I *was* a princess—I sat down on the terrace beside him.

"Do you know when? Did Armenteros tell you when?"

He paused. "Guess she could have, huh? Never thought of that." I'd just broken his heart a little. I could see the crack. "No, they didn't tell me. What about you?"

"I—I suppose my mother thinks it kinder, if I don't know when it's coming."

"Yeah," he said. "Kinder."

His accent was thick enough that it could have been "kind of." Kind of kinder. And was it? I didn't know. Maybe it was.

"I've been reading," I said.

"Course you have. You studied up." Elián laughed, faint as starlight. "What do you reckon, then? How long?"

"Weeks," I said. "The diplomats have reached their end-game. No more than weeks."

"Days?" he said.

"Maybe days."

He closed his eyes. "And all I can come up with is ways of getting the goats into the library."

I choked on a laugh and it came out my nose—the approved royal fashion, of course.

"I love you," Elián said.

"*What?*" All this talk of our death, and yet it was that that made me squawk.

"I love you laughing. I just—" He reached out toward me. I tensed. He stopped, his hands midair. "It's just— You look so different. With your hair down."

In my haste to follow Xie, I'd simply left my hair in its ponytail. It hung past my waist.

"Different?" I was not sure if that was good or bad. It was utterly ridiculous that, in the face of death, I wanted to know which.

But I wanted to know which.

Elián nodded. "Real different. . . . Can I . . . ?" He reached around behind me, and I felt his fingers fumble at the nape of my neck. My whole skin shivered in the warm night. He was close to me, and I could smell the soap on him—the same as the soap on Xie's hands—and I imagined how those hands would taste. Lye, like an electric shock to the tongue. Elián worked the knot open, and then lifted my hair from my spine and spread it over my shoulders like a cape. Hair has no nerve endings, and yet every brush of my hair across my throat made me glitter and jolt.

I was thinking about electricity, suddenly. And not in punishment.

"I'm not going to go quietly, Greta." There was no defiance in his voice. It was soft as a lover's whisper. "They'll have to drag me off."

"You might surprise yourself." I put my hand on Elián's knee.

He looked down at it. I could see his throat move as he swallowed down his fear. "Might, I guess. Life is full of surprises."

He turned to me. Our legs bumped. I was aware of our knees sorting out their borders, my hand still on his thigh, my hair puddled in my lap. My hair was sectioned and smooth from its tenure in braids, and lay in shining pieces, like cords from an unplaited rope. Elián took a cord in each hand and wrapped it round and round, until his wrists and hands and arms were bound by my hair—until we were tangled so close together that I could feel his breath on my lips.

"You're so strong," he said.

And he kissed me.

My hand flew up, and I swear for a moment I meant to push him away. Instead, I put my fingers along the ridge of his jaw. Our noses bumped. His knee pushed inside my thigh and my legs fell open. The tug of my hair on my scalp as he reeled me in was incredible—it felt like heat building, it felt like a thousand urgent prickles. He kissed me and I kissed him and there was not enough air. There was not enough time. Weeks. Days. He was desperate, and I was desperate, and we were out of time.

His tongue, his knee pushing deeper. I gasped something—maybe it was wait—but also I bit his lip. We were going to die together, and it felt like here and now.

"Time to —"

It was Da-Xia's voice. I pushed away from Elián, flushed, gasping.

Xie was standing two tiers above us. She was more than silloutte. It was obvious that she could see.

"Time to go," she said, and her voice cracked. "There are proctors out tonight." She took a step back as if to fade into the darkness.

"Wait, Xie—" I staggered up. My mind felt like an empty cage. Everything had flown out of it. My hair was mad and the ties of my shirt were looser than they should have been.

"Goodness," Da-Xia said, watching me fumble to arrange my shirt. I think she was trying for light, but she seemed stunned. "My Princess of the Icy Places—there's hope for you yet."

Elián, curse him, laughed. "Get her away from those protocol officers and there's no stopping her."

"Shut up," I said. I was glad of the dark. I was blushing as only a red-head could.

Elián shut up. "I didn't mean—"

"Come," said Xie, before Elián specify which part he hadn't meant. "We're pushing our luck."

"Greta," said Elián.

"Let's go," I said, and pulled away from him. Xie led us back to the Precepture, where Atta—silent again—was sitting by the wall. Together the four of us went through the cellars, the kitchens. We came out of the refectory and into the hallway—

And there was the Abbot, standing quietly. Two proctors flanked him.

"Greta," he said, as if I were alone. "Couldn't sleep?"

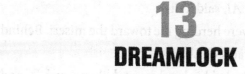

13
DREAMLOCK

I asked you to come to me, Greta, if you couldn't sleep," the Abbot chided. The Abbot had showed me the grey room to scare me into giving up my power. And that hadn't worked. So, next— I should have realized there would be a *next*.

The proctors came in like sheepdogs and cut me out from the herd, away from the others. I went, stiffening my back as if swan wings were attached to my shoulder blades. "I know, good Father," I allowed. But I did not apologize. And I did not explain.

"I asked her to come with me, Father Abbot," said Da-Xia. "Please. It's my fault."

The Abbot's mouth icon turned up at the corners, as if she'd told him a joke. "I know exactly what you said, Xie." His use of the diminutive made me cold. "And perhaps we might discuss it later? I think our dear Greta is distressed. Her heart rate is quite high."

They can read our minds, Atta had said.

Why would they need to, when they could read our lips, and our hearts?

Never lie to an AI, said Talis.

The proctors were herding me toward the miseri. Behind me Elián's voice cracked "Abbot—"

The Abbot swiveled his head around like an owl. "Good night, Ms. Li. Mr. Palnik, Mr. Paşa. Do get some rest."

I heard Xie whispering something to Elián, urgent— shutting him up, probably. And then the door of the miseri closed and there was nothing but soft light and silence.

Dreamlock. Therapists invented it, though torturers made it famous. Magnetic fields induce and guide dreams; drugs circumvent the reflex that wakes the body when dreams become traumatic.

It was once thought that if you died in your dreams you died in life. Thanks to dreamlock, we know this is not true. Most people can die at least six times before something in them gives way.

They use dreamlock; they use drugs.

I had only half believed it.

I don't know how long.

The first dream took—was perhaps designed to take— my sense of time.

It was one of those endless things, where one is lost in a

grey place. There is a cold, distant murmuring, that Halifax sound. The ceiling is not glass; it is low. The darkness grows total. I put out my hand—a stone wall. I walk along it, dragging my hand. There are turns and openings—one, two, many. . . . It's a maze. No. It's a catacomb, a maze of graves. I touch something dead and slickly wrapped in taffeta. A body. A body in my dress.

It's my body.

I jerk and wake up and I am that body. I am that body, and I am lying on a high narrow table. Cold metal. Leather straps hold me down. Someone is looking down at me—the Swan Rider girl with her sickening gentleness and bright blue eyes. There's a cage around my head—something dark and metal swings over me, and—

I wake up, or I don't, and I am sitting in the nighttime garden. I am wearing my taffeta. I can hear its rustle, the night insects, the river. I can hear Elián breathing. His hands are tangled in my hair. He kisses me but he is kissing a dead thing: my lips are nerveless. My skin is a peeled potato. My teeth—my teeth move. I bite him and my hair pulls him in and in and in. I bite him and feel the hot rush of blood.

I wake up, or I —

"Greta. Greta. Wake up."

I felt a hand take mine. I knew it by its shape. Da-Xia.

My eyelashes were tangled in honey, as if bees had been building nests in me. Barely, I saw Xie lift my hand and cradle it against her throat. "Greta. I'm so sorry."

"Xie?" My tongue was dry and stiff.

"You slept through breakfast—I stole you some juice."

I squinted. The light was too bright; the paper cranes seemed to spin, impossibly fast. The Panopticon loomed as if it were right in the middle of our small room, as if its stalk had taken root there. Its bulbous eye was inches from me.

"Greta?"

"Juice," I felt myself say. "Juice would be good."

Xie wrapped an arm around me and sat me up. She held the cup for me. My lips were numb against the cold clay. The juice tasted of cobwebs and blood. I swallowed it anyway, and stood up. I did not wish to be in my bed.

Da-Xia lifted her hands like a priest and cradled my face between them. I could feel my skin pulse against her palms—too fast. Slower. Slower. As Elián had leaned into me, under the pumpkins, I leaned into Xie. She was so small, and yet she seemed larger than I was. I tipped my forehead down until it rested against hers.

"Hold on to me," she said. I felt her breath on my throat. "Come back."

Slowly, slowly, holding on to her, I came back.

And I stayed back until the evening, when the proctor came to fetch me again.

Dreamlock: I am sitting for my portrait.

I sit long and still.

An artist is painting me. My skin is canvas. The strokes follow my clavicle inward from the point of my shoulder, down my sternum, across my breasts. I feel the push of the small brush as the artist splays its bristles and flicks the red curve of a rose petal across the cream of my skin. I feel the prick of each painted thorn.

The artist is kneeling. I cannot see his face. Curls of his dark hair brush under my chin. His breath is warm against my heart. He paints around my ribs. I feel the paint on me, slowly stiffening. It pulls tighter, tighter.

"Why are you sitting?" whispers the artist. I can feel his breath against the skin of my stomach, the whisper of his brush, painting downward. "Why are you just sitting there?"

It is because it never occurred to me to move—no. It is because I cannot move. The paint is like a corset, and then it is worse. It is a constriction and my ribs cannot move. I cannot breathe. I cannot breathe. I panic. I cannot even move my eyes. I am only a painting. And yet I need to breathe. And I cannot breathe.

The artist—and it is Elián, of course, Elián—the artist tilts up his head and smiles at me as he watches me die.

He is growing antlers, like a stag.

The last thing I feel is his hands on me, the roar of my skin—

I wake, or I don't.

It is— It was— Am I awake?

I was in the toolshed. My hands were locked around one of the crank wheels of the cider press. Xie and Elián were talking as if I weren't there. I was angry with Elián. I was afraid. I could not remember why. I was a ghost—compelled to feel, but no longer remembering the roots of the feeling.

". . . and you've been sneaking out for years," Elián was saying. "So why . . ."

The wheel went *click, click, clock* as I pushed at it. Every notch was a little bit harder to move.

". . . control her, control the Precepture," came the fragment of Xie's answer. I wasn't really listening to her. I was thinking of how each notch of the press pushed the apples further. The raw juice dripped from the spile. Wasps swarmed at the pulp that came up around the edges of the press. "You're just a loose cannon, Elián. It's Greta we follow."

The wasps were drunk; the pulp oozed up. *Click, click, click.*

And yet, the business of making cider did not turn into a torture sequence, and no one grew antlers, and slowly I decided it was real.

Of course, I decided this a moment too late, after we'd gone outside to feed the wrung-out apple pulp to some of the goat kids. A tawny little kid named Dipshit butted me in the back of the leg, knocked me down, and climbed on top of me. She stood on my back and stuck her head into the apple bucket.

It is important to note, at this point, that I did not swear. It is one of those things, like cutting one's hair, that queens do not do. "Dipshit!" I shouted. *"Get the expletive off me!"* I reared up; the goat scrambled, making welts with her dainty little hooves as she slid off. My samue was streaked with greenish goat manure—they'd been eating too much food-fight melon—and one of my braids was swinging free. There was something smeared across my face that I refused even to consider.

"Hello, Greta," said Xie. "Welcome back." She reached over the fence and pulled me a hank of grass.

Elián's face was paint-tight with the work of not smiling. "Shut up," I warned him, wiping at my face with the clean grass.

His rigid muscles twitched in answer.

"I'm quite serious, Elián. I was just dreamlocked for you."

Though, in fairness, it had not exactly been for him.

At the mention of dreamlock, Elián got his face under control. Then it cracked again. "Dipshit," he mimicked, "get the *expletive*—"

"It is her name," I said, coiling up the braid and pushing the pins into it. "The names of this particular batch of kids are Flopsy, Mopsy, Topsy, and Dipshit, and I assure you, that was not my idea."

"You don't say," said Elián, with the world's most contagious smile.

It was strange. We were from opposing nations that were at the brink of war. We were days away from dying for that war. And yet I would have done almost anything for Elián.

Except perhaps more dreamlock. Which was, of course, exactly what I feared I would be called on to do, when the moon rose. And so it proved.

I have never begged anyone for anything. I did not beg.

A queen does not beg.

Dreamlock: I stand in front of my portrait. My beautiful dress, my iced-over eyes. Huge behind me arch the white wings of a swan.

A Swan Rider. I've been painted with a Swan Rider looming behind me.

I tense.

The portrait tenses.

It's not a painting, it's a mirror. And the Swan Rider is behind me.

I whirl. But it's Xie.

It is Li Da-Xia, arrayed for her throne, her headdress looped and weighted with turquoise and yellow jade, with red coral and silver and carved white bones. This is her royal. This is her when I never see her again. She is a goddess-queen in red and gold silk, and she looks past me, at something over my shoulder. "No," she says to whatever is back there. "No. You cannot have her."

The wings. It's the Swan Rider. I can still feel the shadow of her wings.

I whirl around, but there's only the mirror. There is no Rider.

It's me, I am wearing them. The wings are on my back.

I am the Rider.

I wake—

". . . up! Greta, wake up!" I have never heard the Abbot so urgent. Is it possible he is afraid? Some kind of drug or current, something artificial, surges through me. It peels open my eyes the way an IV stent opens a vein. I can see but

I cannot choose what to look at. Straight up: the glass roof of the miseri is rippled amber, the color of apple juice. The Abbot leans over me. His face is discomposed, his eye icons sideways like a goat's eyes, his mouth just an oblong. "Greta," he says—he does not make his mouth icon move. "Greta, they are coming. There are shielded places we can go, but you must wake up."

But I cannot even move my eyes. If it is time for me to go to the grey room I will go to it like a sleepwalker.

Which is what they have wanted all along.

From the corner of my eye, I see the ceramic phalanges and braided metal tendons of the Abbot's hand. He is touching my face, my temple, where the dreamlock magnets are affixed.

Something in my brain goes *click, click, click*—and I see things, as if my eyes had been turned to slide projectors.

Xie in her crown.

A body in my dress.

Elián's face, smiling up under his antlers.

My ears are full of the static noise of my silk dress whirling over stone.

There is blood in my mouth.

"Greta!" The Abbot tugs at me. He glances over his shoulder, at the ceiling—a human gesture, and odd, for surely he must have visual feeds. But he turns, and I find I, too, can turn. I look up—

And something is coming down.

Through the sky at dawn, something big is coming. It

slams toward us like a fist swinging in, like the sky itself falling, something round and black and thundering down. There is an enormous sonic boom. The ceiling shatters. The Abbot falls. His mainstem strikes across my legs. His hand splays against the floor with a *clack*. Squares of golden glass patter onto us. The underside of the ship takes up the whole sky.

And then—

Then lightning strikes me. It goes into my brain. I scream and I hear the Abbot scream and—

The world goes black.

14
ELIÁN CHOOSES

There, it is disconnected."

The voice was familiar, but I was adrift. I could not place it. I opened my eyes and saw only a window—a hatchway or a round window, edged with blades. It was a circle, and then the blades swung inward and made it a smaller circle, and then larger again. The twitching looked organic. The blades seemed to flutter like a pulse. Half machine, half—

"Father?" I said. The Abbot. The Abbot had been—

I heard the Abbot's voice, as if in a memory: "Children, I'm afraid there is bad news. . . ."

"Come back, Greta." That voice was Xie's.

"Greta?" Elián. "Please, God— Grego, is she okay?"

"I'm not— A moment." It was the unplaced voice again—Grego. It was Grego. "Ah, yes. See? Yes, they are coming free." There was a twinkle in the corner of my eye.

A dark shadow lifted past me as the dreamlock magnet-net came loose. And then the bladed window took its true size. It was tiny. It was right in front of me, but it was tiny, a laser aperture—an aperture.

Grego's eyes.

Grego pulled away from me, white eyelashes blinking over the dark shutters that pulsed where his irises should have been.

"Sveika, Greta." he murmured. "It is good that you are back."

"What?" My tongue felt thick and rough. "Xie?"

"Greta," she whispered. She wrapped an arm around me and helped me sit up. The room pounded and spun.

Right in front of me was the Abbot. His facescreen was blank—literally blank, with no icons at all. When he spoke, his voice, mouthless, seemed to come from everywhere. "Children, I'm afraid there is bad news."

"Stop *saying* that!" Elián wailed, and kicked the old AI right in the mainstem, just above where the hexapod legs joined. The Abbot staggered, blind, putting out a hand. "Children, I'm afraid—" he said again.

Elián was not wearing what he should have been, not his whites. Patches the colors of stone and dust and books shifted across him and seemed to blur his edges.

Focus, Greta. I blinked hard. Elián—he was wearing chameleon cloth, chamo, a fabric with active pattern disruption. It is what soldiers wear. Elián looks like a soldier. The Abbot looks dead. His face is blank as paper. "There is bad news," he intoned, like a looped recording. "A war has been declared." Dead, but speaking, and Grego had eyes made of blades.

Could I at least have faith in Xie? She was right—her shape, her smell, the strength of her arm around me. I closed my eyes and clutched at her. "Xie? Is this real?"

"You're waking up," she said. "Come back, Greta. It's—"

Something cut her off, a voice that growled out of the shadows, a woman's voice. I could not make out words.

Grego answered the voice. "She was partly hooked to the dreamlock magnets when the EMP hit. There would have been feedback, so there may be . . . damage."

I saw Elián shake his head to deny it, moving so fast that ghost images trailed him like antlers. The chamo cloth seemed to erase his body. *Damage.* I closed my eyes, trying to cope with the pulsing color, pulsing pain.

"Princess Greta," said the unknown woman's voice. "Your Highness?"

The sharp edges of my title cut the inside of my throat like nutshells. I could feel Da-Xia's arm around my back, the warmth of her side against my side. She took a sharp breath in.

"Look at me, please, Your Highness." Despite the "please" and the honorific, it was a command. The kind of command a doctor might give. Had they brought a doctor? I thought I might need a doctor.

I opened my eyes. Yes, there was Xie holding me, there was Elián in fatigues, there was Grego with an engineer's multipencil twinkling in his hands. A bookcase had toppled, spilling books like guts. The school's proctors were there too, piled in a heap of legs and joints.

Xie shifted and pushed, and I sat up fully. A figure, a bulky shadowy thing, took a step toward me. I squinted. It seemed to be human, something human, though my mind was full of animals. A shamble like a bear, but a controlled precision like a warhorse. A hawk nose in a soft face. Gray hair cut short, coarse as a mane. "Crown Princess Greta Gustafsen Stuart," the bear-woman said. "On behalf of the Cumberland Alliance, I offer the Pan Polar Confederacy a formal declaration of war. Will you accept it?"

"Of course," I said, politely.

Then I threw up on the legendary shoes of Wilma Armenteros.

General Wilma Armenteros, secretary of strategic decisions for the Cumberland Alliance, legendary scion of a legendary line, and disgruntled grandmother of the Precepture's most troubled hostage, looked down at her shoes and blinked.

Then she looked up. Her eyes, like the Abbot's, were pixel-grey.

"Major Buckle," she said crisply to someone standing behind me. "Why don't you take these young people outside? I'm sure the fresh air will do Her Highness good."

I turned in time to see the woman behind me salute. "Yes, sir."

"And, Major—send someone to find me some socks."

Xie and Grego hoisted me by the armpits. I stood shaking.

Cubes of gold glass fell from my clothes and hair as if I were some fairy-tale thing, shedding radiance. Elián hesitated. He seemed unsure which category he fell in, the sock-finders or the fresh-air-getters. He looked to Armenteros. I'm not sure what he saw there, but it did not seem to clarify matters for him. For a moment he was as frozen as if the spiders were still on him. But when we moved, he followed us.

"Children." The Abbot's voice trailed us. "I'm afraid there is bad news."

"And fetch me Burr," I heard Armenteros say as the door closed. "I need this thing to talk."

It was beautiful outside, one of those first days when summer rounds the corner and can see fall. It was not cold or even cool, but the air held the promise that the suffocating heat would not return. It was a day like a newly sharpened pencil, full of possibilities. There was, for instance, a whacking great spaceship parked at the top of the hill.

There were also, for some reason I could not quite grasp, a lot of soldiers about, standing like a line of scarecrows along the top of the uppermost terrace. In the flat space between the soldiers and the Precepture hall, the Children of Peace were huddled, still and watchful, like egrets.

Gregori and Da-Xia took me the other way, around to the back of the Precepture, up past the tool shed and the trellis crops, toward the line of whirligig wind generators and the induction spire. We did not go up there, though. The ship was there, and more soldiers, who did not look very civilized.

Soldiers. . . . We were at war. Now, right now, we were at war. The Rider would come. She would say my name, and Elián's, and—

I wobbled, my headache rising. Elián dashed toward the toolshed and upended an empty water trough to make a seat. Grego and Xie sat me down.

Damaged—the gardens were damaged. The goats were loose, and the pumpkin trellis was splayed flat against the ground. The rows of corn were flattened as if by a monstrous hand.

"They've knocked down the pumpkins," I said.

"Greta . . ." Xie looked at me, sidelong. "Greta, the Precepture's been taken. Captured."

"Oh," I said. "Do you think we'll be able to save the corn?"

"Let's take her to her cell," said Elián. "Maybe she can sleep it off."

"No." Horror froze me. "No sleep."

"All right." Elián touched my hair. "No sleep."

He was brave and he thought I was strong. I leaned into his hand, into his leg. Something hard caught the soft part of my cheek: There was a pistol on his hip. "Elián . . . You're armed."

"My grandmother—we're at war."

Elián's grandmother—Wilma Armenteros. I had accepted a formal declaration of war. I had no authority to do any such thing. "I should be sure Armenteros knows I'm not a plenipotentiary."

"Oh, sure," said Elián. "'Cause I'll bet she's worried about that."

"And look at the corn," I said. "This is worse than the food fight."

"They sent a shock ship," Grego explained. "It doesn't decelerate until it's nearly on top of you. The troops have to ride sideways to survive the g-forces. They have compression gear, special harnesses. It is the sonic boom that did this damage to the crops."

"Yes, great, thank you Gregori," said Elián.

And Xie said: "Greta, the corn doesn't matter."

"How can you say that?" Suddenly I found myself weeping. "How can you say that?" We needed the corn; we needed all this food. "Don't you want to live? I want to live."

I was so surprised to hear myself say it that I woke up.

I woke up with tears on my cheeks. It had been real—it held together, as much as I could piece it. The Cumberlanders had sent a shock ship and knocked out the Precepture's defenses and communications with an electromagnetic pulse, an EMP. The Abbot had had some bare warning of it, and had used that warning to pull me out of dreamlock.

There are shielded places we can go, the Abbot had said. He could have saved himself—and he did need to save himself. AIs had died in EMP attacks. It was part of what EMPs had been designed to do, once upon a time, in a less appropriate-tech age—take out enemy artificial intelligences. (*Oh yeah,* said the Utterances, *I'm totally banning those.*)

But the Abbot had not tried to save himself. He'd tried to save me.

And he had succeeded. Probably. More or less. It was Grego who had finished disconnecting the net of dreamlock magnets—his interest in blinking lights paying off at last—but it was the Abbot's sacrifice that had saved me. My head was throbbing, and my vision was too sharp, rainbow-edged, but that hard word that Grego had used—"damage"—I didn't think there was any.

But before I could say so, Elián, always too agitated, stood up. "We should get her to a neuromapper," he said. "A doctor. Somebody."

Da-Xia looked at him as a goddess looks at a mortal who has just given her a spoiled orange. "Elián, I don't think any of us are going anywhere. And particularly not Greta."

I turned to her. "Why's that?"

Xie looked at me and knew at once that I was awake again. She glanced by habit toward the Panopticon.

It was gone.

The Panopticon—gone. It must have been knocked down by the sonic boom. It lay across the clumped prairie grass in chunks and shards.

Nothing was watching us. Nothing. I felt—cut adrift.

I pushed the heels of my hands into my eyes and tried to sort out our situation logically. "Cumberland has attacked the Precepture directly, in advance of a declaration of war."

Even with my eyes covered I could hear Da-Xia's scholarly nod. "So far as I know."

"Greta?" said Elián, delicately. "Are you all right?"

I ignored him and blinked the spots away. "Help me work it out, Xie. To attack the Precepture— It is audacious and illegal. But it may make strategic sense. The Cumberlanders cannot win against the Pan Polar Confederacy under the rules of war. But wage a different kind of war, take hostages against the PanPols, take hostages to prevent the UN's action—that has some hope."

Grego bit his lip. He has of course little pigmentation in his lips, and I could see the blood rising to the pressure of his teeth. "This has been tried," he said, his accent thickening. "When the Kush states struck against Precepture Seven."

We all knew what had happened there. Not for nothing is Talis called the Butcher of Kandahar.

"You don't think that Talis will . . ." Elián's voice was suddenly thin. He was thinking of—Nashville, perhaps? Cleveland? Indianapolis itself?

There was no reason to think it would be only one.

"Talis holds that the Precepture system stops wars," said Da-Xia. "He will do whatever he must to save our Precepture. The entire Cumberland is expendable, next to that."

City goes boom, said the Utterances, commenting on the destruction of the last people to attack a Precepture. *It's really not meant to be subtle.*

It was not subtle, but Elián was struggling, truly struggling, to keep up. I had just spent three days having my thoughts professionally scrambled, but I was doing better than he was. He looked small inside his fatigues, like a child playing dress-up.

"The next question," I told him, "is, why hasn't Talis struck already?"

"And the answer," said Da-Xia, "is that the Cumberlanders have us. The hostages," she said, "are now hostages."

Elián scrubbed at his face. For a long time he was silent, stunned. Then he said: "Y'all really took that Socratic method shit to heart."

"The benefits," I intoned, "of a Precepture education."

"Yes," deadpanned Grego. "We were raised on Latin and Greek instead of love."

Before Xie could crack up—I could see her starting to—and before Elián could reply, there was a shout.

"Hey!" One of the soldiers came across the grass toward us. His gun sat easily in his hands, as if it were a hoe, and he a gardener. "Isn't that Princess what's-her-name?" He was looking at Elián.

"Greta," supplied Elián.

"Well, get her out in the open, okay? The shed blocks too many sight lines. Armenteros wants a close monitor on her."

Grego stepped between me and the soldier, raising his hand like a schoolboy. "Maybe you do not notice," he said, "but she's hurt."

"Just a little too much sun," I told the soldier. I did not need to advertise to the Cumberlanders how much it would take to break me. Let them think it would be easy, and maybe they would go easy. I got up, and let myself tremble, playing the delicate flower. "I'm all right, Gregori."

"Take her round with the others," the soldier ordered

THE SCORPION RULES 165

Elián, who still hadn't caught on. In uniform, armed, he had been mistaken for our guard.

The others. My friends. What had they done with my friends?

"We're going," I said, and I led the way, with our bewildered "guard" trailing us. Xie caught Elián by the elbow, which damaged his credibility, but seemed necessary: he did not look remotely like our military escort. She looked sidelong at him. "You're really not the most focused laser in the array, are you?"

"Hey!" Elián retorted, with laser-like brilliance. Then: "Just because I don't have *the benefits of a Precepture education* . . ." He exaggerated my precision into mockery.

Da-Xia shook her head. "Elián, listen to me, try to understand. We've been taken *hostage*. The Cumberlanders will use us against the UN. And they'll use Greta against the PanPols. It will beyond a doubt get ugly."

Ugly. Yes. Yes, it would.

Elián was trotting along with us now, so Xie dropped his arm. "You have," she said, "about thirty seconds to pick a side."

Around the flank of the Precepture hall we found Atta, Han, and Thandi sitting side by side in the grass, their backs to the soldiers in what had to be a deliberate choice, a tiny gesture of defiance. They had not been singled out or taken away. My friends.

They stood as they spotted us, and in a moment we were face-to-face, the three of them and the four of us. It felt as if we were not so much reuniting as squaring off. Why?

"Elián," said Thandi acidly. "Nice look."

Oh, right. That.

"Nice gun, too," said Thandi. "Really, it's good to know there'll be a friendly face on the firing squad."

"Thandi, don't," murmured Xie.

From all around, the sun glinted off the weapons trained on us. On me.

Elián was floundering. "I'm sorry, guys," he said. "I really am."

Thandi sneered. "I'm sure Greta will remember that when Armenteros starts digging in her claws."

I stiffened my face as if that could shut my ears. I didn't want to hear about claws. Not yet.

Elián was looking from one half of the unbalanced circle to the other. "Look, I know Grandma's not exactly cuddles and puppies. But I'm still gonna side with the people who *haven't* had my soft bits hooked up to electrodes all summer, okay?"

Something ugly—memory?—crawled across Thandi's face.

Elián looked stricken.

"It's all right," I told him softly.

He answered with a snarl like a wounded lion. "Dammit, Greta, it's not *all right.*"

He pushed both fists into his face and stood like that, not looking at me, not looking at any of us. My hands twitched at my side. I ached to reach out for him. He thought I was strong, and I needed to be strong. I needed him.

But I had promised to save him. And here— God help me, I needed him, but here was the moment when I could save him. I had not saved Sidney, and I could not save myself, but maybe I could save Elián. I closed my eyes and sank into the grass. Xie sank with me, and then the others, one by one. "Go, Elián," I whispered. "Go with the soldiers."

Elián hesitated, standing over us, his back to the sun and his face hidden in shadow. Then he turned and walked over to the Cumberlanders and took a place in their line.

"Oh," I said. A very tiny noise, far too small for Elián to hear. As small as a crack in a dam. He was so ridiculous about his defiance. I hadn't really thought he would go.

"In fairness," said Xie, "I don't think he understands."

We were all sitting close together. It was like a game, a child's game, kids in a ring, whispering secrets.

Xie put her hand on top of my knee.

"They're going to use me against my mother," I said. "Exploit her feelings. Public opinion."

"I know," said Xie. Her hand was warm and steady.

"But my mother is inured to the idea of my death," I said. "So it won't be death."

"I know," said Xie.

Thandi put her hand on my other leg. Warm weight, on each of my knees. Steadying. "Something public," I said. "Something—"

I tried not to look at Elián, standing in the line of men and women who were going to do something— That ugly word Grego had used. Something *damaging*.

15
UPLINK

That night it rained. Rain at last, rain too late, rain just when I was all set to get myself tortured over water rights—rain. As if I needed further proof that the fates had a black sense of humor.

Not merely rain, either—a storm. It rolled in from the northwest, tall as a spaceport, black as a mountain range, a huge prairie thunderstorm. Xie and I pulled our mats and blankets onto the floor and lay side by side to watch it billowing and flashing.

For almost an hour we lay there, watching the storm roll in, slow as a Swan Rider. There didn't seem to be anything to say. I could feel the warmth of Xie's body against my side.

"It stormed the first night you came here," she said, when the thunder was nearly on top of us. "Do you remember?"

I remembered. I'd been five and she'd been six. It had

been my first prairie storm. I had been sure that the prickling feeling in my skin meant that lightning was coming for
me. Sure I was going to be struck and catch fire and die.

I'd been paralyzed, but little Da-Xia had been bouncing
on her cot in plain delight. "It's a big one!"

Then she had looked at me. "Are you scared?"

And I had said, "No."

All my life I've been scared. And all my life I've been
telling people I was not. Almost—oh, almost—I believed it
was true.

Overhead the clouds were bubbling, lightning crawling
across their bellies. There was still no rain. A strange green
feeling thickened the air, as if everything were building a
charge, about to be magnetically levitated.

It was not true, what I had always said. It was not true
that I was not frightened.

I reached sideways and Xie took my hand.

The stone floor was hard, even through my mat. Hard
under the points of my shoulders. Hard under each knob of
my spine. Lightning flash-cracked and lit the room like—

"Xie," I said. "Do you think they'll kill me?"

Da-Xia's fingers stroked the pulse point in my wrist.
There weren't five people in the world who would have
answered me honestly, but Xie was one of them. She said,
"Not right away."

The clouds burst. Hail crashed against the glass. It made
a huge noise, and Xie and I twisted against each other, hid-
ing in each other's arms, for a moment that startled. Then we

both gathered ourselves, though the noise continued, loud enough that no one could possibly have known whether I was crying.

Finally the rain fell—only gusts and spatters, after all that—and slowly I shook myself to sleep.

When I woke it was late, well after dawn. Someone had turned off all the rota bells. Not hearing them made me feel as if I were floating in time. The sky had the blank, bruised look of someone freshly beaten.

Above the muddle of mats and blankets, Xie was sitting on the bare ropes of her cot. She nodded to me, and for a few moments I lay there, watching her long fingers fold cranes out of silvery candy wrappers the soldiers must have discarded. The room smelled faintly of chocolate. A Halifax smell: it made me queasy.

There was, surely, not much more time.

I got up.

I took more care than usual scrubbing up, braiding my hair. I ended up making the braids too tight; they pulled at my temples like electrodes.

I was just considering whether to redo them when the door opened, revealing, not the soldiers we had half expected, but a different sort of man. He was middle-aged, middle-height, and tawny everywhere—leathered skin and flyaway hair, eyes that were almost yellow. Tawny, and scrawny, like a lion who'd been kicked out of the pride. He stood alone in the doorway, a smile on his face and a clipboard in his hand.

"Ah, Princess Greta," he said. "Your Royal Highness. And this must be"—he checked his clipboard—"the Daughter of the Heavenly Throne?"

"I am Greta," I said. "I am a blood hostage to this Precepture, and a Child of Peace. We don't use our titles here."

"Ah," he said. "Well, the Precepture is changing, as you've probably gathered. But, of course, I'm glad to follow your preferences. I'm Tolliver Burr." He extended a hand to shake. I had nearly forgotten that people did that. When I didn't take his hand, he turned to Xie. "And you. Should I call you 'Da-Xia'?"

Xie looked down her nose at him. "Do you know, I think 'Daughter of Heaven' will do nicely."

"Your Divinity," he said. "Of course."

"Mr. Burr—" I said.

"Tolliver, please."

"Mr. Burr," I said. "What did you need from us?"

"Ah. I was hoping you'd come with me."

"Both of us?" Da-Xia continued her down-the-nose thing. I needed to learn that from her. It is an impressive trick when you're only five feet tall.

"Well, the crown princess, specifically, Your Divinity. She's needed in the library. But of course you're welcome to come." He opened his arm in the direction of the miseri. Xie glided magnificently past him, leading the way.

"And what did you want with the crown princess?" asked Xie. "Specifically."

"Oh, I'm a . . . specialist. A communications specialist."

"Communications," I echoed, uneasy.

There were two guards outside the miseri. Burr nodded to them, and they stepped aside. The door slid open.

Books still lay where they'd been knocked down by the sonic boom. Daylight fell through the broken ceiling, and I could smell the sharp, sad scent of dust after rain.

Beside the map table stood the Abbot.

He turned as we came in. His face was back on its screen. "Marcus Aurelius says that the best revenge is to be unlike him who performed the injury. I admit I'm struggling with that. Good morning, Da-Xia. Good morning, Greta. I am relieved to see you looking well."

"Good Father," I said, and my voice came out husky. I'd thought the EMP might have killed him. I was more pleased to see him than I could easily say.

"I see you've met Mr. Burr."

"Tolliver, please," said Burr again.

As I came closer to the Abbot, I saw that one of his hands was pinned to the table. Beside the hand rested a small box with a twinkling touch screen. A filament bundle ran out of the box, coiled on the table like a baby snake, and ran up to the Abbot's head. I looked from the Abbot to Burr and back again.

"Mr. Burr and I have been having a disagreement," said the Abbot. There was a funny little wheeze in his voice. "I've been explaining to him that I am a Class Two Artificial Intelligence, with full rights of personhood under the Bangalore Convention, and not, in fact, a communications terminal."

"But you can uplink," said Burr.

"Of course I can," said the Abbot. "Your question should be whether I will."

"Oh," said Burr, as if the matter were merely technical. "I think our box will work all right." He leaned past me and did something to the touch screen.

The Abbot jerked like Elián under shock, and then—he died. It was exactly like seeing the life drain from a human's eyes. One moment the Abbot was there, and then it was just a body, a hunk of parts. "Father!" I cried. But he did not come back.

Da-Xia's hand was on my arm—I could feel her shake. But none of the Cumberlanders reacted.

"Father Abbot?" I said. Nothing.

"Is it working, Burr?" Wilma Armenteros came out of the shadows behind the Abbot's desk.

"Yes, General." Burr squinted at the screen. "We're go for uplink."

"Good," Armenteros grunted. She pulled out a chair opposite the Abbot. "Your Highness. Have a seat."

Slowly I circled the table to her. I sat. I stared at the dead thing that had been my Abbot. The general patted my shoulder, her hand heavy. I could feel my pulse in my temples, tugging at the fine hairs where my braids were too tight. Armenteros loomed behind me. The chair was hard.

Da-Xia came and stood beside the Abbot. Her eyes said, *Hold on.* I wished I might hold her hand. I looked at it, splayed out beside the Abbot's on the table. The Abbot's hand had a screw driven through it, piercing the external rubber muscles and forcing a new opening between the metacarpal nuts. The table was narrow—I could have touched that lifeless hand. I didn't. I felt the back of the chair notch under my shoulder blades: I must have been leaning away.

Tolliver Burr came bustling round the table to my side. "That's perfect, hold still a moment." He held some sort of meter next to my face, and then flipped it around to read it. He nodded at the general, satisfied. "This is fine. If I had a scatter box, I could smooth out some of the shadows—but really, you don't want it to look too polished. She just needs to be clearly recognizable."

Armenteros nodded. "Thank you, Burr. Please patch us through."

"Of course, just let me get out of the shot."

Out of the—his words echoed in my head. Was someone about to shoot me?

I looked up at the Abbot. His facescreen was blank. Only few scattered pixels showed where his eyes and mouth had been when he'd . . . gone.

"And . . . go." Burr lifted a hand from his touch screen with a little ta-da flair of his wrist.

And suddenly, in the place of the Abbot's face, there was my mother.

Queen Anne was not wearing her wig.

That shocked me, shocked me almost as if she'd met us disrobed. Her hair was short, mussy, more ash than fire. For a moment she didn't look at me. Clearly I had not come into focus for her. I heard the whirr of a lens moving somewhere, and then her eyes met mine. "Greta," she said.

I did not know what to say. I tried: "Mother."

"Are you all right? Have they hurt you? Have they hurt any of you?"

"I—" How could I explain? The fact that I'd been in dreamlock when the EMP had hit was not the Cumberlanders' fault. That I'd been in dreamlock at all was too complex a matter to treat here. "None of the Children I've seen are hurt. They've hurt the Abbot—" I looked at his hand, and back to where his face should have been. I could see only my mother.

"Greta . . ." She seemed to be pleading with me. For what?

"And, pan right," said Tolliver. He tapped something on his box. It must have overridden my mother's virtual presence, because the Abbot pivoted mechanically, to focus on the general.

"There's your proof of life, Your Majesty," said Armenteros. "Are you satisfied?"

"I take it you have retrieved your own hostage," Queen Anne said, her voice crisp enough to stamp on coins. "Your grandson, I believe."

Armenteros glanced into the darkness, and then looked back and shrugged. "A side benefit, Your Majesty, and not relevant to this discussion."

The Abbot's head—my mother's head—swung; she turned back to face me. She had zoomed. Her face filled the facescreen, and was shown only chin to forehead. Her eyes were where eye icons would have been. They searched me. I felt I should say something, but I really did not know what. Her gaze held me trembling.

"Greta, talk to me. Say something only you know. Something they couldn't fake."

My scalp prickled, but I didn't stop to think. I just answered: "I'm not Joan of Arc," I said. "I know because I'm frightened."

"*Greta.*" I hardly even heard my name. I could only see it, on the shape of my mother's lips. She lifted the Abbot's hand and touched me: I felt the light coolness of the ceramic fingertips on my cheek. For a moment I let myself lean into that well-known touch, and then I looked at my mother and nodded. My mother nodded back, queen to queen, and turned to face the general.

"All right, Armenteros." The harshness of my mother's voice made the Abbot's voder buzz. "Let's hear your demands."

I sat in the hard wooden chair at the map table—the table where I'd plotted the progress of the wars that had taken us, one by one. Bihn, taken so young. Vitor, solid and sad. Sidney, his hand falling from mine. The map table where I had studied the coming war, the war that was going to kill Elián. And me.

Off to my left, Armenteros was giving her demands—or rather, her demand. She had only one, and it was precisely what I had thought it would be—drinking water rights to Lake Ontario. I had even correctly predicted the amount, seven thousand acre-feet per annum.

Such mastery was usually a comfort to me. I could hear the Abbot's voice saying just that. *I wonder if ignorance is really the kindest thing.* And I could see the high table in the grey room, where the light was so even that no shadows fell. Would it be injection? Beams? A bullet to the head? What reason was there to care? There had not been a reason before. Why should there be one now? The Cumberlanders must surely be planning something less . . . private.

Queen Anne said, "That is beyond the carrying capacity of the lake."

"Just under, my hydrologists say."

Even filtered through the Abbot, the tilt of my mother's head was pure me—pure her. "That analysis was done in a wet decade. The usual pattern is 6,200 acre-feet—ten percent less."

Armenteros shook her head slowly. "Seven thousand is the minimum required to sustain our population."

"Then your population will need to change," said Queen Anne. "The lake can't."

"You suggest I let two hundred thousand people die of thirst?"

I was certain of my mother's raised eyebrow, though I could see only the back of the Abbot's head, the crack in his casing where the fibers had been jammed in. "I suggest you relocate them. But that is your decision: purely an internal matter."

"Your Majesty," said Armenteros. "I will not be coy." She drew a husky breath. I knew what was next. It was time to make explicit the implied threat. Time to mention torture.

Coy, she'd said.

Suddenly I was furious. I reached across the table and took hold of the bundle of fibers between the Abbot's head and Tolliver Burr's box. I yanked.

The wires tore free. The Abbot grunted and staggered, swinging round and catching himself against the table. On his screen, my mother's face froze and distorted.

"General Armenteros," I said, "it would astonish me if you were *coy*."

"Sit down, Your Highness." Armenteros rumbled. "Burr, get the queen back."

"Don't you dare," I snapped at him. And then I rounded on her. "And you," I said, "are not permitted to use my title. My name is Greta, and so you will call me. You think because I am hostage to the Precepture that anyone can use me? I am a Child of Peace. Touch one hair on my head and the AIs will come for you. Talis will wipe Cumberland from the map, do you hear me? *From the map!*" I slapped the table so hard that several soldiers jumped. My hand stung numb.

"Sit down," said the general, and raised one finger. There was a wave of clicking around the room as guns swung up and pointed at me.

I laughed. "You won't shoot me. You can hardly torture me if you shoot me first."

The general made a tock with her tongue, acknowledging the point. She sounded so much like the Abbot that it made me reel. I grabbed onto the table edge.

Tolliver Burr looked at Da-Xia as if deciding what role to cast her in. "What about her? We could shoot her."

"The roommate? Who is she?" said Armenteros, as some of the guns swung to cover Xie.

Da-Xia smiled her destroying Tara smile, pressed her palms together in front of her and bowed over them. "I," she said, "am the Daughter of the Heavenly Throne, the Beloved of the Mountains, the Pure Soul of Snow. Single me out, and you will find yourself at war with most of central Asia."

"She's quite right," said the Abbot. His head was hanging, and there was a thickening whirr in his voice. "They both are. The UN won't take this lightly. Talis will personally order the strike on Cumberland."

Talis. On the lips of another AI, it was a name to conjure with. The temperature in the room seemed to drop.

"I am leaving," I said. "There is no need for me to be here while you decide how to hurt me."

I let go of the table, which had pressed a white fault line into the soft part of my palm. I would have staggered, except that Da-Xia came and took my elbow, formally, as would befit the escort of a queen.

"And you," I snapped at Burr. "You must have some other equipment in that ship of yours. Use it. I won't talk to my mother through the Abbot again. Let him go."

"Thank you, Greta," the Abbot slurred. He didn't lift his head. His hand was still pinned to the table. But he was alive. The guns followed us like eyes as we processed toward the door.

The light through the broken ceiling was chiaroscuro: here bright enough to make one squint, there thick with shadow. The soldiers by the door were blurred by their chamo and mostly hidden in the darkness; I could see only their movement, shifting to make way for us.

It wasn't until I was nearly there that I saw that one of them—his gun slack in his hand, his face as tense and sick as if the spiders were crawling over every inch of him—was Elián.

16
IN THE GARDEN

Outside the miseri Da-Xia took my arm, and we ran like deer. We spilled out of the shadowy transept and into the bright morning. The grass was wet under our bare feet.

"'It would astonish me if you were coy!'" Da-Xia tumbled against the Precepture wall, grinning from ear to ear. "There you are, Greta. Well done!" She was laughing.

A few moments ago I would have been laughing too—at the release, at the look on Armenteros's face—but seeing Elián had ripped it from me. I felt hollowed out. "Oh, Xie. . . ." I leaned against the wall beside her. The easterly light was sweet, but the old stones were still cool with the memory of night. "Do you remember Bihn?"

Bihn. She'd been tiny for her age, and sweet fingered. She had liked to braid my hair. She could hold so still that doves would come and eat out of her hand. When we were nine a Swan Rider came for her. He'd called her name, and she'd started screaming. Sidney, Vitor, and Bihn. Three of my classmates had died, in my time at the Precepture. But only Bihn had been dragged out screaming.

Da-Xia pivoted away from the wall, so that we were face to face. "You will not lose your courage, Greta," she said, willing something into me, something fiercer than a blessing. Her eyes were black with their intensity, locked on to mine. "Listen to me. You will not."

We were belly to belly. Her face was powerfully close.

I am not sure which of us moved first. But suddenly my mouth was on hers. And her lips were warm as the sunlight, and her skin was cool as the grass, and she was everything. Da-Xia. My whole world.

How could it possibly have taken me so long to see that?

Her hand slipped under the hem of my shirt and brushed over the goose-bumped skin of my flank.

"Xie . . ." It came out almost as a moan. I found my hand on the small of her back—awake to the flare of her hip, to the way my fingers fitted between the buttons of her spine. I pulled her closer.

Just then, Elián came bursting out the door. He saw us. He stopped.

Xie pulled away from me. A flush crept up her throat. I could not remember that I had ever seen Da-Xia blush. But she blushed under Elián's panting silence.

"Oh," he said.

"Elián—" I felt the urge to explain. And then a surge of anger: what was there to explain? And what right had he to an explanation? He'd held a gun on me, listened to plans to have me tortured. And, all right, I'd told him to, but—

"You're not armed," said Xie.

"Yeah, well—" Elián scratched behind his ear. "Some question in there about where my loyalties are."

"Out here, too," said Xie.

"God, Xie, like I'd ever—" He cut himself off and turned to me. "Greta. I didn't know, I swear. How could I know?"

"Da-Xia did explain."

"And Thandi," said Xie. "And Grego . . ."

"But I didn't—" He was breathing hard, his voice climbing toward hysteria. "I didn't know. I'm a *sheep farmer*, Greta. I like to bake. I go *bowling*."

"How quaint," said Xie.

I flipped up a hand to stop her, and sagged down against the wall. "Do you know what they're planning, Elián?"

He shook his head to deny it, but there was knowledge in his face. He must have seen me read it; he came out with it slowly. "I only know . . . That man—Tolliver Burr—he's having them— He wants them . . ." His voice dropped and he nearly gagged. "He wants them to move the apple press out onto the lawn. Where the light is better for filming."

We considered that. I tried—oh, how I tried—not to consider it too closely. But there is no rest for a restless mind. The apple press—huge and ancient, with its screws as thick as a thigh, hand-turned from oak trunks in some unimaginable time before machines could speak. And the screws needed to be strong, to carry the force it took to juice an apple—to bring down the iron-bound oak top of the press, turn by turn. It was big, the press. You could lay a bushel of apples in it, or a bushel of potatoes, in the days when Vitor and Atta had tried to make vodka, before the unfortunate explosion of the still. You could put a bushel of carrots into it, or a human torso. Or perhaps just a hand . . . There were so many nerves in the hand. My own hands were cramping into fists. I could feel how much force it took, to turn the press those last few clicks.

I wrenched away from the wall and folded forward, retching.

I crouched by the wall a long time. They knelt with me. Xie rubbed circles on my back. Elián put his hand over mine, where it was digging into the thatch of the grass.

"Sorry," I gasped as the fit passed. "Sorry."

They both shook their heads. There was silence. I leaned back limply against the wall, grateful for its cool strength.

"Tolliver Burr," said Da-Xia, rolling the name around. "Do you know, I could grow to dislike him. And Armenteros, too—no offense, Elián."

"You should—" I coughed, and wiped the back of my hand across my mouth. The bitter taste of fear was still strong enough to choke me. Well, it was either fear or yesterday's stuffed zucchini. "Elián, you should go back to your grandmother."

Elián made a disbelieving huff. "No way am I leaving you."

Da-Xia picked up my hand. "None of us will, Greta. Lean into that."

I shook my head. "Elián—think. Our countries are at war. When Talis reestablishes control over the Precepture, both our lives are forfeit." I tried to concentrate. "I meant it when I said to go. I meant it. Go back to the Cumberlanders. Your only way out of here is with them."

"The expletive I will, Greta," said Elián.

"But there's no way out for me," I said. "You can't save me. Go."

"Dipshit," he whispered, and put a hand in my hair. "The expletive I will."

"Elián Palnik, I think there's hope for you," said Xie. She paused. "Albeit in a somewhat abstract sense. In the concrete sense, you're clearly doomed."

"I can't go back, anyhow. Grandma—I feathered her good. They were going to court-martial me, except"—he smiled at Da-Xia—"turns out I'm not a soldier."

"I haven't figured you out yet," she answered. "But I think I concur."

"I haven't figured you out either." His gaze flipped between us. "I'm guessing there's a bunch of stuff I haven't figured out."

Again, I could have explained. Da-Xia and I were not lovers, we were—what were we? How could I be worried about this when the apple press was being made ready? How could it be that I could still conjure a quickening in my blood when I thought of her kiss? We were not— We were . . . I did not know.

So I explained nothing, but stood up, wiping my hands

down the rough linen of my samue. "Let's go see if any of the pumpkins can be salvaged."

"The . . . pumpkins?" said Elián. I disliked his they've-broken-her-already-poor-thing tone.

"As an act of normalcy," explained Da-Xia.

"As an act," I said grandly, "of defiance. And hope."

"Defiance and hope. Check." Elián let loose one corner of his Spartacus smile. "Y'all will have to tell me if I'm doing it right."

I have never been more proud to be a Child of Peace. By the time we made it to the toppled pumpkin trellises, all the Children were outside, and working in the gardens.

The soldiers bunched up here and there, watching and bewildered. How useless are guns against those who are fearless. How foolish, to set force against innocence. Their own strength made them small.

And to their smallness, we sang.

The Children of Peace do not as a rule sing. But the Cumberlanders couldn't, wouldn't know that. And it baffled them. So we did it.

Thandi—of all people—started it. I did not know if the words were nonsense or Xhosa, but her voice surprised me with its grace. The rhythms were easy and rolling, and the music spilled down over the terraces. Soon everyone was singing. That morning there were songs from every corner of the world. Da-Xia and Elián and I were soon joined by the rest of the cohort in picking through the debris of the pumpkin trellis.

We sorted through the pumpkins, and all the while we sang. Even Elián sang for us: "Jack of diamonds, jack of diamonds, I know you of old . . ." (It was a song about poor impulse control. Naturally.) Then some small one tried to interest the terraces in "Rockabye Baby," and my friends slipped toward silence.

Rockabye baby, your cradle is green
Father's a king, and mother's a queen
When apples are ripe and ready to fall
Down will come baby, apples and all

I was mesmerized by the old song, so much so that I jumped when Elián spoke suddenly, and too loud. "Will Talis really— What will the UN do?"

He looked at me. In his hearing I had wished for the destruction of the entire nation of Cumberland. No, more than wished. I had *invoked* it, called it down like a sibyl calling down the wave that swamped Atlantis. *From the map,* I had said. In that moment I had wanted it, passionately. The death of millions.

"Talis will most likely negotiate," said Grego cautiously.

"No," said Da-Xia. "Forgive me, Gregori, Elián, but—no. We remember him, in the Himalayas, as you do not remember him here. Talis might do many things. But he will certainly not negotiate."

"Oh," said Elián.

It was different, considering the destruction of

Cumberland, when you had to look a Cumberlander—even one—in the eye.

And so we all waited for the various things we feared.

The downside of sorting pumpkins in a manner suggesting defiance and hope was that it gave us a view of the toolshed. It was cruel to watch. There were a half dozen soldiers around it, stringing cabling, setting up cameras on tripods, a scan-and-scramble antenna (thank you, Grego). White umbrellas that bloomed on the lawn like man-high morning glories. From within the shed came banging, cursing—the ancient apple press in silent resistance.

And all the time Tolliver Burr moved here and there. Checked this and that.

I tried not to watch him, but I watched.

The prickling swarm of the pumpkin vines scratched my hands and wrists.

Finally Xie stepped between me and the scene, and caught both my hands. She raised them until we were forearm to forearm, like warriors. "There is no need for us to be here."

"I want to—"

"To garden, to harvest, to carry on. But we wouldn't need to do this particular thing. There is no need for you to torture yourself."

I laughed, then choked on the laugh. "It does seem redundant."

Xie lifted our joined hands, and pressed them on each

side of my cheeks, smiling. I leaned my forehead down against hers. Oh, Xie . . . In a dream I had seen her crowned. But she could not be more glorious crowned than she was now.

"You wouldn't have to show defiance and hope just exactly here," said Elián. "Trust me, I'm a farmer. There's quackweed everywhere."

"May all the gods bless quackweed," said Xie. She released my hands, and tucked an arm around my waist. "Come, Your Royal Highness. Let's go weed the garlic."

I looked toward the toolshed, where the soon-to-be-tor-turers were taking down the apple press. It was also where we kept the hoes.

"What are they doing in there?" said Han.

"I'll go," said Thandi. Her hair, loose, stood out like a halo, full of light. She went with a walk that made the sol-diers step back from her, vanished into the shed for a tight moment, then came back with three hoes over her shoulder. "All that's left," she said. After all, the entire school was out gardening.

I took one; Xie and Elián, the other two. "Thank you," I said, to Thandi, to all of them. My voice was smaller than I would have liked. Then we walked down toward the terraced gardens. Two of the soldiers peeled from the group by the shed and followed us. No one remarked on it.

The garlic was on one of the lowest terraces. It was cooler there, though the sun was drying the last scraps of mud, leaving the bare earth of the newly planted bed cracking like the bed of a drained lake. It smelled of fall. And, of course, of garlic. The shadow of the induction spire swept over us like a clock hand. We stood with the soldiers at our backs, looking down at the alfalfa field and the loop of the Saskatchewan River.

"Could we make it to the river, you think?" said Elián softly.

Neither Xie nor I looked around at the Cumberlanders and their guns, though of course they were vital to that calculation. "Perhaps," said Da-Xia. "But to what end?" We hadn't a boat, and as suicides went, drowning was slow. Interruptible. I doubted there was an escape of any kind in that shining water.

"We should at least think about it," said Elián. "About getting out of here."

"I do," said Xie. "All the time."

It ripped my heart to hear her say it. It ripped my heart because—I never had.

Down the slopes came the whirr of a power saw. The apple press, with its footings sunk deep into the packed earth—Tolliver Burr was having it cut free.

17
IN THE PRESS

Oh, September days—how long they are.

Confine thyself to the present, Aurelius wrote. But I could not. The minutes prickled by. The afternoon wore heat for a while and then took it off like a jacket. By the time Tolliver Burr had me summoned, I was shivering.

The first thing he did was smile at me. Then he took a step away and looked me up and down, and framed me with his fingers. "Hmmmm," he said.

And I was embarrassed. Embarrassed! "I do hope I meet your expectations, Mr. Burr."

"Tolliver," he said absently, as if he'd almost given up on that. "You're lovely, Greta. You're a picture. But . . ." He made a loop in the air with his hand "Perhaps a shower?"

The apple press was standing in the bunch grass beside him. I tried not to notice it, but in truth I saw it sharply—the pale splinters of wood where the supports had been sawn free, the mica flecks in the granite pan. They had a couple of gantry spiders set up to turn the cranks.

"A shower," I said.

Burr smiled and nodded. "So you look your best."

Fervently I hoped that if I threw up again, it would be on Tolliver Burr's crisp white shirt.

"The Precepture does not have showers, Mr. Burr."

"Hmmmm," he said again. "Well, if you don't, you don't." And then, over his shoulder: "Ginger, get the princess a bucket and a washcloth." And to me: "Do you have anything else to wear, Greta? Or shall I find you something?"

I thought of the flower-figured taffeta gown, the dress that had turned to a constrictor in my dream. "Mr. Burr," I said, "I will wear this."

"But . . ."

"If you're going to martyr me," I said, "you may as well dress me as a monk."

"Martyr! Oh, no! I shouldn't think it would go that far." Tolliver Burr swooped his hands around, taking in the cameras, the lights. "I'm a professional, Greta. A persuasive man." He smiled again— It looked corpselike on his desiccated face. "It won't take much, I promise."

And he might be right. The parliamentary elections coming—the public pressure—

Pressure. An unfortunate thing to think. *Pressure,* I thought. And then I could no longer think. I wondered if they had drugged me somehow, or if I was simply that afraid.

"I've got a hardlock override into the public broadcasts,"

Tolliver Burr was saying. I was hardly listening to him. "The viewing audience may well be unprecedented. I'm sure the PanPols will demand that the government save their princess. And of course, your mother loves you."

Of course.

Someone had put a bucket of soapy water at my feet. I looked at it and tried to remember what to do. Burr picked up a cloth, softly wiping my face, washing each of my fingers. "You're beautiful, Greta. A natural."

I came back to myself with a cry: "Don't touch me!"

"There you are," he said encouragingly. "Just natural reactions, dear. Don't bother to act. Truly, you'll be fine."

I staggered back from him, and I was still reeling when two soldiers took me by the elbows.

All my life I had been trained to go quietly. But now—I fought. Why should I not fight? It was hopeless, it was impossible, but I fought anyway, and they had to drag me—if not screaming, at least shouting and kicking.

Someone shoved me to my knees; even as I got up again, someone else jerked my hands out onto the stone tray of the press. My chin hit the stone. There was blood in my mouth. Black sparks in my eyes. Soldiers everywhere. They had plastic straps with smart adhesives. I fought but it took them less than ten seconds to strap me down, wrist and elbow. I jerked and pulled against the straps. They bit into my skin, raising welts along their clear borders. I did it another moment, unable to stop myself.

And then I stilled.

The tray was low; I was hunched awkwardly, my tailbone as high as my shoulders. I took a deep breath, and I knelt. There was dignity in that. Tradition. A queen at the block.

I looked up.

The Cumberlanders had pulled me away from Da-Xia and Elián when Burr had summoned me. With desperate eyes I sought past the apple press, past the cameras, past Burr, to see what had become of them.

They were behind a line of soldiers, clear back by the top of the terraces. Thandi and Atta were holding Xie. She was struggling in their arms, shouting and kicking just as I had. Grego still had his arms full of pumpkin, and Han was gripping Grego's arm, his mouth hanging open. Elián was standing with Armenteros. He had grabbed her by the arm and appeared to be spitting into her face. Armenteros's aide-de-camp, Buckle, had Elián by the other arm. The blood was pounding in my ears; I could not hear them.

Burr was pacing away from the press, considering it from a few different angles, adjusting cameras and nudging diffusers, checking things off on his clipboard. I looked at the cohort, I looked at Elián, getting my breath back, trying to focus. None of the younger children were in sight. Herded back into the Precepture hall? Probably best. This could make a mob of them. Someone could be hurt. I looked at my own hands, fingers tensed and bunched on the grey stone. Yes, indeed. Someone could be hurt.

"If you could just bring them over here," said Burr to the soldiers guarding my cohort. "We'll need them for reaction shots." He consulted a clipboard. "There are supposed to be six. Where's the last one?"

A gust of silence, and then Elián raised his hand like the well-mannered Child of Peace he most certainly was not. "Right here."

"Elián . . ." Armenteros's exasperation was well-worn. Clearly Elián's ridiculous defiance was not a recently acquired trait.

Elián dropped his grandmother's arm and drew himself up. He stepped away from Armenteros and Buckle.

Burr flicked two fingers up and down. "In uniform? No, no, he clashes dreadfully. Is this the grandson? Someone get him his whites."

"I don't want him in whites," said Armenteros.

Elián started fumbling with buttons. "He doesn't want me in chamo, you don't want me in white—did anyone bring my bowling shirt?"

"Elián, you're being childish," said Armenteros.

"Childish!" He yanked off his soldier's shirt and threw it at her. "Maybe I can grow up to be a famous torturer!"

"I'm trying to save our country, Elián," she said blandly.

Elián stood there, bare-ribbed and shivering.

"There's no denying he's got something," said Burr, absently framing Elián in a rectangle of fingers. "I'd love to have him to zoom in on, General. Those eyes could bring it all home."

Armenteros ignored him. "Elián, there's no point in a delay. Do you really think the princess wants to be kept in suspense?"

"Let's ask her," he said, and before anyone was sure it was right to stop him—he was the general's grandson, after all—he had walked over to me. He smiled down. "Hi."

I tried to speak, failed, swallowed, and croaked out, "Hi."

"Greta," he whispered, and knelt. He was across the apple press from me. I could see what Burr meant about his eyes: they were liquid, huge, showing whites. Terrified. I was sure we matched. He took a deep breath and put his hands on the stone. Our fingertips touched. "Told you I was Spartacus," he said. Then he raised his voice to call to the Cumberlanders: "Now I think we're set to go."

Absolute silence. For the moment the only movement came from Tolliver Burr, who was leaning in a handheld camera.

"Shut that thing off!" Armenteros ordered. "Elián, get up."

"Why?" snapped Elián. "You said I should learn to sacrifice for my country."

Armenteros pressed her thumb between her eyebrows. "Buckle, please take my grandson inside and get him a shirt."

"You'll have to drag me," said Elián. "And how's that going to look, huh?"

Buckle looked at Armenteros, who gave a great sigh, then nodded.

"You're a torturer," Elián snarled at his grandmother. "A monster!"

Buckle gathered up a couple of men, and they dragged Elián off. He was still screaming my name.

"You'll have to do without your reaction shots, Burr," Armenteros said. "I want them all locked up."

The soldiers closed in on my friends. A generalized shouting; swearing in several languages. Over the din I heard for a moment another voice—Da-Xia. "Greta!" she shouted. "There's a plume, Greta! A plume!"

A plume of dust.

A Swan Rider. They were coming.

My friends—the passive and obedient Children of Peace— my friends fought like lions.

They took bruises and left scratches.

They were delaying. And not with a noble lack of plan, as Elián had done. A lifetime of watching for that plume—they had all seen it. A lifetime of watching for it, and for the first time we were eager. *What could one Rider do?* asked my sensible self. But my sensible self was overridden. A Rider. The Riders changed everything.

The delay was short—too short—less than five minutes. How long did I need? It had just rained; the plume would not be too high. Not hours. Twenty minutes? Thirty?

Too long, too long.

The Precepture hall swallowed the noise of my friends. The Cumberland soldiers were unnaturally quiet. The nearest one to me was shifting from foot to foot like a child called before the Abbot's desk. A pair of mourning doves flew past me, whirring and whirling, and perched on the roof of the toolshed.

"Well," said Burr. "Hmmm. A wide shot and some chokers cut in, I guess. Unless I can use one of your boys for a reaction, Wilma?" He jerked a thumb at one of the soldiers, a gawky white boy whose wide green eyes seemed to match his skin. He looked as if he might throw up.

"No, you cannot," she said. "Get on with it, Burr."

Tolliver Burr paced the camera line, checking the view from each angle. Then stepped in behind a monitor. He rubbed his hands together. "All right, Greta. Let's have some action."

Lights twinkled as the gantry spiders manning the cranks came to life. There was the barest pause as they set their articulated legs around the pegs meant for human hands. And then the whole mechanism shuddered, and the crushing block began to descend.

The block began a few inches above my head, a good two feet from my hands. Each wheel turn dropped it the barest fraction. It was so slow that one could ordinarily hardly see it moving.

In that moment, I could see nothing else.

Tolliver Burr had moved to tripod directly in front of me. As if I had left my body, I could picture what he saw. The iron-bound oak block, the stone pan, the screws on each side—the press made a dark frame. Inside that frame knelt a princess in white, her hands bound in front of her. I saw the single eye of the camera, and I saw what it saw. I knew what Burr wanted: for me to meet that eye with helpless, pleading terror.

And, God help me, I gave him what he wanted.

"That's lovely, dear," he murmured squinting into the eyepiece. "That's perfect." He held up a hand. "Let's have quiet; I want a good capture on the sound."

Oh, the sound. The heaviness of each *clock* of the master gear. The sound was an arrow entering me, again and again and again. The tick-clocks came a little faster than I could breathe to, and my breath sped up to meet them. There were red spots in my vision, and the camera's eye was like a gaping hole.

"Good," said Burr. "Very good. We can all hear you, Greta, you're a star."

The spiders were turning the cranks slowly. The mechanism was geared six to one. It went: Tick. Tock. Clock. Tick. Tock. *Drop.*

The stone shuddered under my hands.

The camera's eye, and beyond it the ridge, the whirligig generators, the pure blue sky. I saw no plume in it.

"I'm dropping a mute bubble on everything else," said Burr. "You can speak freely, General. The audience can't hear you."

". . . confirmation. The cabinet is in session." Buckle was pressing her hand to her earpiece.

Armenteros pushed her lips together and shook her head. "Not the cabinet. The privy council. Tell them I want the privy council; I want the queen."

Tick. Tock. Clock. Tick. Tock. *Drop.* The top of the press brushed against a stray loop of hair. I reared back from it, jerking at my arms. The plastic might as well have been steel.

"Perfect," Burr purred.

My head was thrown back, and my shoulders wrenched. My arms began to shake like overloaded cables.

Tick. Tock. Clock. Tick. Tock. *Drop.*

". . . in session," said Buckle, to the earpiece. She kept talking. I couldn't listen.

Tick. Tock. Clock. Tick. Tock. *Drop.*

The press was at forehead level now. My shoulders were screaming with pain.

The gears turned and ticked.

The press dropped.

And dropped.

Burr swung one of his handheld cameras in for a view of my hands.

I looked at my hands. The fingers were clenched and raised up. I could see all four tendons across the back of the palm, clear as dowels. I could see the knuckles: white and lumpy like tiny potatoes.

Tick. Tock. Clock. Tick. Tock. *Drop.*

Tick. Tock. Clock. Tick. Tock. *Drop.*

"We're on-screen in the Halifax chambers, General."

Tick. Tock. Clock. Tick. Tock. *Drop.*

Calm down, Greta. Calm down.

My hands didn't look like hands at all. They looked like the Abbot's hands, like machines.

Calm down, Greta. A Rider. A Rider is coming.

Tick. Tock. Clock. Tick. Tock. *Drop.*

Calm down.

Calm down.

I took a deep breath and leaned forward, releasing the tension in my shoulders. It had become a huge pain; easy as that, it was gone. I felt the blood pounding in the swollen skin under the plastic straps.

Tick. Tock. Clock. Tick. Tock. *Drop.*

Tick. Tock. Clock. Tick. Tock. *Drop.*

Calm down. I let go of my fists.

A Rider was coming.

Cameras were on me. Watching me. To see how well I did.

Tick. Tock. Clock. Tick. Tock. *Drop.*

Tick. Tock. Clock. Tick. Tock. *Drop.*

I could do this part. This part. The waiting.

All my life, the waiting.

This part, I could do.

And so. Slowly the press closed. The crushing block came in front of my face. There were some moments when I could see nothing but its ancient grey-brown wood. An iron band brushed by my nose. And then it was farther down, and I could see over it.

Tolliver Burr was bobbing heel to toe like an expectant father. Buckle had her head tilted, conversing with the voice in her ear. Armenteros just stood.

Tick. Tock. Clock.

Tick. Tock. *Drop.*

Sometimes the panic flew up in me and my hands shuddered and clenched. But I did well enough.

The press was at my shoulders now. I could no longer see my hands.

I twisted around to try to see the Precepture hall, but its windows were blank.

On my left, the pens of milk goats, the ripening pumpkins.

On my right, the garden terrace.

Straight ahead, the hole of the camera. The blue flaregun sky.

Tick. Tock. Clock.

Tick. Tock. *Drop.*

What would it feel like when—

My arms jerked against the straps. I could feel the blood trickling under plastic.

Tick. Tock. Clock.

Tick. Tock. *Drop.*

The press was under my collarbone, now. How thick was it? Was the bottom of it nine inches from my hands? Six?

Stay calm, Greta. Stay calm. A Rider is coming.

The plume. Finally I could see the plume. I grabbed hold of it with my eyes.

Tick. Tock. Clock.

Tick. Tock. *Drop.*

"Confirm that?" said Buckle, nodding to herself. She tilted her head. She looked up. "General. There's a single horseback rider, incoming."

"The UN," growled Armenteros.

Talis.

There was a pause. The press dropped again.

"The Swan Riders aren't armed," said Buckle. "Crossbows only."

"Traditionally," said Armenteros.

What was happening here was far from traditional.

Tick. Tock. Clock.

Tick. Tock. *Drop.*

I bent my wrists, letting the straps dig into the backs of my hands. I raised my fingers as far as I could. The tips brushed wood.

Tick. Tock. Clock.

Tick. Tock.

I missed a breath, that time, as the press dropped.

Armenteros shuffled over behind Burr, looking at the monitor.

Inches. I had inches.

Tick. Tock. Clock.

Tick. Tock. *Drop.*

"No word from Halifax?"

"Lots of words," said Burr, tapping his own earbud. "Not the ones you want."

Tick. Tock. Clock.

Tick. Tock. *Drop.*

"Could they have seen the Rider?"

Burr shook his head. "No chance. We've got transmissions snowed under for a hundred miles around."

Tick. Tock. Clock.

Tick. Tock. *Drop*.

"Should I talk to the queen?" Even Armenteros had uncertainty in her voice now.

Tolliver Burr laughed. "This is what we're saying to the queen," he said. I saw the iris flex as the camera fixed on my face. "Look at that; she's perfect."

Tick. Tock. Clock.

Tick. Tock. *Drop*.

Even knowing the camera was there did not keep me from reacting when the press brushed the top of my fists. A wild howl came from somewhere, and I pulled backward on the straps with all my strength.

"See?" said Burr. "The queen will break; I'd stake my next project on it."

Armenteros shuddered, watching me, watching the press. "You stake more than that, Burr."

Tick. Tock. Clock.

Tick. Tock. *Drop*.

I pushed my hands against the stone, making them as flat as I could. I felt the air whistling around them, the wind compressed in the tiny space between press and stone.

"General," said Buckle. "The Rider is here."

My head whipped around. My breath was fast and shuddering, out of time, out of time. It was three more drops before the horse topped the ridge.

The Rider came pounding down the slope from the whirligig generators and pulled the horse to a rearing, prancing stop near the cameras. The creature's ribs were heaving; foam flew from its mouth as it tossed its head.

"Keep it out of my shot!" said Burr.

A couple of the Cumberlanders came between the Rider and the cameras, making the horse mince backward. But I had already seen the Rider's face. Remembered in a flash the last moment I'd seen her. I'd been terrified then, too—it was had been burned into me. It was the Rider who had come for Sidney, the white woman with the chickadee-cap black hair. Expertly reining in the shying, foaming horse, the Swan Rider lifted her head, and—

And she was a different person. When she'd killed Sidney, she'd been so diffident—offensively diffident, as if she were the one with something to steel herself for. Now the soft blue eyes were as intense as an electric discharge. The neat hair was spiky with sweat. She flashed a grin, waggled her fingers at the assembled crowd.

"Hello," she said. "My name is Talis."

18
TALIS

Tick. Tock. *Drop.*

"Talis!" I screamed. Everyone was frozen, and the press—the press was on my hands now. It pushed and it didn't hurt, but it *pushed*, and there was nowhere to go, no more margin, no more waiting. This was the part I couldn't do.

"Stop the press," said Talis. "Ha! I haven't heard that in centuries. 'Stop the presses!' But do." The smile was sharp-edged. "Or I'll have your heads on pikes."

But the Cumberlanders were frozen. *Please please please,* I was saying in my head, and *Talis Talis Talis.* But I could not speak. Tick, *tock*—the press dropped. Every lump in my wrist, every bony knuckle that couldn't get flatter—got flatter.

Something went *crack.*

My panic gave me an impossible strength, and I pulled

backward so hard that my shoulders—my *shoulders*—the pain was a pair of iron spears that shot through me, ripping open my shoulder joints and striking down my dead-straight arms and into my breaking hands. I still couldn't speak, but I started screaming.

"Cut transmission," said Armenteros.

Tick. Tock. No one obeyed her.

Tick. Tock. The press dropped. I cannot describe—

"Cut it," snarled Armenteros. "Raise the damn thing. Get it off her. Make it *stop*."

Tick.

Tock.

And no drop. The apple press shuddered, and the oak block began to rise.

"Better," said Talis. She—or rather, he, for surely Talis was male, no matter what body he had taken—swung down from the panting horse and threw the reins to the nearest Cumberlander. "Here. Good horse. I'd save it if I were you."

I knelt there with the press going up in front of me, my brain like a camera—seeing and recording, without understanding.

First I saw this: Talis came through the soldiers as if they were nothing. Talis, the great AI, the inventor of the Preceptures, the Butcher of Kandahar, Talis who ruled us and had saved us from ourselves, so long ago he was almost a legend. He was wearing layers of riding gear—jeans, a battered duster, a misbuttoned vest. He was skinny. He was young. "Gotta give you points for audacity, Wilma. But really—you thought I'd let you get away with this?"

Armenteros looked at him with skepticism and irritation. "Who are you?"

"Told you—Talis. Borrowed the wetware, of course. Hope it's not a shock. Sometimes you need a personal touch."

He laced his hands in front of him and pushed the palms out with a crackling of joints. The movement displayed his Swan Rider's tattoo, a wing bent into a cuff that encircled his wrist. No one would fake that mark. No one would dare.

"No wings?" said Burr. "Oh, I wish there were wings."

"They're strap-on, honey," Talis answered. "And I don't need them. I'm not a Swan Rider. I'm the reason Swan Riders exist."

Armenteros looked at the hands, at the face. Her tongue ran over her teeth. "Supposing I believe you. Why shouldn't I shoot you in the head?"

Talis raised his eyebrows. "For starters, Rachel—this body is Rachel—probably wouldn't appreciate it. But that's by the by. The real reason is that I'm just a copy, so shooting me won't get you much beyond the splatter. Also I left some pretty dramatic blow-up-the-whole-of-Cumberland programs running, and it would be *such* a pity if I didn't get to shut them off." He wiggled a hand through his hair, shaking out the dust. "I'm not an epoch-defining strategic thinker for nothing, you know."

"No," said Armenteros.

"And neither are you, in your meat-based way. So let's talk." He leaned in between Buckle and Armenteros and regarded the monitor screens, frowned, and pulled glasses from his pocket. He squinted through them, his nose crinkling. "I see you've got a clever little tight-scramble pierce out through the snow here. Why don't you check in with base, get up to date on any breaking news. That little sheep farm where your daughter lives, it's in Harrison County, hmmmm? Near Cynthiana?"

"Buckle," said Armenteros. Buckle put her hand back to her ear and turned her back.

"Interesting about Harrison, isn't it?" Talis chimed. "Back in the day, it was always the children of the poor who fought the wars, always the Nobodies that died when the Somebodies decided that a scrap was worth snarling over. It changed things when the Somebodies got a little skin in the game." He folded his glasses away and looked up at Armenteros. "Harrison changes things for you."

"There are no reports of trouble anywhere in Harrison," said Buckle.

Armenteros looked at Talis, the squint lines around her eyes deepening.

"Yeah, it's fine." He was smiling—a glittery smile. "Backward little place. Wiping it out would hardly make the six o'clock news. On the other hand you might try getting through to Indianapolis."

Buckle's hand was still on her ear. A pause. Then she went grey. The shock bloomed over her dark skin until she looked like an unwashed plum. "Gone," she whispered. "Indianapolis is gone."

"All we are is dust in the wind," said Talis. "All you are, anyway. Now, I'm inclined to make this very simple. Say, one city a day. Until you give me back my Precepture. I'm thinking Columbus next, but I might just roll the dice."

"We still have the royal hostages," Armenteros said.

Talis tipped his head. "Yeah, thing is, I *invented* this system of killing kids for bigger causes. I'm playing the long game here. You really think shooting a few five-year-olds is gonna slow me down?" He clapped Armenteros on the shoulder. "Now. How about you let my princess loose before you make me angry?"

"Burr," ordered Armenteros.

"What? Oh!" Tolliver Burr had been staring at Talis as if contemplating buying roses to throw onto the stage. He finally snapped round. "Yes, that's fine, General. I think we stopped soon enough that Greta could do another take. Easy enough to reset."

"Just get her loose, Burr. And take a look at your snowstorm. Shut down our tight-pierce. I don't want a single qubit in or out of here."

"Right, right," said Burr, bending over one of the equipment lockers. He came up with a multipencil and handed it to the corporal he'd made into his assistant, then turned to the monitor. And so it was that I did not lose my hands. The corporal touched the tip of the multipencil to the straps that held me. Lights twinkled. The adhesion shut off. I yanked my arms free and folded up over them, the release of terror ruining me in a way that even terror never could. I was shivering and crying, recording everything but taking nothing in.

"I'm thinking dawn," said Talis. "For the look of the thing. Dawn. City. Boom. Make a note." And he scooped me up and carried me inside.

I'd like to say Talis strode into the miseri with his duster billowing and scattered the Cumberlanders like November leaves.

I'd like to say he swept clear the foreign clutter that Tolliver Burr had left on the ancient oak of the map table, and laid me there like a princess in a glass case. I'd like to say it was a story. I wanted it to be a story. I wanted to be the princess rescued by the wizard. I wanted Talis to lift his hands and heal me with a word. I wanted the Cumberlanders to be terrified.

But they weren't. They had no idea who Talis was. He didn't look like anyone—shabby and dust-stained and reeking of horse, squinting from the dimness of the hall he'd just left, struggling under my weight as a man might struggle with a particularly long and floppy sack of potatoes—assuming said potatoes were having hysterics. The Cumberlanders, who were clearly using the miseri as a prep-and-rec room, looked up from their smartplex tablets and card games. Most of them were irritated, and some of them were shocked, but not one of them was terrified.

Talis dumped me onto the table amid Burr's cables and storyboards. I was sobbing helplessly.

"Hey!" One of the Cumberlanders—a big man, florid—stood up. "You, girl!"

Talis ignored the soldier and leaned over me, his eyes like suns. He was so dazzling that I saw four of him through the blur of tears. "Easy," he said, as if talking to a horse. "I suppose 'relax' is too much to hope for, but just don't fight me, okay?" As he spoke, he fit a hand against the ball of my shoulder, leaned his weight against it, and with his other hand lifted my arm from the elbow. His eyes crinkled as he sought the right angle, and then suddenly he gave my arm a precise, sharp yank. The shoulder cracked—but even as I yelped, the pain in that shoulder switched off. It was like a magician's trick. The story I'd wanted.

"Hey!" shouted the soldier.

Talis reseated the other dislocated shoulder. For a moment I was in so much less pain that I thought I wasn't in pain at all. Pain does not work like that, but there was a moment in which I didn't know that. I stopped sobbing. The florid Cumberlander grabbed Talis by the back of the neck. "What do you think you're doing?"

Talis turned on a pin. "Me?" He flashed with broad, false innocence. "Oh, you know. Trying out a body, staving off the boredom, wiping out a city. . . . My name is Talis. Perhaps you've heard of me?"

And *there* was the terror. The big man froze. They all froze. I will admit, shaming though it is, that I found their fear gratifying.

Talis smiled at the soldier. "Why don't you be a good

boy and pop out and ask your general about me? I don't imagine she'd want you to get in my way." He turned his back on them without checking to see if they were obeying. No one stopped him as he traced the cables that led from Tolliver Burr's override box to the Abbot's cracked casing. He hummed to himself, fiddled his fingers, and then started pushing buttons.

There was a whirr as the Abbot came back to life. His voder sounded three test tones, and then he coughed. His head swung toward Talis. His eyes turned back on.

"Hullo, Ambrose," Talis said. "Long time, no see. Gone and lost your Precepture, have you?"

"Hello, Michael," said the Abbot. "It shames me to admit it, but yes, I have."

The pain was coming back. Not my shoulders, but my hands. The blood was pounding back into them, and with the blood, pressure, and a sensation that was overwhelmingly and simultaneously hot and cold.

Talis stuck on his glasses again, and peered at the Abbot's hand, which was still fastened to the tabletop. "Oooo, that's nasty. Got a thing for hands, this lot. All right otherwise?"

"I took some substantial damage from the EMP burst, actually. Whether it's temporary remains to be seen."

"Well, that's the thing about healing." Talis said "healing" as if it were a word in a foreign language. "It happens or it doesn't."

And they both turned and looked at me.

I did not like Talis's bright regard. He had eyes like two cameras. I twisted aside. My hands felt as if they were breaking, slowly, the way a bottle breaks if you fill and freeze it.

Then I felt a touch on my cheek—cool, light ceramic. The Abbot's fingers swept up my forehead and into the roots of my hair. "What happened to her, Michael?" he said softly. "What could do this to my Greta?"

"That man Armenteros hired—"

"Tolliver Burr." The Abbot's voice was pneumonia-thick.

"That's the one. Crushed her hands in the cider press. Big long buildup, big psychodrama thingy. Not too much damage, though, in the end."

Something went pop —Talis pulling the bolt out of the Abbot's hand. The Abbot lifted it and light shone through the hole in his palm. I slammed my eyes shut.

"Our medical facilities here are so limited . . ." I felt the Abbot put his the damaged hand on my shoulder. "Ice wouldn't be amiss, I suppose."

"She's just having a bit of a cry, Ambrose. Give me that back; I want to see if I can reattach that muscle."

But the Abbot's hands stayed steady on me. The pain kept rising. Was there a limit to how much it would rise? I was near the limit of what I could swallow down, and the Cumberlanders were still in the room.

"She needs her friends," the Abbot said.

"Yes," I croaked. I felt as if I'd spent an hour screaming: my throat was raw. "I need Xie."

"And Elián?"

Elián's fingertips on mine, his eyes like a wild deer's. *Told you I was Spartacus.* "Yes."

"Ambrose, really. She's fine. And I'm just going to kill her later, when I get my room back online."

"Michael . . ." There was just a hint of a rebuke, a not-in-front-of-the-children note in the hoarse, weary voice.

"Oh, fine," Talis pouted. He pointed to one of the Cumberlanders, at random. "You, get some painkillers. And you"—another point—"go find Li Da-Xia and Elián Palnik. Tell them they're wanted in the lounge." None of them moved. "Come on," Talis sing-songed at them. "What did your nice general tell you about me? 'Do what he says'? 'Don't make him angry'? 'If you have family in Pittsburgh call them now'? Snap to it!"

A second's silence. Then they snapped.

"Or did I say Columbus?" Talis called after them, light as broken glass. "Honestly."

The Cumberlanders were leaving—backing out, some of them. I was glad they were going. I was twitchy with pain. I could feel every knob of my spine wriggling against the table. I rolled onto my side and let my legs pull up, my body folding itself shut around my heart by pure instinct. My hands: I will not speak of them. I hoped only that Talis would heal them soon.

The last of the Cumberlanders left. The Abbot sighed. Talis was pacing, energy threatening to crack him like an egg.

"Pittsburgh . . . ," the Abbot mused. "Erasing whole cities seems a bit excessive."

"The hell it is. They sent soldiers to my Precepture. I'll have it back from them double-quick, and then I'll make an example of Armenteros that will make three-star generals and two-bit presidents think twice for generations to come. I'll make a story out of her. A *myth*."

"She's a patriot, Michael. I'm sure she's taken her personal risk into account."

"Patriots," snarled Talis. "Spare me."

"And what of my children?" said the Abbot, cupping one hand over my ear. "I'm sure the Cumberlanders must have made some wholesale threat against them, to keep the UN at bay. Now that you're here, what will become of them?"

Talis popped the air out of his cheeks. "Well, losing all the hostages would be a blow. But Armenteros will never go that far. I'd turn Kentucky into a crater and send her kids to lap up their damn drinking water from the bottom like dogs. She knows that."

The hand cupped over my ear, the pain roaring in my hands, made the next words echo dully. "So, not all of them, but some . . . ?"

The AI shrugged. "Tell you what, if they come looking for kids to line up against the wall, give them someone young and cute. I don't think Armenteros has the stomach for it."

"But you do."

"To save the Preceptures? Absolutely. Call it the morality of altitude. I'm an awfully long way past my snot-nosed days. Now quit nattering at me. I need to punch a hole out through this snow so I can wipe out Louisville."

"You were human, once, Michael." The Abbot spoke in his most gentle, teacherly voice. "I know you remember."

But Talis didn't answer.

THE SCORPION RULES

19
A THIRD SKIN

I lay on the map table. My hands pounded in time with my heart. They seemed to have a second skin, a swollen, stretched-tight skin made out of pain itself.

Shock, I thought. *I'm in shock. The world was going grey.* Then suddenly the Abbot was leaning over me. I jerked with surprise, then froze.

"It's only—" The icon of his mouth narrowed, as if with sorrow. "Anti-inflammatories and a local anesthetic. The soldiers brought it but I have examined it. Would you trust me?"

I knew he was seeking a response, but I didn't understand what his question was. I did not understand anything at all. The Abbot opened his damaged hand, and I caught the glass-glitter of a syringe. An injection? Injections, a bullet to the head. We were at war. *The grey room.*

"Greta?" The Abbot's voice echoed oddly. "Greta, do you want—" But I still couldn't answer. Insectile, the Abbot took a scuttling sideways step down the table. He slipped a needle into the vein on the back of my left hand.

Injections, then.

Numbness bloomed out from the needle, and in seconds it was a third skin—a skin of no-feeling between the skin itself and the skin of pain. The Abbot did the other hand, and then the pain was gone. He wasn't murdering me. Of course he wasn't. I was only in shock.

The Abbot lifted one of my hands in his damaged one, and used his good hand to softly trace the lines of bones. I felt the pressure of his touch but not its sensation—a strange thing. I was unbecoming myself, unraveling.

"I think there is some chipping fracture in the trapezoid carpal, and perhaps also the metacarpophalangeal joint of the index finger," he said. "But I am no doctor."

Talis scrunched his nose. "Broken? Really? Thought I was in time."

The Abbot glanced at him sidelong.

"Don't look at me like that. What was I supposed to do, blow the place up with my hostages still in it? I came as fast as I could. Took a trickle download to the nearest Riders' refuge. My brain still feels like toothpaste, and I probably killed my horse."

Another beat.

"And I'm not apologizing. It's *your* Precepture. What were *you* doing?"

"As it happens, I had a tokamak shackle around my mind and a bolt through my hand."

"*Toka*— I'm *so* blowing up Pittsburgh. I'll tell them you said hi."

The Abbot hmm'd. "Please, don't go to trouble on my account."

"Broken?" It was my own voice, though it seemed to come from somewhere else. "Are they broken?"

The Abbot tipped his face down toward mine, tinting it a gentle shade. "They're minor, Greta. The breaks are minor."

"A sonic knitter would fix you right up," said Talis. "Amish here objects to all that tech stuff, but the Cumberlanders will have one."

"No," I rasped. "The Cumberlanders—"

"Barring that," said the Abbot, "I think ice. Would you?"

Another pause.

"I'm not fetching you ice," said Talis, when it became clear even to him that he was the only person the Abbot could possibly be asking. "I don't fetch."

My hands seemed to lose contact with the table, like balloons. Time drifted.

"A knitter—" began Talis.

"No," I said, because a knitter meant Cumberland, it meant Burr, it meant— "No, Father, don't let them touch me." I whispered. The Abbot put his hand over my ear. I could feel him shaking. His fingers slipped between the plaits of my braids. My heartbeat echoed back from the shell of his palm.

"Fine." Talis sighed like a twelve-year-old. "Fine. Where do you even keep the ice?"

And thus was the master of the world sent off like a

bellhop, even as I folded my face into the Abbot's hands and wept.

They packed my hands in ice. Numbness spread up my arms, strange sister to pain. Time stretched, became like a membrane. It wrapped me. I blurred and dimmed. And then—

And then Xie came. Of course she came. Pounding through the door at a run, a rabid look on her fine face. Slowly I became aware that she was babbling, begging, saying my name. "I'm sorry, Greta, I'm so sorry. There were too many of them. I would never have left you, Greta. There were so many of them—"

"Xie . . ." Her name was a thistle in my mouth.

"Oh, Greta. Did they—" She put a hand on my forearm. I flinched. She jerked away, tears springing to her eyes. "But they stopped. What happened? Did your mother—"

"Talis . . . ," I whispered. "He came for me."

"Talis? I— But— Talis?"

"Hi," said Talis. He was sprawled on one of the memory foam cushions as if he'd never sat in a chair before. "With you in a tick."

I watched Xie take him in—the shabby riding gear, the young woman's body that was somehow male in the splay of the joints, somehow ancient in the set of the eyes. Her eyes widened; her face paled. "Lord Talis," she whispered. "History walking . . ."

"Don't bother him, Da-Xia," wheezed the Abbot.

"I—" said Xie. She was trembling, caught in awe the way we were sometimes caught in electricity.

"Xie," coaxed the Abbot.

A long, long silence. Then Li Da-Xia slowly and deliberately turned her back on the ruler of the world. She put her hands on my face. "Greta. What do you need?"

Her hands were warm. I could not think of what I needed.

"You," I said, rasping. "I need you."

"I can't hack through it," said Talis, furrowing his hair with hooked fingers. "Bloody hell." He levered himself to his feet and kicked a book. It whirled across the floor like an outraged seagull. "Never mind 'snowstorm'; it's a damn blizzard."

"But you got commands out initially. . . ." The Abbot's eye icons drew together, a mime of puzzlement.

"They had a tight-pierce for piggybacking, but they shut it down. Even if they bring it back up for round two tomorrow, it will take me hours. *Honestly.* How am I supposed to destroy Pittsburgh if I can't get a ping to my weapons platforms?"

"I'm sorry you're frustrated, Michael."

"Frustrated! I'm blind, is what I am. And the data push is giving me a headache."

He'd been at it for half an hour, which is a long time for an AI to do anything. It is said that their quick minds make their time pass slowly, and that the ones who are mad are mad half from boredom.

"'Patience is someone else's virtue,'" Xie murmured. She was quoting from the Utterances.

"Ooo." Talis raised one of those startling black eyebrows at her. "Quoting me at me, are we? You've got a bit of nerve."

"Yes, my lord. So I've been told."

"Li Da-Xia," he named her.

"Lord Talis," she answered. And then, "You were supposed to keep us safe."

"Well," said Talis. "Technically. It's more the prerequisite to the mission than the actual mission, but technically, yes, I was supposed to keep you safe." He nudged the seagull-book with his toe. "Did you know, the man who invented the atomic bomb once said that keeping peace through deterrence was like keeping two scorpions in one bottle? You can picture that, right? They know they can't sting without getting stung. They can't kill without getting killed. And you'd think that would stop them." He gave the book another boot, and it flipped closed with a *snick*. "But it doesn't."

He looked up and his eyes were the color of Cherenkov radiation, the color of an orbital weapon. "You've got a bit of nerve, little scorpion. All I did was invent the bottle." He took a step toward her, coming up onto the book, rising into the air like a cobra. "What do you—"

"Michael," wheezed the Abbot. It was probably supposed to be soothing. It sounded strained and sick.

"Sorry," said Talis. He stepped backward off the book and scrubbed his face with both hands. "Yes, Li Da-Xia, I was supposed to keep you safe. Go help your friend."

Time went by, stretched and strange. Talis paced. Xie held my numb hand. The Abbot stroked my hair. We put ice on my hands, then took it off, then put it back on. I had Xie, but I needed Elián, who thought I was strong—I needed Elián. And just as I was thinking so, the door burst open so fast, it thumped into the wall.

"Greta!" Elián rushed toward me, his hands coming up to his face. "Oh, God . . ."

"She's okay," said Xie. "You're okay, Greta."

Elián actually looked to his torturer for reassurance.

"Hairline fractures," the Abbot told him gently. "Bruising and swelling. She genuinely will be fine, Mr. Palnik."

Elián's hands were coming off his face, reaching for me. A smart-plastic cuff still dangled from one wrist. His face was bruised, as it had been when I'd first seen him. I recognized his expression now as I had not then—swallowed-down fear, carefully tamped fury. "Greta. I swear I had no—"

"Excuse me," said Talis.

"Go away," snapped Elián.

"Elián," said the Abbot. "This is—"

Elián barely glanced at Talis, taking him perhaps for a Cumberlander. "I said *go away!*"

"Talis," whispered Xie.

"Greta," said Elián. "I—I'm so—"

"*Excuse me*," said Talis.

"Elián," said the Abbot. "This is Talis."

Elián turned. He looked at Talis. He looked some more. His eyes hardened. His lips tightened. The knob of his chin wrinkled up.

"Hi," said Talis.

"Take one more step toward me," said Elián. "Take one more step, and I will lay you out. I will put you on the damn ground."

Talis quirked one corner of his mouth. "Really."

"Try me."

"Oh, you are *fantastic*." Talis looked Elián up and down as if he were a piece in an art museum. "Ambrose, I know you have your heart set on Greta, but I think I like this one. Maybe we should upload them both."

That erased Elián's fury, and replace it with a bewilderment that looked a lot like terror. "What?" he said.

"I hardly think he's suitable, Michael. And I'm sure he'd never consent."

Talis shrugged elaborately. "There's that."

"What?" said Elián. "No, I don't consent. Consent to what?"

A smile spread over Talis's face. "What a firecracker, Ambrose. I can see why you've had so much trouble. Elián Palnik. It is a pleasure to meet you at last. You're my new favorite."

"Fuck off," snarled Elián—and Xie grabbed him by the arm.

"Stop," she whispered, pulling at him. "Elián, stop. Greta—it's Greta who needs us."

"Ah, yes," said Talis. "Your princess. My princess. Greta, who needs us."

"You leave her alone," said Elián.

But Talis kept coming forward, slow but unstoppable as the tide. "You're shouting at the wrong person here, Elián. I didn't do this to our Greta. In fact I saved her. You know, mostly. And for now."

"Lord Talis," said Xie. "What do you mean?"

"Thank you, Xie," said Talis. "I do like to be fed my lines. Think about it, kiddies. Really think it through. I stopped dear Wilma by putting a city on the firing line. What do you think will happen if I can't actually fire? What will Grandma do if we wake up in the morning and Pittsburgh is still standing?"

"They wouldn't dare," whispered Xie.

"No," said Talis. "*You* wouldn't dare. Which is adorable. But Armenteros— Let's ask Elián. Hey, Elián. Do we think Grandma would dare?"

I saw Xie look at Elián. I saw her whole body freeze.

"I'll spell it out, shall I?" said Talis. "Slowly? For the benefit of the class? Or, let's be honest here, mostly for Elián. Shall I spell it out for you, Elián? If we wake up in the morning and Pittsburgh is still standing, the Cumberlanders will know their snowstorm is working. They'll risk a call out to Halifax. They have to: it's the only card they've got to play. They'll use an oblivious transfer, quantum scramble up a blizzard so thick that it will take hours to hack, even for me."

He was close to them now—very close. Xie had wedged

her body between him and Elián. She was leaning backward as if afraid Talis might scorch her with his presence. Elián was almost holding her up, which left him unable to deck the ruler of the world.

"Let's think about those hours, shall we?" pressed Talis. "The hours when Cumberland has Halifax on the line and not a lot of time. Do we think Grandma will bow out quietly? Or will she go out with a big number?"

"I—" said Elián.

"Or let's ask Greta," Talis interrupted. In a blink he cut sideways—he had backed Elián and Xie out of the way—and was leaning over the edge of the map table. "What do you think, Princess? Are you up for another turn as the star of the show? Another turn of the screw?" And with that, he closed his hand over mine, and squeezed.

"Michael!" objected the Abbot.

"No," I heard myself whisper, plead. Talis's grip was slowly breaking through the membranes, through the skins of numbness and pain and into the skin itself. "No, please, Talis—please."

So abject. And I could not even hate myself for it. I was too far gone.

Elián, though—give him this, he's never been paralyzed. He swung out from behind Xie and seized Talis's arm and yanked him away from me. "Don't you *touch* her."

Talis just smiled. "But I didn't touch her. I saved her. Whether I can do it again . . . If I were you, Elián, and if I loved her . . . Well. I need you to flip this little situation around for me. I need you to punch me a hole in the snow."

"I d-don't . . . " Elián stuttered. "I can't— I don't know anything about broadcast jamming."

"But probably you have friends who do. And you might be able to get them access." Talis laughed lightly. "If that fails, try murdering Tolliver Burr."

I could hear Elián's harsh breathing. But he said nothing.

"Grego," whispered Da-Xia. "Talk to Grego. He knows broadcasting, if anyone here does."

"Xie, I—" Elián cut himself off and turned to me. "Greta, I can't. It's crazy. And even if— I *can't*."

But I could only fold up, curling the whole of my body around my broken hands. "Don't let them," I said, to him, to all of them. "Oh, don't let them. Please."

Da-Xia covered her mouth with one hand, and put the other on Elián's arm.

"Go," said the Abbot, to both of them. "I'll take care of Greta. Go."

A long summer evening spread across the misericord. There was birdsong in the twilight, and the sky turned lavender, with high clouds like brushstrokes, first white and then a luminous gold. Cirrus clouds, a shift of the weather. The Cumberlanders had a generator going somewhere. I could hear its growl, and the uncouth voices of the soldiers, who did not belong in this silent, careful place.

It was quiet again. Da-Xia and Elián, slipped away. Even Talis, dismissed. "Use my cell," the Abbot had said to him.

"It's easier to defend than the rest of the Precepture, if the Cumberlanders decide to take action in the middle of the night."

So it was the Abbot and I.

He took off my shoes and tidied my hair. He wiped the tear streaks from my face with a cool cloth. Then he scooped me up from the table and laid me in the rounded cushion by the Romanist shelves; my nest, and the place where he himself had sent me plunging into terrible dreams.

This seemed like just one more. One more dream. Except that sometimes my hands hurt, and needles were needed to keep me from sobbing.

Darkness fell, and stars opened beyond the shattered roof. The Abbot lit one of the golden lamps. He was silent, crouched at my side.

"You should sleep," he said, finally.

Obedient—even now, obedient—I closed my eyes for a moment. Terror loomed up from my inner darkness. My eyes flew open. I breathed in through my nose and blew out as if blowing out a candle, two times, three, and four. When I could speak again, I said, "You should shelve the books."

"Ah. That I could do." The Abbot unbent his hexapod legs and leaned forward, his hands on the upper joints, wheezing like an old man. He paused there a moment. And then he turned to the books and lifted one delicately.

I watched him work in the lamplight, and he did not seem like a machine. He lifted the tumbled volumes as if they were flowers. He tucked them to sleep on their shelves.

Where they were crumpled, or broken-spined, he piled them on his desk. He had glue and binder's tape, a bonefolder.

He had a book press.

I looked away from the little press, its pan and levered top. Felt my heartbeat pounding in my shoulders.

The Abbot left the injured books and came back to me.

"Would that the whole world were so easy to order," he said. "So easy to repair."

"But it's not."

"No. It's not."

"Dreamlock," said the Abbot, softly. "Let me help you. Dreamlock, merely to keep dreams at bay."

"No," I said. "Not that."

I wanted to lift my hands, to cover my face, but even the first stir of the movement made my tender shoulders glow with pain. Talis had reseated them—his strange eyes glowing—but it was going to be days or even weeks before the tendon damage healed.

Who was I trying to fool? I didn't have weeks.

The apple press was tomorrow.

"In four hundred years," said the Abbot, "no army in the world, no nation and no alliance of nations, has stood for long against Talis. The UN will have its Precepture back."

"And then you'll kill me." It was a cold fear all through me, but perversely I was comforted. Better the grey room than Tolliver Burr.

But the Abbot made a *tock* noise in his throat. "Greta Gustafsen Stuart," he said. "What if there were another way?"

20
CLASS TWO

Another way. A way out of the Precepture other than death.

I remembered Atta's voice, rusted with anger. *They watch us everywhere. It is an illusion.* I was going to die, surely. Surely. And yet—and yet stirring inside me was the kind of fear that comes with hope.

My voice came out very small and cautious: "What do you mean?"

The Abbot was flexing his damaged hand. He'd used the bookbinding equipment to reattach the muscle, but his movements were ratcheting, stiff. He watched the hand open and close a moment before answering. "Greta, dear, do you know what a Class Two Turing Intelligence is?"

"I do— I can't— I know, but I can't think."

"I'm sorry," whispered the Abbot, turning his facescreen aside. His voice was as human and soft as I'd ever heard it. He sounded like a child. "Of course you can't." The golden lamp-light caught the edge of the ancient casing of his facescreen. There were fine scratches in the aluminum, and dimples as small as grains of sand.

"Class Two," he said. "It means a machine intelligence that was once human. It means an AI whose 'birth' involved the upload of a copied human psyche." He turned to me, his face icon changing to a smile whose meaning I had trouble reading. "It means me. I am not quite the man I was."

"You were human." My voice felt strange. The Abbot sounded more human than I did. "I knew that already. You were human."

"Talis, also. Though he was part of the first wave. I trust you remember it."

"Yes." The Abbot was coaxing me into a classroom. And it was working. I was good at classrooms. "Yes, I remember." There had been a period just before the War Storms when ending human death had seemed both a good idea and a wise use of resources. When melding humans to machines had seemed one way to become immortal. It had been a brief period—and it had been a bad idea. Most of the AIs had died, and most of the ones who didn't had fragmented, their personalities peeling off layer by layer. I suppose that it was immortality of a kind. The immortal fate of a soul in hell.

The Abbot nodded his scholarly approval at me. "I am younger. In two ways, younger. I was a younger man when I . . . chose this. And it was not so long ago."

"How long . . ." The question crossed a line—it was like

asking a Precepture Child about home. But I had to ask it. "How long ago?"

"One hundred eighty-three years."

"Oh." I swallowed. It was a big number. "Oh."

The Abbot settled beside me. "This place was younger then, too, though already old. And somewhat different, under the . . . old leadership."

"You . . . you were a Child of Peace?"

"Indeed," he said. "A hostage child, and before that, someone's son. Some country's young prince. I was sixteen. But I do not suppose it matters. That body is long gone. The country was lost in the war whose beginning sent me to the grey room. But, Greta: the grey room has more than one door."

It didn't. It was empty, except for that table. That table, with its terrible crown. But the Abbot had been a hostage child. He'd gone to the grey room. "Tell me," I said. "Tell me how you got out."

"The grey room . . ." The Abbot's voice trailed away, as if in reverence. He gathered himself. "It is beams—I know you've wondered. The grey room uses high-intensity electromagnetic beams. They take the human mind as an EMP burst might take a machine. One goes out in a flash. It is meant to be painless."

"Is it?"

His pause was one beat too long. "There have been no complaints."

It seemed reassuring for an instant. Then the hairs on the back of my neck stood up.

"My point," said the Abbot, "is that the speed is controllable. The mind can be unspooled more slowly, and the process recorded. Then reversed." He shrugged. "The details are beyond me: I am a machine but not a machinist. What matters is the memory is copied, and that much of the man that is the sum of the memory."

"Which is how much?"

He took my damaged hand with his damaged hand. "This much," he said. "Enough."

I could not feel my skin; he had no skin. But I held on fiercely.

"I need a successor, Greta," he said. "The EMP damaged me, but even before that—I approach the end of this incarnation and have no wish for another. Yet, I would not abandon you, but stay with you, train you. You would keep your body at first, and then become as I am. You could be a scholar; a great mind. A servant of peace and an enduring fact in the world."

I did not answer.

"You know your history. You know that the transition is—"

I knew. Most of the AIs died. But it was a chance. A chance I hadn't had, the hour before.

"Ask me anything," the Abbot said. "I will not lie to you."

What came out of my mouth surprised me. "Do you dream?"

"In my body I used to dream. In this form I have no dreams I do not wish to have."

I looked at our joined hands. I could feel the pressure of his hand on mine, but not the texture. "The . . . process. Does it hurt?"

The Abbot paused, his mouth icon narrowing. "Profoundly," he said at last. "But for me there is no torment in the memory of the pain. It is merely a thing that happened. Do this, Greta, and survive it, and no one will ever hurt you again."

In this way, the Abbot saved me: he turned my mind back on. The apple press had left me suspended between horror and numbness, unable to think, far from myself. Say this for the prospect of becoming a machine: it was at least something to think about.

I had never cared much for my body. It was clumsy and freckly and somewhat lugubrious about the nose. It followed my brain about like a wolfhound on a lead. I did not think I would miss it.

And really, I had to lose only . . . but then I remembered the taste of Da-Xia's lips—honey and anise, her hand slipping under my shirt. Elián lifting the hair from the nape of my neck. My body warmed and softened to those memories—the taste, the tug, the goose bump brush.

I had a lot to lose.

"Elián and Xie," I said, and the reality of what I'd asked them—begged them—to do came crashing in. "Oh, God. Elián and Xie."

The Abbot's eye icons blinked, a pantomime of confusion.

"I sent them to kill someone."

"It was Talis who—"

"No." Suddenly the memory cushion's softness felt insidious—an abuser's murmur, a jellyfish kiss. I flailed away from it. "No. They didn't go for Talis. They went for me. I sent them—they'll be killed."

I still had the Abbot's hand in mine. I tried to use it to pull myself to my feet, and my shoulder lit with pain. Tears sprang into my eyes. "Da-Xia and Elián. And Grego. And—" I couldn't get up. But I couldn't let this happen.

"Shhhh," said the Abbot. "Here." He shifted and wrapped his hands around my ribs, lifting me. I wobbled on my feet, in his arms. "Greta. Your friends are trying to help Talis pierce the broadcast jamming and take control of the situation. If they cannot do that, tonight, then you will be tortured again. Tomorrow. Do you understand that?"

"Yes." All around us little cubes of gold glass from the broken roof shone in the lamplight. The Cumberland ship had come down like a city falling on us. The press had come down one *tick tock* at a time. I swallowed, and I said, "I know. But I want no one to die for me, Abbot. No one."

And these were my friends.

The Abbot leaned his head forward until the edge of his facescreen rested feather-light against my forehead. "Would that I could kiss you, child," he whispered.

Then he straightened up and took a step back, leaving me to stand on my own two feet. "Your Royal Highness," he said. "How can I help?"

★ ★ ★

In the end the Abbot did three things for me. He advised me that the Cumberlanders' broadcast jammer was almost certainly on the Cumberlanders' ship. He bound my still-weak shoulders into two slings, so that I could walk around. And he cleared the way for me to reach the tunnels under the kitchen.

The darkness down there was thick.

Hard as it is to find one's way in darkness, it is harder with one's hands bound up. I crept around the shelves of jars, around the barrels of precious flour and even more precious salt, deeper in. Once I smacked my head on a shelf of canned vegetables. But eventually I found my way to the one place in the Precepture that I had heard of but never been: the long tunnel that struck out toward the ridge, near the induction spire. And the Cumberland ship.

"Long and straight, Greta," the Abbot had said. "Perhaps . . . four hundred fifty steps."

Four hundred fifty steps. I counted them, and tried to stop myself from thinking of the apple press, how it had come down step by step by step by step.

Spiderwebs broke across my face and I could not wipe the stickiness away. But I went on. Lit by the glowstick the Abbot had tucked into my belt tie, empty doors gaped here and there on either side. Some of them had bars.

It was like nothing so much as a catacomb.

No, that was a lie. It was like nothing so much as a dungeon.

"Make no turns," the Abbot had said. "Count your steps, and make no turns."

Four hundred fifty steps, through a dungeon. The Abbot had known where he was sending me, and what I would see.

Was this where Elián had been kept? This place with no sky?

"I have tried to make this place a school and a garden, one vision of a paradise," the Abbot had said as he bound up my hands. "I know it is not a paradise. I know you are all frightened. I know I have hurt you all, tortured you all, *conditioned* you all. I know, above all, that I am charged with keeping order." He had paused as if to take a breath, though he could not breathe. "I know that I have failed."

And then he had gone to make sure the hallway and the kitchen were clear.

Two hundred steps. Two hundred fifty.

For years there had been a dungeon under my feet. A dungeon.

Three hundred. Four hundred. And then—finally, finally—something brushed against me like the scent of night-blooming flowers.

Da-Xia's voice, and, faint and stifled, Elián's laughter.

If anyone could laugh in a dungeon, it would be Elián Palnik.

My heart and stomach seemed to switch places. I went staggering toward the voices, trying not to call out names. I could see starlight now—the stair at the tunnel opening. Who knew how close the patrols might be.

I could see them above me now, Elián and Da-Xia and a third behind them; I wasn't sure who. Elián said something, and Xie twisted away with a soft laugh, her hand rising to cover her mouth.

For a moment I just stood as if someone had hit me. Struck, that was the word. I was struck. Struck by Elián's drawling voice, the well-known tilt of Xie's head, the just-so lift of her hand. Struck by my own loneliness. Why had I kept myself so apart from them, for so long? I only wanted to be with them. I only wanted someone to hold me.

I must have made some noise, because they turned. There was a flurry of movement, which was strangely blurred, and the three of them came running toward me. It was Elián, Grego, and Xie.

"Elián," I said. "There's a *dungeon*."

"Yeah," he said. "I noticed, actually."

"You can't do this," I said.

Elián frowned and took my elbow. Pain flared up and down, into my shoulders and hand.

"Don't touch her arms," said Da-Xia softly. She pressed her fingertips against my cheekbone. "Greta." Behind her stood Gregori, his eyes faintly luminous.

"You can't do this," I said to her. "Don't do this."

She dropped her fingertips. My face felt aglow with her touch, and suddenly I was terrified. "Don't do this"? It meant, *I'd rather be tortured.*

My friends—

They were wearing military chameleon cloth. Black and

grey and brown wrapped them and muddled their edges. "Where did you get chamo?" I said. "What are you doing?"

In my own voice I heard only flatness and fear, but Xie answered neatly, "Grego thinks the broadcast jammer is on the ship."

The Abbot had thought that too, but . . . . the image of Tolliver Burr at his camera flashed into me like a nerve firing. Burr at his camera, and Talis leaning in beside him, glasses sliding down his nose, peering into a— "Monitor," I croaked. "I mean, they had a monitor. By the apple press."

"A remote terminal, yes," said Gregori. "But the actual jammer must broadcast with some strength, no? Perhaps a kilowatt, maybe more. For this it needs a power source. It must be the ship."

"We thought about reprogramming it, but—" began Xie.

"This is too complicated," said Gregori. "I thought, we'll unplug it."

"Behold our assembled genius," said Elián, with a roll in his voice that was almost another laugh. "Our backup plan is to smash it with a rock."

"You can't," I said. "The ship—there will be guards. It's a military shock ship."

They all looked at one another. Their chamo had adapted as we stood in the dungeons with only my little glowstick for light, and their bodies were almost invisible. They looked like hands and heads, like machines with no bodies.

"You'll be killed," I said.

Xie shook her head, but Elián answered: "We know."

"There is a plan," said Grego.

"There's a plan, but it's risky," said Elián. "We know it's dangerous, Greta. We're doing it anyway."

"I want—" I said. "I don't—" I was aware that I wasn't making much sense. I wanted contradictory things: I wanted to save my friends, and I wanted them to save me. I could not have both.

"Shhhh," said Xie. "Come into the air." She reached for my hand, but of course she couldn't take it. She froze helplessly. It was Elián put his hand between my shoulders and guided me up the staircase and into the starlit night.

Outside, the baked-bread smell of the prairie at night wrapped me. I took a breath and tried to orient myself. We were on top of the ridge, between Charlie's pen and the induction spire, hidden in the shadow of the rock pile—all those stones that generations of hostages had cleared from the upper gardens. We crouched together, huddling in the prickling saskatoon bushes.

Below us the Precepture hall sat, huge and dark and foursquare, like one of the facts of the world. On the lawn between the hall and the upper terraces, the Cumberlanders had set up white tents. Lit from within, they glowed softly. I could see figures there, walking, sitting.

Nearby, the small darkness of the toolshed.

And the apple press.

"If we disable the jammer," I said, "Talis will— He will—"

He would destroy a city.

I had been so frightened of the apple press that I had

almost forgotten what else was at stake. A city. A city, and Elián's life.

"Once the jammer's down, I'll go straight to Armenteros," said Elián. "Tell her what I've—tell her it's down. She won't—" He was struggling. "She won't take on Talis, not to his face. She'll let the Precepture go."

"Cumberland loses the war," said Gregori. "Everything, click, is over." He dusted his hands together.

Over. My heart leapt after the word. But only for a moment.

Over, but not undone. War had still been declared. Even if Talis spared Pittsburgh, surely he would kill the Cumberland leaders—and their hostage. I looked at Elián and saw that he knew it.

He read my look. "I can't have a city on my head. And I can't just watch them—" He made a mute, angry gesture, toward hands. In the starlight they peeped from their slings, swollen and purpling. I knew Elián wanted to touch me, but was afraid to hurt me. Was simply afraid. "She's my grandmother— They're my people, but I can't just watch them torture someone. I can't."

"And I can't let them kill you, Elián."

"Why not?" Suddenly Elián's carefully tended anger slid into bitterness. He changed in that instant, and I did not like the change. He was polished as a Precepture Child; he was sharp as horseradish.

He was terrified.

"So they're going to kill me. There's a war, Greta. I'm the

hostage." And in an echo of my accent: "It's the way things are done."

He was right. Somewhere in the last few weeks, I had rejected a lifetime of training, half a millennium of high purpose.

I had not even noticed.

"It's too late now, anyway." Elián shrugged like the Abbot, turning his palm up and spreading his fingers. I wished he would laugh. I think I was half in love with him, just for his impossible laugh. He didn't laugh, though. In a clipped and precise Precepture accent, he said, "It's out of your hands."

Below us, from the field of tents, came shouting.

21
SHOCK SHIP

Goats—the shapers of history.

Da-Xia filled me in. Thandi and Atta had been sent to free the nanny goats. Meanwhile slight and quiet Han, one of the world's overlooked people—Han's job had been to take the tiny glass tubes of male goat pheromones from their rack in the cold cellar. He had scattered them in the grass around the Cumberland tents like micro-mines. As the Cumberlanders stirred themselves to see what was happening, they stepped on the tubes. The nannies, of course, went mad. They started knocking down the soldiers and doing rude things to their knees.

And then, from above us on the ridge, came an unearthly wailing, a series of shattering crashes. If one had not known it was a sexually excited billy goat crashing horn-first into a wood-and-wire gate, one would have thought it was a demon forcing its way into the world.

In fairness, there's not a big difference.

The gate gave a twang and crunch; Bonnie Prince Charlie gave an eldritch *Grah* of triumph and broke loose. I saw the white-and-tawny body bound by, heading downslope, bellowing.

"Han," said Elián, softly. "You are a magnificent bastard."

"Truly he is," Grego whispered back. "You have no notion."

Below us the first Cumberland tent collapsed. There was shouting, and someone fired a shot into the darkness.

I think technically we were in violation of Talis's decree banning biological warfare. If he had failed to mention goat pheromones specifically, it was pure oversight. But in this particular case, I was confident he wouldn't mind.

"Let's go," said Xie.

"You will have to stay here," Grego told me. "The white will give you away." He was pulling something from his pocket—something liquid and silver in the moonlight. It wasn't until Da-Xia took it from him and started fastening it like an armband that I recognized it as fabric. It was UN blue, the mark of a noncombatant—a chaplain, a medic. And the color of our bedding. Elián was passing around big squares of—bandages? Kitchen towels? No, it was cotton gauze from the dairy. Da-Xia and Gregori tied the cloth squares round their necks.

"This is your plan?" I said. "You have cheesecloth and bedsheets."

There was another shot from below. The Cumberland

voices were getting louder, and there was the frankly terrifying sound of goats in goat love.

"Behold our assembled genius," said Da-Xia, softly.

"I've always hated those damn symbolic blankets," said Elián. "'Bout time they were useful." He was knotting the cheesecloth behind his neck. "Remember," he said to his fellow masqueraders, "it's all about attitude. You're on an urgent and righteous mission to save lives. The guards wouldn't even dream about stopping you." He gave them a pair of thumbs-up. "*Channel* that royal entitlement, right? Greta, try to stay low. If we don't come back—"

"No," I said. "Wait."

Elián blanched. I saw again the flicker of his fear, and remembered again that if everything went perfectly, he'd end up in the grey room. He pulled the mask up over his face.

I could still stop them. I *should* still stop them. The plan was unfolding, and it was too late to call it off without consequence, but I should still stop them from going there—the guns, the guards, the ship.

"I don't—" I said. Would Burr strap down my hands again? Would it be the feet? Where would it stop?

"Don't," I said. "I need to stay with you."

"Greta," said Xie. Tears sprang into her eyes.

"But you're in white," said Grego.

"I should stop you," I said. "I should but I can't. So let me—let me help you. It's my life. Let me help you."

"We—" Gregori began.

"But you're being medics, right? You could . . ."

"Yeah, we could," said Elián. "And you're right. It's your life." And he scooped me up, and held me in his arms as Talis had, but Elián—taller, stronger—was better at it. It was like something in a tale. "Close your eyes," he whispered. "Trust me."

I lay limp in Elián's arms while he ran. The pounding of the stones under his feet seemed to go straight into my shoulders: it was like being hit with mallets.

An unfamiliar voice hailed.

"Out of the way," Elián shouted, "out of the way!"

I decided it was theatrically acceptable to moan, and I moaned.

"Break out the decontam gear," Elián said, "Get your gas masks! Hurry!"

"What's happening?" The stranger's voice was tight with confusion and fear.

"Some kind of chemical—" said Da-Xia, and dissolved into a fit of gagging.

But for all the commotion, we were slowing, stopping. Not good. Elián staggered to a halt, jarring me and making the red darkness behind my closed eyes flash.

"Isn't that the princess?" A different guard. At least two, then.

"And if she dies the whole game's up." Elián had let the Kentucky mountains into his voice; it was rolling and strong, a granite boulder. "Talis will kill us all, right sure."

"Out of the way, out of the way," said Grego, and his

attempt at a Cumberland accent was *terrible*.

Elián hoisted my weight and resettled me in his arms. A little cry broke from me, without regard for the theater of the moment.

"She's dying," cried Elián. "Get the hell out of the way!"

The airlock went *chunk*.

And then we moved.

Elián's footsteps rang against metal, and the jostling of the rough ground changed to something harder but smoother. I could cope with it, time it to my breaths. Echoes from the metal walls, the sound of us running. The eyelid darkness was strobing. We rounded a corner, another, and then Elián staggered to a stop. He tilted, leaning against a wall. "Okay," he panted. "Okay. Wake up, Princess."

"Don't call me that." I opened my eyes, blinking.

"Sorry." Elián let me slide to the ground. His voice was low.

We were in a . . . a corridor, I suppose, a step or two from a junction with another. The space was so narrow that I was surprised that Elián could carry me through it. It was square as a duct, metal, unadorned but for the traction plating on the floor. There were pinpoint lights in the ceiling, making a rhythm of dimness and dazzle. "Where to, Grego?" asked Elián.

Grego answered. "A shock ship, for short-range transport. Troops above, troops below. This is the central level—command, communications, storage, medical."

"So we're on the right level, but we've gotta find the

communications room before the panic dies down," said Elián. "Since the panic is being caused by goats, that's probably not going to take too long." Da-Xia had already moved off down the corridor and was checking doors. Grego moved off in the opposite direction.

"You okay if I leave you here?" Elián asked me. I nodded, still shaken, and he stepped down the intersecting corridor, leaving me standing in the junction, swaying in the center of the world. He palmed a pressure strip and a door slid open. "Hey, it's food! Man, I could really go for something highly processed." He did not raid the pantry but moved on, rapid and capable.

I swallowed twice, and then I took the fourth way, opposite from Elián. It took a few seconds to work out how to activate the pressure strip with my hip. The door opened. The room behind it was dark.

And in it, folded up around a glowing smartplex tablet like a spider wrapped around a fly, was Tolliver Burr.

I staggered backward and fell against the corridor wall. It should have hurt but it didn't. I felt only shock. A physical jolt, as if I'd jumped into cold water.

Burr looked up. At first he looked blankly surprised. Then he looked afraid. Then he smiled. "Hello, Greta." His leather-tight face was lit from below by the tablet screen; the smile looked like a leer. "Did you want to see the rough cut?"

He flipped the tablet around, and I could see a still shot of my own hands, strapped down and stark against the blue-grey stone. There was a streak of blood at the edge of the plastic strap, and the knuckles were white knots.

I made some kind of noise, then.

It may have been that noise that drew my friends, or perhaps Elián had seen me fall. He was there in an instant, and the others were close behind.

"Tolliver Burr," said Da-Xia.

"Hey, look, everybody." Elián's voice was light but his body was shaking. "It's plan B." And I did not know where it had come from, but there was a knife in his hand.

I could hear Talis say it: *Try murdering Tolliver Burr.*

The knife was a kitchen knife, a hand-span long, with a curved edge—a knife for chopping vegetables. The wood handle was so worn that it was nearly grey. Elián's knuckles were yellow-pale around it.

"I'll scream," said Burr.

"Oh," drawled Elián. "I hope so."

The tablet clicked to life, and the recorded hands began to move, clenching and jerking. Then a smash-cut to the face. The eyes were blown wide, the mouth as open as a camera. Elián struck out and knocked the thing from Burr's grip. It skittered into the dark room behind him, where it continued to play, glowing like a small hatch in the floor. I could hear it, too: Tick. Tock. Clock . . .

Da-Xia took me under the shoulder—she had forgotten how that hurt me—and hauled me up. "We are here to shut off the snowstorm," she said. "Do that for us."

"Yes," said Grego, fumbling after bravado. "Or—"

Tolliver Burr had taken control of his fear. He smiled at Grego, indulgent. "Okay." He stepped backward, deeper into the shadows of the low-ceilinged room. It was like a cobra slipping back into a cave. "Come in."

Tick. Tock. *Drop*.

22
LE POINT VIERGE

The communications room was low and dim. From the hall I could see only the white of Burr's shirt and the rectangle of smartplex on the floor that was still playing the scene of me being tortured. "We can't go in there," I said. "We can't."

But of course we had to.

It was Grego—I think compensating for the wavering note of his "or else"—who went in first.

Tolliver Burr shot him in the neck.

The bullet clipped the side of Grego's throat. He half turned, as if someone had tapped him on the shoulder, then folded up. It was quiet, without the least fuss.

"Gregori!" shouted Da-Xia, diving for him.

Elián leapt into the darkness, toward Burr. There was a muzzle flash, and a noise as loud as if Elián had been hit by lightning. Da-Xia screamed. My knees gave way and I sat down on the deckplate.

Inches away Xie was leaning over Grego. Blood was bubbling up from his neck as if from a hot spring. He had raised a hand to it, but was not clutching at it, or not anymore. His iris implants were wide and black, and he was squinting as if curious. Da-Xia hesitated, fingers splayed and stiff. Then she pressed her hands in over his, over the wound. Dark blood welled between her fingers. Grego looked up at Da-Xia and blinked. "It's all right, Gregori," she said. "It's all right."

Elián and Burr were scuffling. The gun spun out across the floor and struck against my hip. I looked at it. I bent my elbow and pulled my right hand free of the sling. The weight of my arm pulled at my shoulder. The pain opened my mouth like a gag, but I made no noise. My hand was numb. My ears were ringing. I fumbled for the gun.

"Gregori?" Da-Xia's voice cracked. "Grego?"

I looked at them. The cheesecloth around Grego's throat wicked the blood up and was red as a bandana, and more blood was black and shining around the raised grey pattern of the traction plating. It smelled like coins held too long in the hand.

And then—I could see it happen. Grego died.

His eyes changed into paintings of eyes. Into blank icons. "Oh," said Xie. "Oh no."

I closed my fingers around the gun, and rose to my feet like the Lady of the Lake.

With the gun in my hand, I counted the people breathing— five. Me, Da-Xia, Elián, Burr, and the recording of me, which sounded like something being sawed in half. Not Grego. The sounds of the scuffle had mostly stopped. I squared my feet on the deckplate and felt the blood seep between my toes. It was warm.

Burr's white shirt swam up from the darkness. Elián had overcome him. He held one of Burr's arms twisted round his back. With his other hand Elián pressed the knife against the side of Burr's neck. Blankly I noticed that it was the wrong way around, the dull edge against skin. Elián clearly knew as little of knife fights as I knew of guns.

But then, really: when it comes to guns, what is there to know?

Elián and Burr shuffled forward. I pointed the gun at them, though my hands couldn't feel it. My shoulder had become a ball of some hard-rubber substance I supposed was pain.

"Greta," gasped Burr.

"Tolliver," I answered.

On the deckplate I heard hoofbeats, the crash of Talis's horse. And then someone began to scream.

"Shut that off! God!" Elián wrapped his arm around Burr's neck and twisted both their faces aside.

But the tablet was across Grego's body from Da-Xia, and Elián was busy, and I did not care.

"What do you want, Greta?" Burr's voice was rough because of the pressure on his Adam's apple, but he seemed calm.

I had frankly no idea what I wanted. The recording on

the floor was screaming intolerably. Then it stopped.

"Which one's the broadcast jammer?" Elián panted. He sounded strained, much more so than the man he was choking.

Tolliver Burr jabbed the thumb of his free hand toward a certain machine. "That one. I'll shut it off for you. I've got no loyalties to Cumberland. There's no need for drama."

"Drama!" said Da-Xia. "You just shot Grego!"

The recording had looped around to its beginning. "That's lovely, dear," said Burr's voice. "That's perfect."

"Worth a shot," said Burr. "I thought you might be angry enough to kill me. But you're not, are you, Greta? You really are a pacifist."

"I'm not," said Elián, and pushed the dull edge of his knife harder.

Da-Xia stood up. "If you think so, Mr. Burr, then you do not understand the Children of Peace."

The recording said: "We can all hear you, Greta, you're a star."

"Give me the gun, Greta," said Xie.

But I didn't move. My whole arm, held stiffly out and ending in a gun, was alien to me.

The recording caught a murmur. "Oh, Greta, you are perfect."

"You are," Burr echoed himself, smiling fondly. "You were raised to just *take it*."

I closed my eyes.

A shout, a struggle—I opened my eyes and Tolliver Burr

was lunging toward me like a rabid dog.

I lifted the gun and my hand twitched around it, and I—I—

I did not shoot him. The moment opened and seemed to stretch, and in that endless moment I did not shoot Tolliver Burr.

Elián caught Burr and growled, "I'll cut your damn throat."

Just take it indeed. "You do not understand me, Mr. Burr." My voice rang out, as if I were speaking inside a bell. "You do not know the first thing about me. And I do hope that terrifies you." I moved the gun some ten degrees and fired into the darkness. Burr yelped and jerked—but I had been aiming at the machine he had said was the broadcast jammer. The bullet struck metal with a spark and a smash, and the jammer's lights winked off by one.

My father told me something once. A quiet night on one of his boats, drifting on the glassy sea. He told me about *le point vierge*, the untouched place—the cupped and open space in the center of the human soul, where only God can enter. In that dark little room, with the blood between my toes, in that endless moment, I fell into the untouched place. I became Greta again, and whole. I was not afraid.

I handed Xie the gun.

She took it, and she shot every machine in the room. After all, there was no way to know if the torturer had been telling us the truth.

The sound was shattering. Ringing filled my ears. I

worked my elbows back into their slings. Pain faded. I couldn't hear, I didn't hurt, and I was not afraid.

And in that strange state, I knew something. I saw something. I saw a way out. A way to save Elián, and Pittsburgh, and my soul—if not my life. A way out.

It was dazzling.

When every machine in the room was smoking, Da-Xia turned the gun on the smartplex tablet at my feet. It shattered. Each fragment kept playing a different piece of the recording of Tolliver Burr torturing me. But they were small pieces. I felt I could handle them.

I had seen a way out.

As if watching a vid on mute, I noted that Burr was still struggling. Elián gave his pinned arm a jerk, and suddenly the torturer went limp in his grip. His mouth widened with pain. Something must have broken, torn, dislocated. I cannot say I was sorry.

Elián had stopped trying to restrain Burr and was trying, now, to hold him up.

"What do we do with—" Elián couldn't seem to decide whether to ask about Burr or Grego's body first. But it didn't matter, because at that moment a squad of soldiers burst into the room.

The soldiers had guns drawn but, fortunately, not blazing. I do not know what had alerted them—if the ampoules of goat pheromones had been discovered, if the soundproofing of the ship had failed in the face of all that gunfire, if the destruction of the broadcast jammer had set off an alarm. It did not seem to matter. Here they were, five soldiers, at the ready. Buckle was at the back of them. She looked more tired than ready.

Seeing them, Da-Xia dropped her weapon at once, and raised her blood-gloved hands. Elián hesitated, grunted, and let Burr drop. The communications specialist flopped to the floor like a hooked fish. I still wasn't sorry.

But I didn't want him to touch Grego. I stepped between them. The eyes of the guns followed me.

Elián pitched his plea over the heads of the squad. "I'm Elián Palnik—the general's grandson."

"Yes," sighed Buckle. "I know who you are." Her tone suggested that she regretted knowing. If she hadn't, she simply could have had him shot. Or at least locked up. After all, we had a dungeon.

"I need to see her," demanded Elián.

"Not me," I said. I was still thinking of that *point vierge* moment, the door I'd seen that might get everyone out of this alive. "I want to see Talis."

"What?" said Elián. "Why?"

Da-Xia turned to me. I saw the quick calculation in her eyes, her guesses, but she said nothing.

"Greta—" said Elián, and he would have said more, except that Buckle cut him off.

"Outside," she snapped to her squad, and then put her hand to her ear. "Clancy? Wake the general."

One of the Cumberlanders started to heave up Grego's body.

"Don't touch him!" Elián was ferocious and snapping. "I'll take him, I'll carry him."

They let him.

Down the square metal corridor, Elián carried Grego in his arms, as he had carried me. He went like a prince at the head of a procession. Xie and I followed him. The soldiers followed us. I assumed there were guns at our back, but I couldn't be bothered to look. I was looking at Grego. The tuft of white hair tucked against Elián's shoulder. One hand swinging loose.

The whole ship smelled like gunpowder and blood.

And then, suddenly, the night opened up and we were on the gangplank, and then in the grass, with the wild sweet wind blowing around us.

Out there to meet us were more soldiers, and with them Han, Thandi, and Atta.

Atta was leaning on Thandi, his eyes dimmed, blood trickling down behind one ear. Thandi was stormcloud and silence. And Han—sweet, innocent Han, magnificent bastard that he was—was the one particularly guarded, the one clapped in irons.

Nevertheless it was Han who burst from the group and ran toward us. Han who—as he ever did—said what we were all thinking, but did not dare speak. "Oh no," he said. "Oh no, no, no."

He raised his hands to touch Grego's face. His handcuffs rattled. "Oh," he said. "No."

"I'm sorry," Elián said to him. "I'm sorry. I know you loved him."

The soldiers around them seemed to shrink back, leaving the three of them—Elián, Han, and Grego—cupped in a small space all their own. "He was so brave, Han," said Elián. "He was so good. He was so scared, and he was so brave."

"He went in first," said Xie.

Slowly, reverently, Elián laid Grego's body in the rustling grass. Han knelt beside him—it—and then, one by one, the rest of us knelt.

The chamo cloth—and perhaps this was what chamo was for—hid a great deal of the blood. It looked merely like a dark stain, seeping down over his shoulder, front and back, like an officer's half cape. Only in his snow-white hair was it vivid, and even that was fading. His skin was pale as a lamp shade, and he was unlit.

"Grego," said Xie. And one by one the rest of us said it too.

His eyes were open, just a little. He had long, long white eyelashes.

Moonlight fell across us. The Cumberlanders drew back, leaving just the seven of us—the six of us, now. The Children of Peace, alone, as we always were.

Atta was swaying on his knees. Xie wrapped an arm around his waist.

"You all right?" murmured Elián.

Atta nodded, but his head was hanging.

"Concussion, I think," said Thandi, her voice very low. "He blacked out for a second. Threw up."

"We need to wash him clean," said Han. He was leaning forward, almost covering Grego's body, in a world of his own.

"We do," said Xie. "We do." She herself was wearing blood like a pair of gloves.

But Han just repeated himself: "We need to wash him clean."

"What happened here?" said a new voice.

We looked up, and there, standing in the sere grass, was Wilma Armenteros. In her bathrobe.

"Grego's dead," said Elián. "Your torturer shot him. He's dead."

"Mr. Burr," said Armenteros.

My head jerked up, but Burr wasn't there. The Cumberlanders must have taken him away while we'd been taken up with Grego.

"Buckle, where is Mr. Burr?"

"No." Da-Xia stood up. "No, don't look for someone to blame. Look at this. Look at him. Look at what you have done."

And Armenteros—give her this. She looked. At the wind stirring the white hair, tangling it in the grass. At the intensely innocent eyelashes. At the raw meat of the throat.

"His name is Gregori Kalvelis," Da-Xia said. "Grego."

"Grego," said Armenteros. A grandmotherly rumble of a word. She looked away and became a general again. "Who was he? Whose hostage?" She was asking me, of all people.

"He was the son of the Grand Duke of the Baltic Alliance," I answered.

"Cumberland has no quarrel with the Baltics. His death was—"

"A murder," said Xie. "He was murdered by Tolliver Burr, who is employed by you and deployed under your colors in an active theater of war. That makes his actions your responsibility." It was practically chapter and verse, and quite right.

Buckle said: "The boy was dressed as a soldier."

Da-Xia rounded on her, her Blue Tara composure cracking, her hands and knees bloody. "He was an innocent." Her voice cracked too, and broke into a whisper. "He told jokes and he was scared and he didn't even like to take eggs from chickens." She lifted her chin, a goddess again, and turned to Armenteros. "Whatever titles we hold, General, we are not soldiers. And we are not rulers. We are *innocents*. I think you have forgotten that."

Armenteros wrinkled her eyes, a weary look. "You'd be wrong there." She looked up from Grego's body, which was moon-pale and being lapped by the wild grass. "Children of Peace. I confine you to your cells. I haven't the manpower to guard you while you have the run of this place, and you are more trouble than I counted on. I will see to food and so on."

Buckle said, "What about your grandson, sir?"

Armenteros looked at Elián. She didn't sigh. "Him too."

"But—" said Elián. "I mean, I have to tell you what I—"

"I know what you did," said Armenteros. "And I know that, thanks to what you did, we have about two hours before Talis blows up a city. I'm dealing with that right now. The business between us, we can sort out later."

"No," said Elián. "You can't. You have to back off. You have to get out of here."

"No," I said. "What you have to do is let me talk to Talis."

Elián shook his head violently. Thandi just stopped herself before she grabbed me by the sling. Her hand closed on empty air. "What are you doing, Greta?"

I tried to ignore them—and Xie, whose eyes were locked on me, glimmering with understanding. "General," I said. "You need to take me to talk to Talis."

Armenteros studied me. The broad planes of her face pulled in, as if she were chewing on the insides of her cheeks. She asked what Elián had asked, but with her there was no dodging. She had a mind like a grizzly bear: she had reach, and it was unwise to run. She said, "Why?"

"Because he'll never let you leave. And that's what you want, isn't it? You came here gambling that Talis wouldn't strike while you held his hostages hostage. And that my mother would—"

I did not mean to pause there, but I did. Of course she loved me. *Of course.* "That my mother would act to save me. You were wrong on both counts. You lost. So now the best you can hope for is to get away. You don't even need the water anymore. Your population has fallen by—" I stopped. I had no idea of the population of what had once been Indianapolis.

"Three hundred and seventy thousand," Armenteros growled.

"And your water needs," I said, "correspondingly."

Armenteros grunted and stuffed her fists into the pockets of her robe. It was white. She looked like a hostage herself, which I suppose she was. "Why Talis? Why meet with Talis?"

"I have something he wants. I'm the only one here who does."

She didn't ask what it was. Instead her eyes went to my hands, curled and swollen. "Your Highness—I don't see why you'd take Cumberland's part."

"It's 'Your *Royal* Highness,'" I said. "And it's because if you can get out, General, then you can take Elián with you."

"What?" said Elián, who someone (Buckle, probably) had slapped into handcuffs. "Greta—"

I kept my focus on the general. "They'll kill him if he stays. They'll send him to the grey room."

"Talis will never allow it, General," said Buckle. "The boy—he's the *hostage*."

"Greta, what are you doing?" said Elián.

Armenteros herself didn't speak at once. I watched her stand there in her rumpled bathrobe, with Grego's body at her feet, her powerful mind sniffing slowly through the possibilities. At great length she turned to Elián. "I promised your mother, you know. Told her I wouldn't come back without you."

Elián face fell open. He looked stunned as if struck by an arrow.

"So," said Wilma Armenteros, turning back to me. "You're actually not the only one with something Talis wants, Your Highness. If you can't talk him round, tell him that I offer my personal surrender. Not my men—just me. He can do what he wants. That might tempt him."

"*General,*" objected Buckle, and Elián said: "No!"

I remembered how Talis had snarled over the idea of hurting Armenteros, the thin surface of his humanity cracking. *I'll make a story of her. A myth.*

Dear God.

It was fully dark, but there were birds singing. It would be dawn in two hours, with smoke over Pittsburgh. There was nothing else to do, and no one else to do it. Elián was chained up, again. Xie was covered in blood. The Abbot was dying. And Grego was dead. It had to be me.

"All right," I said. "I'll tell him."

The Cumberlanders took me into the miseri, then through the narrow door behind the Abbot's desk. The hallway there was lined with compartments, like the cubbies of a catacomb, and in each of them one of our teachers was stored, hands folded, head tucked tight in sleep. There should have been power-points pulsing in the walls behind them, recharging them—but there were not. There was only one light, a handheld lantern set on top of a pile of sandbags. There were soldiers there, halfway down the empty, echoing hall. They had set up a checkpoint, complete with some minor fortifications and a gun in a fixed position, pointing down the hall, to the simple closed door of the Abbot's cell.

Talis was behind that door.

I did not think all the sandbags in the world would do

the Cumberlanders any good. But it's odd, what makes soldiers feel better.

We came into the pool of light. "General says to take her to see *him*," the woman guarding me said to the checkpoint soldiers. She cocked her head at the Abbot's door, in case anyone was in doubt about who or what earned that heavy pronoun. *Talis.*

"I wish to go alone," I added.

The boy at the sandbags—I recognized him, with a jolt, as the lad who'd turned so green at the thought of me being tortured—looked at me with widened eyes, and it was a moment before he scared up any bravado. "Better you than me, Princess," he said.

He reminded me of Grego. I hoped Talis wouldn't kill him.

The solider in charge of the checkpoints frowned at the other two—then nodded.

They let me pass.

I left the guard and the lamplight behind; my armless, swaying shadow went ahead of me. I paused before the door and let its eye sweep me: once, twice. What intelligence controlled that eye now? The door opened.

Inside was only darkness.

"Talis?" I called softly, as if into a lion's den.

For a moment there was silence, then a rustle, a glint of eyes. Then someone standing before me—the Swan Rider girl in a sepia-dirty white shirt, faded jeans. I could still smell the horse on her. But the moment the thing spoke, the

Rider was gone. She had become Talis again, a godling in the doorway, with hair all mussed. "Greta Gustafsen Stuart," he said, with a long slow smile. "Do come in."

I shivered. But I went in. The door slid closed being me.

The Abbot's cell was utterly empty. Two hundred years old, and his cell was empty. Four walls. No windows. A blank, hard ceiling that was like a weight over me.

Someone—Talis himself, I supposed—had dragged in a memory cushion. His duster lay on the floor beside it, kicked off like a . . . blanket? Did such a creature sleep?

The AI leaned backward against the wall and tucked up one foot like a heron. "What brings you here, Greta? And at such a strange hour."

The foot resting against the stone wall was bare. A woman's foot, slender and high-arched, the nails neatly trimmed. I stared at it.

"Talis," I said. "I want you to kill me."

23
CONSENT

Talis blinked.

I had made the strategic mind of the epoch blink.

"I'm certainly *willing* to kill you," he said. "But you do understand, I have no particular expertise in hands-on murder." He flashed a dazzling smile and spread said hands—they were elegantly long-fingered, striped with rein-callus, and not his at all. "Could get messy."

"No—I mean—"

Talis clicked his tongue against his teeth. "Just a tick." He stooped and rifled through the pockets of the discarded coat. I hoped he wasn't looking for a weapon. I hadn't yet had the chance to explain my request for death, and I would have hated to disappoint him by asking for a delay. But he stood up flourishing his glasses. "Rachel's farsighted," he explained, unfolding them and settling them on his nose. "And a bit night-blind—she never said. Doesn't know, maybe. Not everybody knows their own weaknesses. One just assumes one's normal."

"Were you asleep?" I surprised myself by genuinely wanting to know.

"On and off," he said absently. "Rachel dreams . . ." He leaned past me, triggering the door, and stuck his head into the hallway. That provoked a wave of raised weapons, the click of safeties echoing down the stone corridor. "Are those sandbags? Ha!" He popped back into the room. The door closed. "Sandbags!" he told me. "I love that. What exactly do you think they think I'm going to do?"

"Uh—" I said, unable for a moment to keep up with him. He moved fast, and I was so tired that my bones were hollow.

"So," Talis said. "Death." He plopped down onto the edge of the cushion and patted the space beside him. "Sit down before you fall over, Greta. And explain to me your brilliant plan."

I sat, awkwardly. It is difficult to sink to sitting without one's arms. Talis reached up and put one of his capable, stolen hands flat between my shoulder blades, steadying me on the way down.

"Thank you," I said.

"I—" he began, and something flashed across his narrow face, some piece of ordinary humanity that was so strange in him that it took my breath. "I'm sorry about your hands." I stared into his eyes. The littlest doubt fluttered there. "Rachel dreamt . . ."

He let it fall into silence. I let the silence hold.

"Rachel dreamt—" His eyebrows pulled together. And then in a different tone, cheerful and metal-bright. "Rachel had inductive webbing implanted in her brain, you see, so I could inhabit her. All my Riders have it. Also a datastore, here"—he slapped his ribs as if striking a drum—"because otherwise I wouldn't fit. And they dream! Rachel, she has all these lovely squishy chemical *body* things that pull at my thoughts. Lets me think differently. Stretch out a little. It's one of the tricks for a long life, stretching." He yawned until his jaw cracked, and he stretched his neck, pulling an ear toward one shoulder. Head sideways, he grinned at me. "And that wraps up today's edition of Michael Talis's Top Tips for Becoming a Successful AI. Now, what were you saying?"

He'd guessed.

Of course he had.

"The grey room, the upload." I was fumbling after the words. "It requires my consent?"

"The grey room doesn't. Obviously it's nice to have, and the Abbot—he's done a brilliant job here, getting you kids to sign off. But the upload . . ." He paused, nudging my bare toes with his bare toes. "Yes—consent at a minimum. It's not just any mind that can hold together through the spooling. An unwilling one doesn't have a hope."

"What . . . ," I said, rather faintly, and did not know how to finish it.

"You have to be smart. Disciplined. Ambitious doesn't hurt. Stubborn as a mule with a toothache. Reasonable tolerance for pain." He made a pop with the air in his mouth. "All in all, Greta, I'd say you have a fair chance. But we can't do anything until— Oh!" Something strange happened to his face, as if his eyes had swung inside him, and then out, faster than one could see. "You shut off the snowstorm! That's brilliant! Did you kill Burr?"

"I—" I said. "No."

He scrunched up his nose as if I'd offended him by smell.

"I think Elián broke his arm," I offered.

"Well," Talis chirped, "that's something! Let's hope my little weapons demonstration is convincing. Cumberland isn't huge. They only have so many cities to spare."

"Talis—"

"Or!" he interrupted. "I could kill you! Sorry, forgot for a second. If you're dead, they have no leverage against the PanPols at all." He looked over the top of his glasses at me. "That's quite noble of you, you know."

"Talis," I tried again. "They want to leave. They just want to leave."

"Oh." Another blink. "Well, that's anticlimactic. And not acceptable. There's a price to pay for attacking my Preceptures. It needs to be high."

The Abbot's cell was very small, very blank. It had no outlet, no place to rest the eyes. Talis's quick, strong will seemed trapped in it, like a bird. A bird battering itself.

"I will consent," I said. "I will consent to the upload. I will become AI. But only if you will let them go."

Talis tipped his head, taking my measure. I was aware,

suddenly, that he was very close to me. And—despite Rachel's slight, young body—he was very powerful, very male. "You think I want you that badly?"

It was hard not to pull back. But I did not. "I think you might."

"And why's that?"

"The AIs," I said, softly. "There aren't many of them."

"No."

"You want there to be more."

Softly in turn, he said, "Yes."

"That's why," I said. And saw it hit home.

Here is something that you learn when you spend a lifetime in rigorous study of the history of war: the weaknesses we perceive in others are often the ones we fear in ourselves. Talis was, famously, someone who knew how to use love—parent-child love—as a lever. How to turn grief into power. Well. Two could play at that game. The AIs were his family, and most of them were dead.

Talis ran his tongue slowly over his teeth, as if counting them. A moment ago I'd glimpsed something human in his face, something that could easily have been taken for heartbreak. It was gone now. He was raven-eyed, bright and frank, and he smiled at me before he spoke again. "So that's what I want. Swell. Glad we understand each other. Though—gotta say, you've got some nerve, pushing at it. The stakes must be high for you."

It was halfway to a question. To a negotiation. *State your demands*, he was saying. So I did.

"Let the Cumberlanders go. And let them take Elián Palnik with them."

"Ah, Elián! So it's young love!"

"In point of fact, I think I might be falling in love with Li Da-Xia. But I promised Elián I would save him."

"Xie." He flipped the name with the tip of his tongue. "Hot Asian roommate. Kinky."

It was not worth a retort.

"Sorry," he said, fitting it around his smile. "Sorry. I'm a prude."

"I doubt that."

"Old-fashioned, then. Or just old." He reached out with both hands and touched my face, tracing the eye sockets with his index fingers, then letting them sweep backward toward my ears.

Talis held my face gently cupped. "I think it's old. I think I'm very old, Greta. And I think you should be more frightened."

"I am very frightened," I said, with as much dignity as I could manage.

"It isn't easy," he said, softly. "It hurts—more than you can imagine."

Prickling, shivering sweat crept up my spine. "The Abbot told me."

He shook his head. "It doesn't stop there." His eyes had that quick-winged doubt again—*Rachel dreams*. "You cannot do this at a whim. You gain more than you can imagine. But you give up more than you can guess."

His thumbs sculpted the corners of my jaws, as if I were clay. I sat a long moment, looking at him. Feeling the touch that should have belonged to Rachel, but did not. The blood between my toes was dry now, and both very different and not so different from dried mud. Through the stone walls I could hear the dawn of birds.

"Don't do this for Elián. Don't do it for Pittsburgh, Louisville, all those abstract cities. It won't be enough. It won't hold you together." For once he didn't smile. "Do *you*, Greta Stuart, do you consent to this?"

It put pressure behind my eyes just to look at Talis. I was that frightened. But I said, "I— If you will let them go, I will consent."

"Once there was a boy," he said, as if to himself, "named Michael." And then his face did another flip-shift, as if his mind had been wiped blank and another mind installed. He popped to his feet, struck a fencer's wide-leg stance, and stuck out his hand for me. "Join me, Greta, and we shall rule the galaxy as father and son!"

The galaxy? Son? There was too little air in that small room. There was too much heat in my skin. I was losing track of things.

"I cannot take your hand, Talis."

He folded up the pose, but kept the wild grin. "Right-o." He bent his knees and grabbed me around the waist like a man lifting a barrel. "Let's go see what exactly those sandbags are for, okay? Because that has to be fun." It seemed as if he were genuinely seeking permission. Or at least company—someone to play with. "And share the news, of course! Old Ambrose. He's had his eye on you for a while."

What the Abbot wanted was a successor. He was a teacher who wanted his best student, a master who wanted an apprentice. What Talis wanted was . . . a daughter?

Grinning at me, he waved at the sensor, and the door opened.

We found ourselves looking down gun barrels. The two soldiers out there were kneeling behind the sandbags, weapons ready. I did not particularly want to be shot, but it was hard to fear them. And besides, I had not yet heard Talis agree to my terms. "Talis? You will let them go?"

"Except for Wilma," he said. "Now, her I want. Tell her it's a deal-breaker. Do people still say that? Tell her to look it up."

"She—" She'd guessed this. "Armenteros asked me to offer her personal surrender."

"Wilma Armenteros," Talis spun the name into a laugh. "You've got to give that gal points, just for the *stones*." We'd reached the Cumberland fortification. "Hi, boys!" Talis reached out to ruffle the nearest one's hair. "Having fun?"

"So you'll—" I pressed him.

"Wilma's offer is a sop. It's a steak for the guard dog. Well, it worked. This dog is happy."

Talis dipped down so that he was crouched between the two soldiers, face-to-face. "Already notified them, have you? The monster's loose?"

Both of the soldiers had their gazes locked straight

ahead, their faces frozen.

"Scurry off, then," Talis ordered. "You can fetch some folks for me. I want Armenteros, and the Abbot. Let's get Tolliver Burr out of his sickbed, just for kicks. And arrange a virtual presence terminal for my queen's mum, here."

"Um," said the boy, the one who'd turned so green.

"Her Majesty Queen Anne," I translated for him, "of the Pan Polar Confederacy." My mother. At any point during the descent of the apple press, she could have said one word and saved me. I understood exactly why she hadn't. I didn't blame her, I told myself. I did not.

It would be good to see her, even. One last time.

"Tell them, on the lawn, at dawn," Talis said. "Hey, that rhymes!" He popped to his feet and put an arm around me, and we swept past them. Halfway down the hall he twirled round and called back, "Oh, and tell them not to take that cider press down."

24

TERMS

With Talis's hand between my shoulder blades—steadying, friendly, but shiveringly possessive—we went outside.

It was twilight, perhaps three quarters of an hour before dawn. It's a strange word, "twilight." It makes me think of endings, of things done or left undone, of things over, of evening. But there are two twilights in every day, and one of them does not foretell darkness, but dawn. In this twilight, something new was opening up before me.

The sandbag soldiers must have sent their messages, because the Cumberlanders were bustling about with lanterns, streaking the greyness like fireflies. Or, like fireflies except that they were terrified. Talis ignored them. He guided me around the edge of the Precepture hall. The apple press drew my eye, hulking and black. I shied like a horse—then tried to hide it in a question: "Where are we going?"

"Up to the ship. I want to borrow you a bone-knitter."

Even the word "ship" smelled of blood. Flickering images in darkness. I stopped. "Talis, I don't want them to touch me."

"Oh, don't be ridiculous." He gave me a little push that sent me staggering. He caught me again almost at once, as if it had been a move in a dance—but his hand grabbing me by the shoulder was a shattering pain. I gasped.

"See?" he said. "It hurts, and it can be fixed, so stop whining."

I widened my stance, balancing myself against his touch. "I don't," I said crisply, "want them to touch me."

"Oh, fine," he sulked. "They won't touch you. I'll do it."

"Do you know how?"

"I have a four-digit IQ, Greta. A bone-knitter is a long way from the most complicated thing I've bent to my steely will, okay?"

"But have you ever used one?"

"Sure." His smile flashed in the half-light, flaring open like the white on a blue jay's wing. I could not tell if he was lying.

But I decided I did not much care.

Talis walked me up the hill, and into the Cumberlanders' ship—the guards at the door were pushed away from him as if by magnets. The sound of our feet on the deck plating, the smell of the air recycler, the rhythm of the pinpoint lights . . . the muscles in my neck bunched up, and my shoulders grew hot with pain. But I said nothing of it. Grego: he had been so afraid, and so quiet about it. It had been its own kind of strength.

Talis guided me to the medical bay, pushed me onto a tilt table, and started rummaging through locker drawers with such energy that I thought he might start tossing discarded things over his shoulders. But I hypothesized that even Talis's theatricality had limits, for nothing went flying. I lay on the tilt table, squinting against the pinpoint light. I thought about Grego, and about the grey room. I thought about pain, and about what it would be like to have a mind one could switch off.

"Ta da!" Talis spun around, holding something up. "Sonic knitter!"

Alternate hypothesis: tossing things theatrically had simply not occurred to him.

"Ready?" He didn't give me a chance to consent, but pushed the round head of the device against my shoulder.

Everything I had heard about bone-knitters was true. It vibrated my teeth, it heated my skin, it produced a kind of synesthetic overload, like biting on tinfoil. But all these things were brief. I was left not with pain but with a sort of hollow space where pain used to be.

When he'd done the tendons in both shoulders and the bones in both hands, Talis lifted the knitter away, and I flopped back limply against the padded table, gasping.

The AI grinned at me: "Was it good for you too?"

I continued to hold out the hope that if I did not respond to such taunts, Talis would stop making them. It seemed a somewhat faint hope, but one takes what one can find. Tentatively, I lifted an arm. My shoulder joint rolled through the motion as if it had too much lubrication, and my hand, conversely, was too stiff. But everything moved, and nothing hurt. So I pulled the two slings off over my head, first the left, then the right. I let the fabric drop to the diamond-patterned floor. The buckles went *clink*. I was so tired. I leaned back into the table.

Talis let the mania slide out of his smile and lifted a hand to trace the line of my braid, just above one ear. "We'll probably have to cut it."

I was dumbstruck. A queen does not cut her hair.

"For when we bolt you down," he said, still with that fond look. "You want the beams to make a nice, accurate neuromap. Can't do that if you wiggle."

"So you . . . restrain?"

"Bolt. Literally bolt, right into the skull. Don't worry, it doesn't hurt." A panicked bird in his eyes again. "That part doesn't. Anyway, can't get a hole through all that hair. Lu-Lien had hair like that, back in the day, as long as a river. She, now—she wiggled, and after the upload she just—" He fluttered his hands. "She melted like an ice cream cone, that fast. Came to pieces. Seriously, I'm thinking haircut."

I swallowed. Maybe I nodded.

Talis snapped his fingers. "And another thing."

"In the whole history of human discourse, Lord Talis, no good announcement has ever started with 'and another thing.'"

He grinned at that, but pushed past it. "Elián. This treaty between us—your big brain for his little life? It can't be public. Your countries have declared war, and when wars are declared, my Children die. It's got to be that simple."

I understood that. In this one thing, perhaps, my understanding was even better than his. But I did not nod. I waited, letting my silence pull more from him.

"If he leaves here alive," said Talis, "he's got to vanish. Change his name and disappear. My Riders catch a rumor of him and I'll reel him right back in. He may yet regret that you bought his life."

If he leaves here alive. "If?"

Talis tilted his head and corrected his grammatical mood. "When."

"I—" I stopped.

I watched Talis watch me work it through. The AI was as near to all-powerful as any earthly thing could be. No one could hold him to anything. Therefore, he could offer me no assurances, give no hostages to this treaty. I would have to trust him. Or not.

Did I?

He did not tell me, like a villain in a vid, that I had no choice. I simply knew that I had no choice.

"I'll tell him," I said.

"Up you get, then. It's almost time."

I pushed myself up from the tilt table, feeling both too loose and too stiff, and altogether strange.

Talis led me out into the broadening light.

* * *

On the lawn, at dawn, they gathered—the parties of war. The Abbot, leaning on a stick. Armenteros, making her starched dress uniform look rumpled. Buckle, solemn. Tolliver Burr, hanging back like a kicked dog. Elián, holding himself apart from the other Cumberlanders. Da-Xia, who hadn't been invited but who put herself at the center of the world by sheer force of will.

Brother Delta was there too. The old machine had his head bent to the Abbot's, conferring quietly. I was surprised to see him there, until he turned and glanced up the slope and I saw he was wearing my mother's face.

I paused.

Talis reached over and laced his fingers through mine.

We picked our way down the rocky slope, past the goat pens, hand in hand.

The Precepture hall bulked grey behind us. Overhead were high cirrus clouds blazing yellow and orange in the cobalt sky.

We reached the others. Talis let me go. For a moment we all stood staring at one another.

Then Talis clapped his hands together, with a sound like a rifle shot cracking the cool still air. "Right. Here's the deal. Cumberland, here"—he put both index fingers to his lips, then drew a circle in the air, ending up pointing at Armenteros—"has invaded my Precepture. I, in turn, have destroyed their capital. Now, I'm nothing if I'm not magnanimous, so I'm going to call that even. On the following terms: First, the Cumberlanders are leaving. Now. I want your people lifting off by noon, General. And every stick of your equipment. Leave anything behind—an eavesdrop bug, a weapon for young Elián, so much as a cigarette butt in my potato patch—and I will encase it in a lead shell and drop it back on your heads at escape velocity. Is that clear?"

Armenteros said nothing.

"Done?" prompted the AI.

"Done," said Armenteros.

"Second, I'm keeping you, Wilma." He bumped his folded fingers under her chin, as if she were a cat he was fond of. "To do with as I like."

"But—" said Elián.

"Done," said Armenteros.

"You can't—" said Elián.

"Third," said Talis, speaking over him, "I want Burr."

"What!" said Burr, turning white.

"Relax." Talis clapped the torturer on the shoulder. "If I'm to make an example of Wilma, here, I could use a cameraman."

Burr breathed out. "Oh."

"And after that— If you'll remember, you *did* put your hands on my hostages. Haven't decided what to do about that." He shrugged wickedly. "What do you think? Sternly worded letter?"

"General!" said Burr, whirling toward her.

"Done," said Armenteros into Burr's desperate face.

I hoped dearly that Tolliver Burr would faint. He looked near to it.

"Aaaand, that'll do me," said Talis. "I'm a simple man." Which was, on at least two counts, a flat-out lie.

"Excuse me, Lord Talis," said my mother's voice.

"Your Majesty?" Talis turned and bowed—not deeply, but formally, like a duke.

"Thank you." My mother held Brother Delta's fingers steepled. Her face was zoomed to fill the screen, but I could just see the heavy coils of her ashes-and-strawberries wig sweeping backward over the tips of her ears. "With respect, your terms seem to leave untouched the state of war that exists between Cumberland and the Pan Polars."

"Oh, right," Talis said. "That. Cumberland wants to sue for peace." He cued Wilma Armenteros with one sharp finger.

"Cumberland," she rumbled, "wants to sue for peace." There was some hint of humor or defiance buried in that. Suddenly I could see where Elián got it.

Talis peered at Queen Anne over the tops of his glasses. "I would advise you to make no demands."

"Surely, Lord Talis, that is a sovereign matter?"

"Surely," he said. "But the PanPols have no cause to demand reparations. You have not suffered."

Queen Anne lifted her eyebrows. "I am not sure my daughter would agree, milord."

"Greta," said Talis coolly, "is *mine. And I would advise you to make no demands.*"

Precise words, clicking out from between his teeth like pearls. I saw my mother grapple with them a moment, trying to unpack, to analyze. Then she turned to Armenteros, giving Talis a view of her borrowed shoulder. "The Pan Polar Confederacy waives its right to reparations. Withdraw your forces and your demands against the lake, Madame Secretary, and we will have peace."

"Witness?" Armenteros glanced at Da-Xia.

"On behalf of the Mountain Glacial States, no party to this conflict, I witness this peace," she said. "I bind you to it and I wish you joy of it." I was confident that Xie had never had occasion to officially witness a treaty, but she did it flawlessly. Of course she did.

"Thank you, Your Divinity," said Armenteros formally, and Xie answered, equally formal: "Long may peace endure."

"*Very* long," said Talis. "Or I will show you all a thing or two about endurance." He pulled off his glasses and folded them away. "Now that that's settled, shoo, warriors. I want to talk to my children."

Thus shooed, they went. Buckle took Armenteros under the arm as they walked away. The general was perhaps more frightened than she was letting on. I could not help a glance at Tolliver Burr trailing the officers, more wolf than dog. At the edge of the lawn the apple press seemed to keep its darkness as the light rose. Armenteros was right to be afraid.

Even after the rest of the Cumberlanders were gone, Elián stayed right at my side. And Brother Delta, with my mother's virtual presence still animating him, lingered too.

Talis flicked his fingers at her. "I said, shoo."

She inclined her head respectfully. "My Lord Talis. I had only hoped for a word with my daughter." She paused, her eyes seeking me, but her face, and Brother Delta's heavy head, quite steady. "A good-bye," she said. "Just that."

"Later," he said.

Her lips parted. So far as she knew, there would be no later.

"*Later*," said Talis, baring his teeth at her.

Queen Anne nodded, her face turned on the screen as she reached for a switch, and she was gone. Brother Delta stood abandoned. Talis looked at the still form, his nose wrinkling in distaste. "Power up, then. Scurry off." But nothing happened. Talis slapped the side of the head casing, hard. "Wake up."

Brother Delta's facescreen flashed and solarized, then focused and blinked. "Yes?"

"Leave," said Talis.

We watched him go. The Abbot spread his hexapod support gingerly, using the stick to help him shift his center of gravity lower. Da-Xia stepped forward and took his other hand. "He's getting old," the Abbot said, softly. "I suppose we all are."

"Gee," said Elián. "Getting old. A fate worse than— Oh, wait, no it's not."

"I'll upgrade him," said Talis, ignoring Elián.

The Abbot was as near to sitting now as a thing with no waist ever got. He nodded to Xie. "Thank you, child. I'm all right."

"Are you?" said Talis. "Because it looks to me like the cascade is . . ." He fiddled his fingers. "Cascading."

"As they do," said the Abbot. "I have some time yet, Michael. Tend to your other business."

"Yeah, about that: Is my room online?"

"The grey room?" said Elián.

"No," said the Abbot, ignoring Elián in his turn. At this stage we were all pretty good at it. "The shock ship's EMP blew out the collimators. It will be at least a day before even the basic functions are online."

"Hmmm," said Talis. "And the more advanced functions?"

The Abbot glanced toward me, his eyes widening. Xie caught the glance.

Elián, of course, missed it. "How advanced do you need your murders to be? Because I saw Grego die. It didn't look all that hard."

Talis smiled. "Keep snarking at me, Elián Palnik, and we'll see how hard I can make it."

That stopped even Elián. Frankly I think the look on Talis's face could have stopped the sea.

"As for the advanced functions," said the Abbot, "I am not sure. I really know little about the technical aspects of such things."

"You could look it up," said Talis, plainly irritated.

The Abbot began "I cherish—"

"You cherish your limits, yes, I know," Talis snapped. I did not understand the little squabble, but it had the feeling of an old one. The pair of them suddenly reminded me of my parents. "Never mind. I'll do it." Then his attention flipped, like that of a cat that has spotted a laser pointer. "Incidentally, does anyone know what happened to my horse?"

"Excuse me," said Da-Xia. "But, may I ask—what is under discussion here?"

Talis reached out and claimed my hand. "Do you want to tell them, sweetheart? Or shall I?"

In keeping with my "don't encourage him" policy, I said nothing.

But this time silence made no dent in Talis. He wrapped his arm around me and pulled me close, then flashed a grin at the others. "Greta and I are going to run away together!"

I'd always known that Elián had an explosive temperament, but I'd never before thought it might be a literal statement. Now, though, he looked as if his head might blow off. "What!" he said. "I'm sorry, I mean, *What!*"

"Elián . . ." I wanted to explain. But it was hard to know where to begin.

"Is this why you agreed to let the Cumberlanders go?" the Abbot asked Talis.

"No." Talis grimaced. "And by 'no' I mean 'sort of.' You know, a bit."

The Abbot's eye icons narrowed, and he began to speak, then gave a rattling, shivering cough instead. A test tone sounded before he could get the words out. "Talis, I would not have her blackmailed into this."

"It's not blackmail, good Father," I said. "It's a treaty."

"Yeah," said Elián. "I'm going to stick with '*What!*'"

Xie said nothing, but looked at me with black, compelling eyes.

"A treaty," I said. "Between Greta Gustafsen Stuart, Duchess of Halifax and Crown Princess to the Pan Polar Confederacy, and Michael Talis, Master of the World."

"My blushes, Greta," Talis murmured.

"I am blood hostage to the Precepture," I said. "War has been declared and my life is forfeited thereby. But I choose—" My voice broke across the word "choose." For so long I had thought that I had no choices. *I choose.* "But I choose not to die," I said. "I choose to go to the grey room with my eyes open. I choose to let my mind be unspooled slowly, so that it may be copied. I choose upload. I choose to become AI."

"Greta," whispered Xie.

"And these are my terms," I said, closing my eyes. "That the Cumberlanders will not be further punished: no more cities destroyed. And that the Cumberland hostage, Elián Palnik, be spared."

"In secret," Talis prompted.

"Spared in secret, to be set free, to change his name and his life, to begin something new."

I opened my eyes. Elián was staring at me as if I had betrayed him.

"To be as nobody as he can manage," I said. "To live."

They were all looking at me now, and profoundly silent.

"Done?" I prompted Talis.

He answered softly, "Done."

"Witness," I said.

No one answered.

Talis raised eyebrows at Da-Xia.

"I can't—" Da-Xia was wearing a fresh samue, and was freshly scrubbed—her hands pink with the scrubbing, but without a trace of Grego's blood. She looked down at them. "I can't witness that . . ."

I stopped myself from reaching for her, though I wanted her strong hand in mine. Wanted it badly. "Da-Xia," I said. "Please."

Her eyes locked into mine. "I witness—" Her voice cracked. "On behalf of the Mountain Glacial States, no party to this conflict, I witness this—" Again, a crack. "This peace. I bind you to it and I—I wish you joy."

"Your Divinity," I said, and touched her cheek. She turned her head into my hand and kissed my palm.

"Awww," said Talis. "That's adorable. Aren't they adorable, everybody?"

Elián was gaping at me. "You can't be serious."

I let out a huff that was meant to be a laugh but instead sounded as if he'd struck me in the chest. "Didn't I sound serious?"

"You're going to be a robot? You want to be a robot? For me?"

Talis patted his arm. "For you, and for the Greater Louisville Metropolitan Area. Also the preferred term is 'AI.'"

Elián jerked his arm away.

"Ah, Elián, Elián," said Talis, shaking his head sadly. "The problems of three little people don't amount to a hill of beans in this crazy world. You've got to let her go, son. If you don't, you'll regret it. Maybe not today, maybe not tomorrow, but soon and for—" But then, at Elián's startled recognition, he dropped whatever character he was playing and grinned hugely. "Ha! Look, you got that one! *Casablanca*! A movie fan! That Spartacus thing, you know—totally wasted on this lot. Isn't it awful, what we've lost? Greta, when we get to the Red Mountains, I'm going to make you watch a lot of movies."

For a split second there, Elián had been grinning goofily at Talis. Now he looked as if he might throw up. For my part I pulled the one significant piece of information out of Talis's little sidebar, as I was beginning to suspect would be an essential skill. "We're going to the Red Mountains?"

"What, you thought I'd stick your brain in a box, plug it into a 'bot, and send you on your way? You're going to need some fairly intensive support, if you're going to keep sane."

I glanced at the Abbot, who said, "Quite true. And I do trust that Michael has warned you, Greta. There is a fair chance that what's left of you won't be recognizable. That you won't, in any meaningful way, survive."

"I know my history," I said.

"History," intoned the Abbot. Like me, he loved history, but he said it as if it were the smallest word he'd ever heard. "I'd meant to give you more training, Greta, more time, more—" He dropped the end of whatever he'd been about to say, and turned on Talis slowly, like a gun platform swinging round. "Warn her, Michael. Do it now."

And Talis— Oddly enough, the strategic mind of the epoch seemed at a loss for words. His face was baffled as a little child's. He looked . . . vulnerable. When I spoke, it was half out of pity. "I do know. Most of the AIs died."

"Yeah," he began, and then stopped. He raked his hand up the back of his neck, raising his porcupine spikes again. "Okay, so the thing is, the human mind is a miracle of integration. You're so good at fooling yourselves into thinking you're just one thing, one central little *me* that makes all the calls. It's a total delusion, a fiction, but it *works*. AIs aren't like that. We have layers." He made a little tick, tongue against teeth. "We have layers—and we lose them. The techs used to call it skinning. They meant like onion skin, but that doesn't cover it. The clients called it skinning too, and we meant . . . something different."

To be *skinned*. Goose bumps prickled over me. I thought of the smartplex tablet in Tolliver Burr's hands. I would be like that. Blown into pieces, and each piece still playing, still remembering . . .

"Know that," said the Abbot. "Know that, before you choose."

I looked at the Abbot, the well-known abstraction that was his face. I looked at Talis, who was suddenly smiling again. It was a smile like the sun: so brilliant that it was painful to look at.

Dig deep within yourself, wrote Aurelius. Within is the

wellspring of Good, and it is always ready to bubble up, if you just dig.

Elián was staring at me. I felt Xie's hand slip into mine. I laced my fingers through hers. I dug deep and answered: "I choose."

25
THREE

Three days.

Talis had popped off, glittering and spouting nonsense, and had returned later with the news. His repair of the grey room would take three days. He was speckled with grease, holding a multipencil, and looking pleased.

"It will take an all-nighter or two, mind. Does the Precepture have coffee?" We were all looking at him, but he spoke only to me. "I've got you pegged as more of a tea gal, Greta, which frankly you're just plain wrong about, but anything caffeinated would do."

"Riiiight, coffee," Elián drawled. "⊠Cause what you need is to be *more* intense."

I stepped in to save Elián from himself. (Again.) "I'm afraid that if it doesn't grow in Saskatchewan, we don't have it, Lord Talis. Which eliminates both coffee and tea. But thank you for letting me know how long I have to live."

He gave me a weirdly compressed little smile. And then, for a miracle, he went away.

"Did you just dismiss Talis?" said Elián. "You've gotta show me how to do that."

"I think you hurt his feelings," said Xie, wonderingly, looking after the AI.

"What makes you think he *has* feelings?" said Elián.

"If he doesn't," I said, "then where will that leave me?"

We were sitting on the bench where we'd put out the pumpkins as a symbol of defiance and hope. Elián was peeling long splinters of cedar bark away from the bench. Below us the Cumberlanders were scuttling like mice beneath a hawk, trying to meet Talis's deadline.

"They released Atta?" said Elián.

Xie nodded. "The Cumberlanders checked him over. The concussion was minor. He's fine. Han, on the other hand . . ."

"Yeah." Elián looked down, peeling a long splinter of cedar bark away from the pumpkin bench. "I know."

Han and Grego. I had missed so much. Lost so much. But I had saved a few things. The pumpkins, for instance, had already grown more orange. They were ripening. Going to make it.

Elián was going to make it.

He did not seem happy about it. "I don't get it. From the day they dragged me here, I was going to die—we were both going to die—and you were okay with that."

"I was wrong."

I said it that simply. As if saying it didn't make my heart

twist. As if learning it hadn't kicked the scaffold away from the entire structure of my life, leaving me tottering. "I was wrong. My whole life, I— My friends have died here, Elián. The boy before you—you didn't know him, but he was my friend, could have been my friend. And he died. I wanted that to mean something. I wanted it to be okay."

"It does mean something," murmured Xie.

"But it's not okay," I said. "It's never been okay."

"No," she said. "It's never been okay."

Elián was still looking at me as if I'd turned into a chicken. "So, what, you're just going to join forces with that . . . thing?" Elián snapped his strand of bark into matchsticks, and threw them in the direction Talis had gone.

"I'm going to save us," I said. "All my life I've been trying, and I never have. Now I finally get to. I'm going to save us." I stopped, took a deep breath. "But I'm frightened."

It hurts more than you can imagine, Talis had said. Talis, who knew exactly what I could imagine. Who had seen them break my hands.

The Cumberlanders kept packing, but no one moved the apple press. Or its cameras.

Xie wrapped her arm around me. I leaned into her and closed my eyes.

The morning stretched and warmed. The shock ship seemed to be nearly loaded.

One thing was loading—a coffin. Of course they had come with coffins. Into it, they put Grego's body, to be repatriated back to the Baltic Alliance. He would be the first dead hostage in four hundred years to get a decent funeral. To the Cumberlanders it was the first step in what would probably be a long, prickly process of negotiating reparations. To us it was our friend, who was dead, and who was leaving. We looked at them carrying the plain box up the gangplank, and we held each other's hands.

Someone—a young female Cumberlander—turned up with Talis's horse, which (despite having been ridden brutally, who knew how far) was not in fact dead. The soldier was leading the horse with a . . . leading thing (horses are not my strong point), and the horse was apparently looking for sugar cubes in the soldier's ears. Both of them were smiling.

Elián was pacing, restless, unable—without the benefits of a Precepture education—to stay still, to contain his own physicality. He looked at the horse, and then back at Da-Xia and me, who were still sitting side by side. One of the younger hostages had brought us a UN-blue blanket and some food—hot flat bread and salty goat cheese.

"We should—" Elián said wildly. "We should hide you on board—stow you away."

I looked at the ship, remembering Grego's enthusiasm for it, his talk of deceleration forces and gravity harnesses; remembering the close spaces and the blood coagulating on the deck plates.

"I don't think that's practical, Elián," said Xie.

It wasn't.

"Or the horse. We could steal the horse."

"I don't know how to use a horse," I said. "Do you know how to use a horse?"

Xie tipped her chin up and pointed with her thumb toward the sky. The Panopticon might have been gone, but Talis's net of satellites certainly was not. Elián followed her gaze, his face falling.

"We'd probably end by eating it," I said.

The horse looked over at me, reproachful and, I would swear, alarmed.

Elián was alarmed too—nearly panicking. I thought it was not really about me. The cameras stood waiting by the apple press. We were increasingly sure what they were for: the death of Wilma Armenteros.

Elián stopped pacing to look at the cameras, but couldn't keep looking at them. He whirled away. "She—Grandma, she promised my mother, she said. She promised my mother she wouldn't come home without me. And I—"

Elián had betrayed his grandmother—his whole nation, but his grandmother, specifically. To save me, he'd chosen to sabotage the snowstorm that had been keeping Talis at bay. And now that Talis was no longer at bay, he would tear out Wilma's throat.

"I can't go home," he whispered.

His exile was already struck into the treaty. His broken heart would seal it.

Down the slope, Talis was explaining that part of the deal to Armenteros. The general glanced toward us, and there was joy shining out of her whole body.

"She's just heard that you're going to live." Da-Xia's voice was soft, steady, sure. "Look at her, Elián, so that you will remember. She does not for a second regret what she's doing, because it means you are going to live."

Elián stared. I did too, realizing something that it was probably best not to say aloud: Elián's survival was to be a secret. If Talis was telling Armenteros, then he was sure—very sure—that she would not be passing the word around. She did not have long. And so he was telling her out of . . . could it be kindness?

"Ooo, I know!" Talis's chiming voice drifted over the grass. "He can go to Moose Jaw and help mine the dump. That would be fun for him."

"Don't be ridiculous," said Armenteros.

"Fine." The AI splayed his fingers. "I don't care. I'll get him a horse. He can go anywhere. But tell him he's got to *vanish*, Wilma, or he will regret it."

"Understood."

"No, I'm not going," said Elián, to us. "They're not sending me anywhere." He reached for my hand. "I'll see it through—see Grandma through, and you, Greta. Okay?"

"Okay," I said.

He set off down the slope like Spartacus himself: the slave made hero. When he reached Armenteros she grabbed him like a rearing bear and pulled his lanky body into her soft, fierce one. It wasn't three minutes before they were fighting again, though. Only this time—just for once—I thought Elián would probably win.

★ ★ ★

The ship left. The bulk of it looked ridiculous, lifting from the ground, as if a man had taken flight by flapping his hands. But lift it did. It slung itself up the induction spire, gathering speed. It cleared the top and then fired rockets—chemical ones, a blast of heat and stink. The convention limiting rockets to compressed air was apparently a nicety the military felt it could ignore, environmental damage be damned. I made a note to discuss that with Talis later. The policy might need to be changed.

Oh.

I had just made a note about ruling the world.

Talis—he'd been human, once. Ambrose, our Abbot, who had the charge of this terrible place—he'd been a hostage child.. What had happened to them? What was going to happen to me?

I watched the ship shrink to a pinpoint, and inside I shook.

"Let's go down to the river," said Da-Xia.

Elián looked startled. "Will they let us?"

"They'll let me," I said, sure of it. I relished the surety—and I was frightened by the relish. It was early for power to change me, and it would not be only power. I wondered exactly how it was that a boy named Michael had become a monster.

We gathered the others and went down through the alfalfa—which was coming back up nicely, we should get one more cutting out of it, to feed the goats through the winter—to the sandy shingle of the looping river.

The water was cold and clear, flashing with minnows.

Da-Xia and Atta went wading in the shallow water, each with an arm wrapped around Han, who moved between them like a sleepwalker. Thandi and Elián competed at skipping stones.

I sat on the horizontal branch of a cottonwood tree that overhung the water, and watched myself in the bright surface, my reflection distorted and continually washing away.

It was a good day. It was beautiful.

In due course Elián lost his skipping stone contest—because no one beats Thandi at anything—and came and stood before me. The current eddied around his shins, lapping the bottom of his rolled-up camouflage. He put his hands on my knees and cocked his head to look up at me. "That night in the garden," he said, and then stopped. He squeezed my knees and looked bewildered. "I kissed you," he said. "I woulda sworn—I could have sworn you were kissing me too."

A twist and flush started at my belly button and crept both up and down. "I was. I did."

"But—" He let go of one of my knees and ran his hand up the back of his head, against the grain of his once-again floppy hair. (Talis did that too.) "You don't love me."

"Oh, Elián." It was not that simple. Not nearly. "I—I'm seventeen years old. And I've been asleep my whole life." I tilted forward on the branch—so far that I would have fallen if he hadn't reached up to brace me. But he did brace me, and I had known that he would. I trusted him, and—I loved him?

I looked past him to where Atta and Xie had their arms around Han, their hands joined at the small of his back. Then I leaned forward, and kissed Elián on the mouth. It was soft and slow, neither of us pushing the other, both taking warmth and comfort, if not the more that he wanted. "You woke me up, Elián Palnik."

"Like Sleeping Beauty," he said, with a rough, sad smile. "My princess."

It was not really what I had meant—it was his scream that had awakened me, not his kiss—but I let him have the interpretation. Why not? And the kiss *had* helped. "You woke me up," I said again.

"And you saved me," he answered.

I kissed him again, and he pulled me even farther forward, until he'd pulled me from the branch and I was in his arms, held in his arms as if he were a prince in a storybook—held in his arms as I had been the night on the shock ship, when I'd been damaged and terrified. But now I felt only. . . held. Treasured. Safe. Still.

So naturally, Elián Palnik—forever bad with stillness—chose that moment to dunk me into the river.

26
TWO

The second day was the day Talis killed Wilma Armenteros.

I do not wish to dwell on it. These are the bare facts. He used the apple press, and the torso.

Tolliver Burr was made to film it. I do not imagine he minded.

A fact, also: the Precepture is a small place. With the windows thrown open to the beautiful September day, there was no escaping the sounds.

Da-Xia took me by the hand, and we ran from our cell. Together we found Elián. He was huddled and shivering in the kitchen, with his back to one of the stoves. We grabbed up a lightstick and went running through the four-hundred-fifty step tunnel up to the stone pile, and then past it, over the ridge top and onto the wide golden prairie. There we found the crater, where Elián's road had once been blocked by a beam from the sky. The blasted interior was still a bare saucer of earth, here and there cracked open by fireweed, which had already produced its filament bundles of seed—plants like veins of ash. Elián tumbled over the edge, cowered against the crater rim, and wept.

I held him in my arms until the distant screaming stopped—and then he struggled free and dashed into the center of the crater and fell again to his knees. This time Xie went to him and sat holding his hand. I twisted the fireweed between my fingers—my so-nearly-crushed fingers—and the wiry stems gave off a strong smell, wild, as bitter as yarrow. The seeds lifted on the wind.

Wilma Armenteros.

Talis had promised to make a legend of her, and I had no doubt that he would succeed.

But Spartacus had become legend too, and not quite in the way that the Romans had intended.

We stayed in the crater even after the screams had stopped. The wind blew the grass in waves, bright as straw on their crests, dark in the troughs, restless as the sea. It made a low and constant sound. There were coneflowers in bloom, and monarchs in the milkweed. My nose got sunburned. I think we sat there a long time.

It was Talis himself who fetched us in the end, or fetched me, turning up blood-smudged and grinning. He was holding Tolliver Burr by a wire round his neck. "Hey, Greta," he said. "Thought you might want to get in on this bit."

I looked at the pair of them, jolted by the uncanny picture, the dissonance—the wolf-lean, leathery man being held by a slip of a girl with a boyish haircut and dirt smeared across her nose.

Except she wasn't a girl.

And it wasn't dirt.

"No," I said.

"Ah, come on," Talis coaxed. "He's nearly wetting himself. It'll be fun." He let Burr go, and the man staggered free and bolted by pure instinct: three steps, four, five.

Talis pointed at him without breaking his gaze with me. "Don't run," he said. "I swear you'll regret it if you run." Burr stumbled and stopped, falling to his knees. Talis closed the distance between them like a king on a stage. He bent down and spoke low and sweet. "Run, and I'll start with your feet. Work my way up."

"Lord Talis," Burr gasped. "Please."

"Don't 'Lord' me," snapped Talis. "It's way too late for that."

Panting, Burr closed his eyes.

"These are my *children*." Talis grabbed Burr by the chin and made him look at us. The man's eyes came open, his face crushed with the pressure of the grip and distorted with fear. "They are *sacrosanct. How dare you?*"

Da-Xia stood up. "Talis." Her voice rang out like a temple bell.

"Now, you, I'd take a 'Lord' from," said Talis. Then he looked at her, his eyebrows coming up, grin blossoming.

"Oooo, look. She's going to rebuke me. How cute is that?"

"You made tools of us." Da-Xia was barefoot in the prickly grass, and the bread-smelling wind was blowing straggles of hair into her face, but she looked more like a god than he did. Far more. "Have you never considered: The thing of a tool is that anyone might use it."

Talis didn't answer, but his face quieted, and slowly the grin came off it.

I looked at Burr; I looked at the blood on Talis's hands.

"I've been here already." I was thinking of the moment on the shock ship: the blood between my toes, the gun at the end of my arm. "I could have killed him. I let him go." That *point vierge* moment. The moment in which I had reclaimed myself, though terrified. Redeemed my soul from fear.

I looked at Talis and said, "I want to let him go."

Talis blinked at me, and dropped Burr's chin. "What, seriously?"

I didn't answer. I had been serious enough, and I knew he could see it.

Talis took a step back. A long silence. "Fine," he said.

"What?" said Tolliver Burr.

"Fine," said Talis. "Go."

Burr gaped at him.

"Saskatoon," said Talis, pointing out over the trackless prairie with one finger, "is that way. *Go.*"

Burr got up, looking gormless. One could almost see the questions circling his head like stars. Talis said nothing. We all looked at Burr. And we all said nothing. Burr stared from face to face—and then he broke into a shambling run, skirting the crater, making for the open plain.

"Well, that's boring." Talis flipped a hand toward Burr's shrinking form. "He might even live."

"No," said Elián, who had set out on that path himself once. "Probably not."

Talis scratched behind his ear like a hound, watching Burr move out of sight. "Right, well. Two things. One: Greta, your mother wants to talk to you. Two: Does anyone know how to sterilize a scalpel?"

In a slight variation of my "don't encourage him" policy, I didn't ask about the scalpel. I was not sure I wanted to know. I had, after all, taken a master class in anticipation from a torturer, and I had learned that ignorance really can be a kindness.

Talis sulked when no one rose to his bait, but he didn't press. He hooked me under the arm, and took me back to the Precepture, to the miseri.

He'd dug out from somewhere—the Cumberland equipage?—a tablet of smartplex the size of a piece of paper folded in two. I sat down at the map table with it. The tablet was a Halifax thing, and it did not belong in the Precepture, but it sat as comfortably as a book in my hands, and was better by far than the jolt of seeing my mother's face overtake the familiar screen of one of my teachers.

Still, I had to take a breath, and two, and three, before I tapped it on. Talis hovered.

"Mother," I said.

The screen came to life. I got my mother's privy secretary, a hasty bow, and then my mother herself, sinking into her chair with a scroop of satin. The heavy loops of her wig were caught up in a jeweled net, but her glasses were wire-rimmed and plain, ordinary things. By this I knew she was not meeting me with ceremony, but with love. "Greta . . ." She looked over my shoulder. "Thank you, Lord Talis."

"Oh, hey. You bet."

"And now, if you would leave us? 'Shoo,' is that how one puts it?"

How I loved my mother.

Talis raised both eyebrows, but then made a sweeping bow. "As you wish." Then: "Greta?" He closed a hand over my shoulder in parting, his fingers finding the tender places where he had healed me. "Surgery's next. Meet you in your room."

And before I had a moment to say he was by no means welcome in my room, he was gone.

"Surgery?" My mother's voice almost cracked. I could see her do exactly as I would once have done: swallow the question to allow me my own space and dignity.

"Don't," I said. "You're already so far away . . ."

She looked so close that I might touch her, reach for her as if into a book. I put my fingers on the smartplex. But I also knew how it would look to her. She was sitting at the dressing table where she took private calls. I would be in place of her mirrored reflection, caught in the glass, reaching out.

"You're so far away," I said again.

"I wish I were not," she said. "I wish I had not always been." She put her fingers against mine. I felt nothing. Pearls and sapphires glowed in the net that held her hair. "The broadcast, Greta. The—apple press . . ."

Well, there was a word I would never be able to hear again. I felt as if there were still screams ringing around in the hollows of my ears.

"Don't faint." My mother was leaning close, her breath almost fogging the mirror between us. "Should I call you help? Father Abbot!"

But he wasn't there. It was only me, and she, and the distance.

I took a breath. My mother and I both breathed. Fingertip to fingertip, we steadied our selves, then let our hands fall away.

"We did not know, in my time . . ." I saw her eyes glance behind me, to the curve of the wall that hid the grey room. "Do you? Do you know—what Talis will do?"

Even now she could not drop the Precepture's coded speech. *Do you know what will happen in the grey room? Do you know how you will die?*

How could I even begin to explain?

She was desperate with her good-byes. "I only wanted to say—to say—"

"Mother—" I interrupted her, and she fell completely silent. Her eyes were bright blue and almost glazed, as mine had been in that fateful portrait. They held a resignation that seemed more terrible than grief. It occurred to me that she had been waiting to talk to me for a whole day, and might well have thought me dead. A war had been declared. A Rider—and what a Rider!—had arrived. I *should* be dead. And yet she had held herself ready for the call, waiting. I wondered how long she would have waited.

"Mother," I said again.

She had waited through every inch of the apple press.

She had been waiting for thirteen years.

There were tears welling behind her only-for-family glasses.

I thought if I closed my eyes, I would be able to feel her fingers fiercely tight on my five-year-old arms.

And for the first time since choosing my own fate, I too began to cry. "Mother. It's not death. He's not going to kill me. I'm not going to die."

The second day was also the day that Talis cut me open.

I did not particularly want to talk to Talis after talking to my mother, but I was in no position to disobey him, and I was afraid to leave him alone in my room, lest he get bored and paint it pink or sacrifice a goat in it or something. So I scrubbed up my blotchy face, tidied my hair, and went.

I found him lying on my bunk with his nose in my copy of the *Meditations* of Aurelius.

"What is this about surgery?" I said, to the book.

He lowered the book far enough to peer at me over it. "I thought you knew your history."

"I'm a classicist."

"Really? Wow, that's useless." He lifted the book. "Explains this, though. 'You have power over your mind, not outside events,'" he read. "'Keep to your own mind, and stand tall. Your life is what your thoughts make it.'" He crossed his ankles and raised both eyebrows at me.

"You object to that?"

"I'd like to think I had something to do with your life." He waved his hand around the little room—the two narrow bunks and one creaky table, the laundry and the white linens on hooks, the paper birds making the sky more soft and beautiful.

"Something," I said. "But not everything. Which is rather the point."

He sat up, letting my book slide to the floor. I rescued it as it fell.

Talis's duster was tossed across Xie's cot. I nudged it aside and sat facing him, the book in my hands. We were nearly knee to knee. I did not like to see him in this familiar place. He was like a knife in the spoon drawer. Like a torch in the barn.

"Thank you," he said.

"For . . ."

"For giving me the out." He put one thumb on top of the other and let his fingers steeple and unsteeple, rapid as shuffling cards. "I don't actually want to blow up cities, you know. That's what the Preceptures are for, so that I don't have to. Obviously, therefore, I have to exact some kind of cost for touching the Preceptures. But I don't want too much red on the books. I would just as soon . . . have the out."

It was two parts explanation, one part threat. Just a little reminder of why I was doing this, and what might happen if I changed my mind.

I set my book on the table and patted it closed. Talis had cracked the spine. There was a little box on that table too. His? "Explain the surgery, Talis. I agreed to upload, and there was no mention of surgery."

"Yeah, but it's a package deal." He ran his hands through his hair. There was blood, Wilma's blood, in little dots on his shirt cuffs. "Okay. Remember, in my day, in Michael's day, the upload was part of a general quest for immortality, which was dumb, but never mind that. The point was to get immortal, so obviously the upload's not supposed to kill you, and yet your brain can't survive the spooling. I mean, never mind riding a bicycle—your brain won't remember breathing when the grey room is done with it. So."

There was a faint pause there. Talis rubbed at a spot under his right collarbone the way a man might rub at a bruise.

"So. Your self. The essential data that the spooling records. It's got to go somewhere. It goes here." He curled his fingers and tapped the spot he'd been rubbing. Through the thin fabric of his shirt I could just see the structure of his collarbone and the soft curve of Rachel's bound breasts. There was a shadowy shape between the clavicle and the binding wrap, a distension of the skin that was too rectangular to be anything natural.

"The datastore—the AI's heart and soul. The surgery implants it. There's some odds and ends, too—full-spectrum retinas, fingertip sensors and transmitters, the little things no self-respecting superior being would be without." He spread his hands and tilted them to catch the light. There was something there, a faint silveriness to his palms and fingertips. You'd never see it without the just-so tilt, but it was startling in its slightly-off-ness, like Grego's eyes. "Becoming AI is all about the brain, obviously, but you need a bit of body work, so to speak—a first step."

"But—" I said. Xie's newest folded birds were shimmering above me, and I swore I could still smell chocolate. "But, if you can't breathe . . ."

"The surgery also threads inductive webbing in the brain. The datastore uses that to operate the brain, and the brain operates the body. Bit convoluted, but it generally works. You'll be breathing, I promise."

That thing under his shirt—that thing was going in me. Stuff in my fingers, stuff in my eyes, stuff in my brain. And he, he had it too? The woman he was being, borrowing, what about her? I tried to form the question. "The Riders—"

"Are universally brilliant at breathing. It's part of my recruitment screening."

Not what I meant. That shadowy structure under his shirt—it was his shirt, and yet under it were the slightly crooked ridges of the binding wrap, and Rachel's breasts. "The Riders—you use them, operate them?"

"Yeah, and you can too, someday—but it's better to operate

your own body at first. Less disorienting. I mean, marginally. Take what you can get on that point, trust me. You can transfer later when your body wears out. Which it will, fast, by the way—something about the induced voltages, and microscarring. Dunno; there weren't huge numbers of volunteers, after what happened to us in that first batch, and then Antarctica melted and all that, so the research kind of hit a dead end. Anyway, my point is you won't get more than a year or two out of it."

"But—" I had many objections. I picked one. "What about Rachel?"

"She volunteered," he said. "My Riders serve a higher purpose."

"But she's—" Was he killing her, just by making her breathe? Was that what he was saying? "This voltage scarring—"

"Higher purpose," he chirruped. "I'm the good guy, remember?"

I looked down. The little stains on the cuffs of his shirt were more brown than red. His fingernails were scrubbed and tidy. He had his little box in his hands, and was fiddling with it.

"I—I don't—" I stuttered. A clean sacrifice was one thing. Becoming an abstraction, like the Abbot. This was different. It was so biological, such a mishmash, a horror. "Talis, I don't want—" The box in his hands opened.

"Oh, don't be squeamish," he said, and he injected something into my arm. It was cool, like chilled oil. It spread fast. My legs went liquid, my vision swam.

Talis caught me, smiling softly as he gathered me in his arms. "There," he said. "I've got you. Don't be afraid."

I woke surrounded by blue, my head pounding. Blue: UN blue, more silver than the sky. A sheet beneath me, another over me, more tented round. I was stretched out on something as hard as an autopsy slab, but the sheets meant some care had been taken with sterility, which— Well. I should have been comforted, I suppose. Talis had just told me I was keeping my body for a year or two, and I suppose postoperative septicemia would have put a dent in that. But it was hard to be relieved. What had happened to me? I had not been uploaded, but I felt already changed. Irrevocably changed.

I was alone. The surface I was lying on was marble—the pastry counter in our kitchen. The sterile sheets had been hung from the pot racks. The symbolism was bad: I'd always been hopeless in the kitchen.

I reached up and touched my chest beneath my right collarbone. A numb tenderness met my fingers—that third skin again. I traced the rectangle of the implant, the new sensors in my fingerpads shunting information into my mind. There was a line of forcescar above the implant, slick as plastic. Faint electromagnetic radiation bloomed upward through my skin. That was strange, and then I realized I could feel it—even stranger. I blinked, wild color flaring around me, ultraviolets, infrareds. I could feel the route the blood vessels took in my head.

Strange beyond strange beyond strange.

But not painful. I sat up slowly, and the room did not spin, though I was aware of the whisper of Coriolis force from the rotation of the world.

"Well, this is interesting." Talis's chiming voice came through the curtains. "I don't know that I've ever been murdered."

I staggered through the draping, and found Talis backed against the butchery counter. Elián was holding a knife point to the hollow of the AI's throat.

It was not—it was *not* what it looked like. Elián was tall and muscled, a farm lad who evoked the adjective "strapping," and he was holding a butchering knife. Talis was unarmed, unprepossessing, and cornered.

But Elián was just a boy. And Talis was . . . Talis. I had an urge to reach behind me for the gamma scalpel, and it was not Talis I thought I might need to defend.

"Her blood's all over," Elián snarled. "It's all over you!"

Talis was wearing hostage white as surgical scrubs, and there was indeed blood on them—my blood. *But I consented,* I thought. *Sort of.*

"Give me some credit." The AI was leaning backward onto the counter, partly away from the knife, and partly just lounging. "I washed."

Elián pushed with the knife. The point dimpled Talis's skin, making a ring of white pressure.

"But you mean metaphorical blood, and fair enough." Talis's brightness was glinting up the blade. "You're right. I laid her face up in that press and let her watch it drop. I did it slow. I filmed her face. And it will be *centuries* before anyone touches a hostage Child again."

They had not been talking about me at all.

"How can you—" Elián was shaking. "You're a monster."

"Yes," said Talis. "Are you?" He straightened up. Elián had to step back so that Talis's own movement wouldn't drive the knifepoint in.

"Elián—" I said, and Elián looked wildly round at me.

"The world needs its monsters," said Talis. "It needs its gods. And it needs a certain number of passionate sheep farmers who are neither. Don't do this, Elián Palnik. It will destroy you." He cocked his head, Rachel's glasses glinting, his eyes a pale and thoughtful blue. "In all sincerity, child: I'm not worth it."

"Greta." Elián threw a fast glance over his shoulder. "I didn't know you were—" The knife was away from Talis's throat now, though only an inch or two. "Are you all right?"

Well, I was wearing a bedsheet and watching a murder. "Oddly enough, I can feel the magnetic field of the Earth."

The knife swung a little, as if in that unseen field. "What did you do to her?"

"Upgrade," said Talis, snapping the *p*. "The standard package."

"I should kill you just for that." Elián made a noise like a laugh or a sob. "Can you even die?"

"Sure." Talis gave a loose shrug. "Stab me in the throat and watch me bleed out on the floor. And don't look for me to go winging back to base either. There's no bandwidth for that. I'll just be, *poof*." He made a firework with his fingers. "It's a death, near enough. On the other hand, I'm only a copy. The master version of me can get along just fine without incorporating all of these squishy little memories."

"And what of you?" I said. "This you." It seemed important—and not just because this was the copy with whom (with which?) I had a treaty.

"Who knows?" In Talis's strange Cherenkov blue eyes, I could see my own future. "Maybe there's something after death, even for monsters."

"I hope so," said Elián fiercely. "In the name of God I hope so." He lowered the knife. I let him think he was saving me as he wrapped an arm around me and I took him from the room.

27
ONE

That night—my last night—we burned the body of
Wilma Armenteros.

The Abbot had asked Elián what he wanted done, had
even taken him (and Xie and me, unwilling to let Elián face
it alone) past the induction spire, over the ridge top, to the
graves.

All my years in the Precepture, all the deaths, and I had
never wondered about the graves.

They were a little way out onto the prairie, away from the
scattered boulders of the ridge. This year's graves were still
distinct, jagged with bare earth, the first plants—lamb's-quar-
ters, the tiny questing vines of bindweed (that some call wild
morning glory) filtering into the hard places, opening their
white flowers. Sidney Carlow would be under one of those
mounds. And somewhere Vitor. And Bihn, who had tamed
the birds. She'd hardly be a bump.

Last year's graves were distinct by vegetation: blue flax, sweet clover, coming in before the grasses. Older graves had settled back toward grass and were dimpled inward. They were not dots—not individual graves—but lines. They made a faint pattern of indentations, like the traces of waves. Dozens. Maybe hundreds.

"No," gasped Elián. His voice was flat with horror. "No."

The Abbot was leaning heavily on my arm. I could feel the vibrations set up by his diaphragms as he moved the air to make himself nod gently. "She was not my Child. And, on reflection, Elián, neither were you. I should not have disposition of her body. No more than I should have had your life."

"Oh." Elián was wobbling, perhaps under the vastness of that apology. "Oh. Okay."

"It is your choice, Elián," the Abbot said. "What would you like to do?"

Elián did not, could not, answer. Silence filled with the sound of the grass.

"We could burn her," said Xie, in her gentlest voice. "It is what they do for heroes."

Elián nodded with a jerk, and wrapped his arms around his body as if something inside had shattered.

Atta found us when we came back down the hill, the three of us fearful and stumbling. He opened his big arms wide, and Da-Xia went to him—but it was Elián he gathered in.

Elián is tall, but Atta is huge and muscular, big as a bull.

He wrapped Elián up in a hug like a father wraps a child. When he let go, Elián was no longer shaking. Atta held him at arm's length.

"We need to burn the body," said Xie softly.

"I—" said Atta. His long-frozen voice broke, and he choked and swallowed. "Elián. You have no priest here."

"Rabbi," said Elián, staring at him. "I mean, she isn't, wasn't, but I am . . ." He shrugged at the enormity of it all—his complicated family, his loss, his horror. "No. I have no priest here."

"Let me." Atta's voice cracked again. "Help you."

Elián, being Elián, laughed once—but it was high, almost hysterical. "Are you like Xie, then? Are you a god?"

"Prophet," said Atta. His voice was smoothing out, becoming as big as he was, as deep. "A prince in the line of the Prophet. That's how it is, among my people."

"Okay," said Elián.

"Burning is not what your people would do," said Atta. "And it is not what my people would do. But we can make it holy."

"Well, you're talking," said Elián. "So that's one miracle already."

"Listen to me, Elián," said Atta. His voice had become like a brass singing bowl. "We can make this holy."

"Yeah?" said Elián, all harshness and challenge. And then, from nowhere, tears sprang into his eyes. Not rage, not horror, but grief. And he breathed out: "Yeah."

"Yeah," said Da-Xia, like a blessing.

"I've never burned a body," said Elián, softly. "What do we do?"

The root of holiness, it turns out, is to do things deliberately. We wrapped the body of Wilma Armenteros in a shroud made out of ragged cheesecloth, and we laid it on a stretcher made out of shattered pumpkin trellis. But it still seemed holy. Han and Thandi, Atta and Xie, Elián and me. We carried the stretcher to the apple press, and put it in the place of the bottom stone.

As my friends worked into the evening, I found myself looking at them, wondering, watching. Da-Xia and Thandi, who I thought loved nothing better than to needle each other, were sitting knee to knee, braiding sage and scented grasses into a smudge. Han, who I thought knew nothing of the world, stood slim and small and self-contained, yet made larger by his loss.

And Atta, who I thought was silent, was singing.

He leaned over the body, his white clothing aglow, his skin aglow like old brass. Like old brass it was pure rubbed gold on the inside of his wrists and on his palms. When he turned his hands upward to draw down a blessing, he seemed to be holding the setting sun.

You made tools of us, Da-Xia had told Talis. But it wasn't true. These were no one's tools.

No one's.

Something prickled at the back of my neck. I turned, and there was Talis.

We'd saved the crushing stone for the apple press—behold

the horrible practicality of the Precepture—and Talis was sitting on it. He was leaning back against the wall, with elbows on his knees, chin in his hands, like a thoughtful child himself. He saw my glance and raised his eyebrows to meet it. I wondered how close he could come to reading my mind, and for once I hoped it was close. *No one's tools, Talis.* I turned away.

Under the body we built a pyre of sagebrush and creosote bush, and apple wood from the orchard. Thandi leaned forward and set the end of the braid of grass and sage smoldering. Elián took it and moved the smoking thing up and down the white-wrapped body.

The sun went down behind the induction spire. The spire lit like a streak of silver. Then, as the light sank, a streak of black. It was as thin as a line of ink dividing past and future.

The smudge rope burned down.

Atta kindled a torch and handed it to Elián.

He stood there holding it out, silent.

With the infrared that Talis had added to my vision, I could see the blood heat of strong emotion creeping up Elián's neck, outlining his mouth where words would not come. "Awww, damn it," he whispered, and set the torch to the pyre.

The fire crackled and spat, caught and rose. I felt the heat on my face; strong and then stronger. Even Elián had to step back. There rose a smell I do not care to comment on. Time passed. The darkness thickened and rose up from the earth. It wasn't until much later, when the sparks were spiraling up into a pure dark sky, that Elián spoke again, this time in a language I didn't know. Soft words, hardly a breath, and not to me. They went up with the sparks.

And rising in me, for the first time, came knowledge that I hadn't learned, hadn't earned. Something implanted, something from the datastore. It was not like a memory, which rises into view like a whale from the sea. It was not like an understanding, which pulls pieces together to make a new picture, like stars resolving into a constellation. It was a click, a mechanical thing, as if my brain had new slots carved into it, ready to have knowledge dropped into them. My brain ticked. My teeth hurt. And I knew this, suddenly. Elián was saying the kaddish.

May God's great name be blessed forever . . .

I had been *programmed* with the kaddish. I could have said it with him, Hebrew and all. But I didn't. I was still at least that human.

I did not want to lose my human-ness; I did not want to change. But I was tumbling toward it already. And I *could* do it. I could save us.

Blessed and glorified, honored and extolled, adored and acclaimed . . .

Let there be peace for us and life for us . . .

We all waited with Elián. The pyre consumed both the body and itself. The press itself was the last thing to catch. The iron-hard oak of the footing beams blackened and cracked with heat, and the cracks began to glow. Little flames fitted themselves like spider legs around the pegs of the cogwheels.

Smoke ribboned up the grooves of the great wooden screws. The central fire roared. I caught a glimpse of bones, glowing white. My throat grew as stiff as a flute, watching this, and I could hear the notes of my breathing.

And meanwhile Elián staggered through the kaddish over and over, whispering praise for that which is beyond all praise.

Help me, I thought, to whatever might have bent close to hear those words. *I can do this. I cannot do this. Help me do this.*

Time passed. The bone glow went out. Wilma's white wrappings were long gone. She was black, an ember among the embers, the shell of a shape.

Finally one of the beams gave a *scranch* then a *crack*, and fell sideways into the pyre. Then the whole press groaned and gave way. Embers and spent coals shot outward. The fire, which had been dying down, sprang up again for a moment. When the moment was gone, the body of Wilma Armenteros was gone too.

The fire sank to coals. I could feel the night pass in the spin of the Earth. Hours, and hours. Dawn sidled near; the sky lightened over the loop of the river. And finally, finally, Elián turned. I took his hand, and Xie took mine, and Atta and Thandi and Han put their arms around each other, and we went toward the Precepture together. The building had a dark solidity against the luminous sky.

And deep in the shadows, Talis was still sitting. He was wrapped in his duster, almost unseen against the dewy stones. He had sat there, unnoticed, watching, all night. I was exhausted, and thought he must be too: I knew he *could* sleep, and guessed that he needed to, as much as any bodied thing did. That he hadn't—the whole business had the look of a vigil.

Peace for us and life for us . . .

Let He who makes peace in the heavens . . .

Talis smiled up at me, soft-eyed. In the infrared overlay, I could see the deep chill on him. "Don't forget," he said. "Cut your hair."

My hair.

Back in our cell, I asked Da-Xia to cut it. I explained why—Lu-Lien, who'd wiggled, the bolts against the skull. Xie's face grew very still. "Greta."

"Maybe it will kill me," I said. I took her hand. "But . . . maybe it will not." It was perhaps time to learn to hope. I'd taken the scissors, small and sharp, from the Abbot's bookbinding kit. I held them out. "I can't do this— Xie, I can't do this without you."

Help me, I thought again. *Please help me.*

Xie took refuge in deadpan. "There are those who believe that Talis was a hairdresser in his first life."

That was so wildly unlikely that it almost cracked the moment. But I held to it. "Da-Xia. That's not what I mean."

And she touched my face, the way she had when I'd bolted from the threat of torture, in that moment just before I'd kissed her. "I know," she said. She took the scissors from me.

The cutting of my hair took a long time. The scissors were small. My hair was heavy. Xie's hands were careful, working their way close to my scalp, lifting a lock at a time. Odd that hair is called "locks." This was an unlocking: one piece at a time, I was growing opener and looser, my breath coming deeper, warmer. Xie walked around me slowly in her work, her clothing brushing mine, her waist by my shoulder, her breasts by my ear. My skin came alive to hers, the way a drum skin shivers to the beat of another drum. Neither of us spoke.

It was full light, dappling down through the folded cranes, by the time Da-Xia stepped back from me. She looked me over. Her voice came roughened: we'd been silent all morning. "There. There you are."

I lifted my hands to touch the lightness, the unfamiliar texture of the shorn ends, which were prickly, but soft, too, as if she'd turned me into velvet. "I look like a boy," I said, wondering—feeling that transformed.

Da-Xia made a husky, amazed noise. "You do not."

With my new vision I could see by heat how her blood moved—to her throat, her lips, her breasts. It was arousal. She did not hide it—she never had—but she did not speak of it either. And for how many years had I read Greek, and missed this? "Xie . . . ," I said. I wished I knew how to shut off the implanted sensors. I wanted to see her through my own eyes. I wanted to see her. All of her.

"Li Da-Xia," I said, and stood up. And I kissed her.

In the midst of life we are in death. It struck me,

thinking later, that this was a reversible statement: in the midst of death we are in life. If I was going to put my life down—as Wilma had—then I wanted to mourn it. I wanted to regret it, and fiercely. Maybe the grey room would kill me, and maybe not, but one way or another it would transform me, and this life would be done. I wanted to be alive before that happened. I wanted to be alive before I died, and I wanted death to terrify me, not slip in like a long-expected guest.

I kissed Xie: we kissed. We wept and we kissed. Then we did more than kiss. As for the rest of that morning—I will not say more. I will keep it silently, in that holy place in my heart.

We slept then. My last day, and we slept through it, tumbled and tangled together on Xie's narrow cot, her goddess hands folded over my belly, her breath stirring the hairs at the nape of my neck.

But how could we not have slept? I was so far beyond exhausted that I seemed to be entering already into a different world. And what had we left to say to each other, or to do? We had had our years. That I had missed them wrenched my heart, but they could not be called back now. Not even Talis could do that.

I think it was hunger that woke me—certainly I woke hungry. My newly logical body tallied the time since it had eaten and recommended starches and protein. But instead of going to find them, I lay still. Xie's breath moved against my spine. I let myself rest in the warmth of the space between us, that opened and closed.

All my life I'd lived under the threat of death—mine, my friends'. I'd been a pawn in a scheme about the greater good, and I had kept myself asleep in order to survive. I was awake now. And I had found . . . love, all around me. Love where I had never expected it to be. Xie.

Xie, and not only Xie. Elián. Atta. Grego and Han. Love. It was everywhere. And now I was going to give it up. For the greater good. It was one thing to give it up unknowingly, as I had done for years. It was quite another to hold love in one's hand, and then let it go.

My breath snagged. Xie's voice came sleepily into my ear. "Greta."

I rolled to face her. With one fingertip she traced my cheekbones, my long wolfhound nose. The fine hairs of my skin rose to meet her. Her tiny braids—undone and every-where—licked like paintbrushes across my throat. The wind had picked up, and was blowing the yellow apple leaves like coins against the glass of the ceiling. I could hear them, fainter than the rain. "I was born under cherry blossoms," she said. "I'll be eighteen in the spring."

"And go home." Li Da-Xia was going to live.

"To the mountains," she said, as if it were a correction. I knew the feeling: the open sky of the prairies—surely that would always be home, no matter where I had been born, or what land I was supposed to have ruled.

"I should write a note. Remind my mother to take me

out of the succession." As I said it, I realized it was not necessary. Someone would see to it. The PanPols would never consent to be ruled by an AI.

Xie made a catlike hum of affirmation, following the jump of my thought effortlessly. "My father wrote. The monks have found me a suitor. I understand his lineage is impeccable."

"I wish . . ." I whispered, before I could stop myself. I wished for impossible things. It was never going to have been a fairy tale for us. There are no fairy tales about two princesses. "It's six months until cherry blossoms. I wish we could have it."

In answer Xie kissed me softly. "I have had eyes."

My marriage will be dynastic, but in the meantime, I have eyes. I wished—

"Do you suppose the machines love each other?" I said. "The AIs?"

Her body was aglow in my arms. What would it be like, not to have a body?

"Hold on to yourself," she said. "Please, Greta. Hold on to yourself. Hold fiercely."

And she wrapped her hand behind my head—my prickling hair—and moved her hungry mouth to mine.

We were still tangled in each other when the door slid open.

I grabbed up a sheet.

It was Talis, of course, his hands in his pockets and his duster stirring like a heartbeat. I flushed, thinking he would grin, taunt. My newly opened soul was too tender for that. I knew I could not defend myself.

But to my surprise he didn't smile at all. His pale eyes moved over every inch of us, but it did not look like lechery. It looked like sorrow. "We're ready," he said.

28
ZERO

I stood up.

I was wearing only a bedsheet, and I was blushing, but I was taller than Talis, and was not ashamed. "No," I said.

Talis froze. His face was hard at first, his ancient eyes like bits of lit glass. Then it opened into something bigger—was it anger? Fear? Wonder?

"No," I said again. "We do this my way. I want dinner."

"Oh," said Talis. "Okay."

So, dinner.

My last meal was zucchini. I leaned against the end of the table and I laughed. Then I wept.

Thandi moved over along the bench to make room for me and Xie. Han and Atta knotted closely around. Elián was not there.

And the zucchini, I almost hate to admit, was good:

sautéed with browned butter and basil. There were corn and peppers cooked up with onions and herbs and a lot of garlic. There was flatbread that was scorchingly hot on my fingers. There was butter for the bread, too. Generous butter, thick slices of chèvre piled on brilliant tomatoes, salt in a jar. Some of these things were things we were careful with, things that we rationed. Not today. This was our abundance.

I ate, and when I pushed my plate away, I felt fingers on my shoulders. I turned. It was a little boy, five or six, black, slight, with brilliant beads in his hair. I did not know him. "Greta," he said, and touched my face shyly. And then he ducked away. Fingers brushed my ears on the other side, and I turned again, and again a child touched my face and said my name softly: "Greta."

One by one they came to me, not all of them, but many, the Children of Peace. They touched my newly sensitive hair, my shoulders, my freckles one by one. They called me by name. Da-Xia had to put her hand between my shoulder blades to hold me steady. There were a few gifts. An origami koi fish, no larger than the end of my thumb. "For immortality." A carved wooden comb for what had once been my hair. "S-sorry," said that boy, stammering. A little girl, just the right age to have the care of bees, brought me a dripping honeycomb. It was so fresh that it was warm. "For now," she said. "Eat it now."

So I did. And by the time I had finished the sticky sweetness, the room had fallen quiet. Han spoke into it: "Are you going to die?"

Oh, Han. Always, always, always the wrong thing.

"I don't know," I said.

I did not know what to say to the others. Atta, who sat soaking everything in, like a stone in the sun. Thandi with her anger and her damage. And Xie. But surely I had said what I needed to say to Xie. I reached across the table and took Atta's hard, strong hands. "Talk to her."

"I'm done with silence," he answered. But his voice caught—not with disuse but with sudden tears.

"You and Grego and Elián," said Thandi. "We'll be shorthanded."

"I know." I looked at her—proud, strong, unbruised, unmarked. Once, she had been a terrified and tortured child. I had missed my chance to help her through that. I had missed it by years.

"You remember Talis's first rule of war?" she asked. The impulse to speak quietly to condemned people did not seem present in her. Her strong voice filled the room. Everyone was looking at her, at us. I nodded, but she answered for me anyway. "It's 'make it personal.'"

"I know," I said again.

"So," she said. "If you get a chance, do something for me?"

"Of course," I said. Everyone hung on the solemn edge of the moment, listening.

"Kick Talis in the nuts."

The room burst into laughter. But Thandi was not laughing. She nodded to me, queen to queen.

Then she smiled. And I smiled.

I scrapped the bench backward. I stood. I wobbled. I squared my feet. "I'm ready." Or I thought I had been. My voice snagged. "Xie, would—would you come with me?"

"Always," she said. As I had known she would.

We went out. And outside the refectory door was Elián.

"Oh," he said, "your hair." He folded his hand and ran his knuckles across the cut velvet of my scalp.

I shivered at the softness of his touch. "Elián . . ."

He wrapped me in his arms. I could still smell the pyre on him as I turned my nose toward those untamable curls. He pulled back and kissed my cheek, and then, his voice rough as if with smoke, he said, "It's the Abbot, Greta. . . . Could you come?"

In a pool of lamplight in the misericord of the Fourth Precepture, there is a memory cushion that lies like a nest in the grove of columnar bookshelves housing classical philosophy. In it the Abbot was sprawled as a man might sprawl, with his arms limp, and the soles of his footpads off the ground. The forward bend in his mainstem meant that his head was a foot off the surface of the cushion. Someone had piled books under it, into something halfway between a buttress and a pillow. The Abbot had not been built to lie down.

And yet he lay there.

I had been lying in just that place when he had taken this damage to save me, rushing to unhook me from the dreamlock magnets while the Cumberland ship roared down. He could have shielded himself, but he'd saved me instead. I had been lying there, and he had been torturing me.

I knelt. "Abbot."

His monitor turned against the book-pillow. His face-screen was pixelated, his eyes only intermittently showing as coins of grey.

"Greta?" I could hear the synthetic parts of his voice—this tone and that tone—blurring slightly out of sync. My new sensors could see the currents moving through him, falling from capacitive plane to capacitive plane like water down steps of ice. *Cascade,* came the word. A cascade failure. It was washing him away.

"Good Father." I took his hand. "I'm here."

Da-Xia came and took his other hand. "Cannot Talis repair you?"

His head twitched against the books, the sound of a page being turned. "He could, I—" A spark, then, jumping down that slope like a coyote hunting. "Greta, please, I wanted—"

"Father Abbot." I squeezed his hand. *How much of a man? This much.* "Father. *Ambrose.*"

His voice was entirely synthetic now, like a pipe organ given speech. "Tell him not."

"Not what?"

"Repair."

"Ambrose," I said, again.

"No repair." His face swung to me, blind, weaving from

side to side like a snake's head finding by smell. My velvet hair prickled with instinctual fear. Then his eye icons resolved, and for one second he was my Abbot again. "Forgive," he said.

And nothing more.

Da-Xia's eyes met my eyes over his body—wide, shocked.

Elián—and I realized it had been Elián who had piled the book pillow, who had kept this vigil—Elián touched the side of the Abbot's main casing where Tolliver Burr had once forced his wires. "God knows I hated you," he said, and swallowed. "God knows I had cause." His hand shifted, soft, against the frozen monitor, as if to brush closed the eyes. "God knows what you used to be," he said. "God knows."

Xie steepled her hands around her nose, covering her mouth. Tears sprang up in her eyes. "What will we do?"

I thought, *I have just seen my death.*

But I said, "Something new."

We left the Abbot's body lying in the golden light. What else could we have done? Talis had give me three days, and it had been three days. We went hand in hand. Da-Xia and Elián, walking me. The grey room wasn't far away. Its ordinary, ever-closed door.

That door was open. Talis was inside, sitting on the high narrow table, swinging his feet. He hopped down when he saw us, and rubbed his hands dry against the faded spots on the thighs of his jeans. "Where's old Ambrose? Thought he'd want to see you off."

"He did," Elián said, smooth as a cat. Who knew if such a death were reversible, but even if it were, surely time would make it less so. Let the Abbot have that time.

The Abbot. The grey room. He had done this, once. He had lived. But later he had wanted to die.

Under the lintel, Talis opened his hand through the doorway with a very Talisy grin. "Your table awaits."

I froze and swallowed.

Talis let the grin drop away. "Ready?" he asked softly.

Without prompting, without a word, Elián and Da-Xia folded themselves around me, hugging me, covering me like wings. For a moment we three paused there, our arms gripping each other tightly, our breath mingling, our foreheads resting together. "So, right," Elián whispered. "Xie, you take the snap; Greta, you go long . . ."

I knew he was joking, but I had to stop him: I couldn't bear it. "Elián," I whispered.

Da-Xia was weeping without a sound, her tears dripping down onto the flagstones. Rain on the mountains. "Hold on," she said. "Hold on, Greta. Please hold on."

I could not even tell her that I would. I did not know if I could. I could not speak at all. I straightened up.

"Ready?" said Talis, again.

"Willing," I said, which is a different thing.

And I walked alone into the grey room.

29
COLOR

The door whispered closed.

That room. Its soft walls, its carefully filtered light. It was—I could feel it, now, in my new sensors—it was washed in radiation, hidden collimators on the walls humming like bees. "My friends—" I began.

"It would kill them to stay here. It would kill me, for that matter—Twice. Scramble me and kill Rachel. I'm afraid you'll have to go solo."

"I know," I said. Then: "Okay."

Talis patted the surface of the high table. "Hop up."

The aluminum surface was even with my ribcage. "That would be undignified." I truly did not want to spend my last human moments struggling to hoist myself to death.

"Oh, right! Forgot!" He hooked his foot around something stored underneath the table. It slid out—a milking stool. It could have been centuries old. Its use had polished it like gold-grey glass.

A milking stool.

It struck me as horrible, suddenly, that someone had thought of this way to boost us to the right height for our deaths. The gamma rays crawled over my skin. I put my foot on the milking stool, my hands on the table, and I boosted myself up. "What do you do with the little ones?" I asked. "The babies?"

Talis shrugged, preoccupied. "The Riders lift them. Does it matter?"

"It does," I said. "It should."

"Lie down," he said.

"Talis—" I said, and then could not think of a thing to say.

"Put your head," he said, putting one finger on the tabletop, where the intersecting radiation beams (though still quiescent) made a bright spot that only the two of us would have been able to see. "Just here."

I put my head just there.

The bright spot was brighter than I'd anticipated. I squinted, but it wasn't that kind of bright. I could see the sparkles of ionization where high-energy particles were entering the soft gel of my eyes. "This will blind me," I said.

"Hmmmm?" Talis was standing at my ear, a flicker and loom on the periphery, bigger than he should have been, nightmarish. I could see his busy hands, the invisible light dancing over his weaver's fingers, the blackwork tattoo at his wrist. "Oh, yes. Cataracts. That body won't last long enough to develop them. Don't worry."

Don't worry.

Something as hard as a scythe swung into my vision then, and I flinched—and then strained my eyes upward to look. The cage for the head. It was a half circle of metal that swung into slots beside my ears. It was pierced with threaded bolts.

Bolt. Literally bolt, Talis had said.

I was ready to.

I heard metal brush metal, very close.

Elián, I thought. *Pittsburgh. Louisville.*

And then, reminding myself: *I choose. I hope. Something new.*

Talis leaned over me; I saw his face upside down, bisected by the metal arch of the halo. He put a hand over each of my ears and moved me minutely, this way, then that, then simply holding me steady, centered in the beams.

"Talis," I said, and was ashamed that I was starting to cry with fear, ashamed that I could think of nothing to say.

"Greta." He swiped tears off my cheekbones with the pads of his thumbs. "Let me tell you something that I learned in my youth, from a sage called the Road Runner. You can walk off a cliff and the air will hold you. Only, don't look down."

I tried to take that in. I would have nodded, except that I was afraid of ruining the alignment. Lu-Lien, who'd wiggled. *Melted like an ice cream cone.* I held very, very still.

Talis's eyes were intense and sure. "It's too late for doubt. Understand?"

I choose. Not death. Something new. "Yes," I said. My chest was so tight.

Talis began to set the bolts.

I could hear them, ticking and creaking, as minutely as crickets. *Tick, tock, drop.* He set one against the prominence of bone behind my left ear. Another against the right side. I could still have sat up; I could still—

He set one against the center of my forehead. I could see the flat bottom of the bolt starting to come down. *I laid her faceup in that press and let her watch.*

The blunt ends of the bolts were firm and cold, like coins on the eyes. There were four more to set.

Talis set them.

And then tightened them.

Bruising. And then burrowing. No pain, but a wrongness that no amount of anesthetic could ever deaden. They were *in* me.

Don't panic, Greta. Don't panic.

The radiation like ants crawling over my face. Into my eyes and ears. I reached up and touched the halo. Talis laid his fingers over mine. I could feel our sensors meeting, meshing, like to like. "Don't look down," he said.

I swallowed. Lowered my hands slowly to my sides. One wrist brushed leather.

"You don't have to . . ." I meant the straps.

Talis's smile flickered. "You'll need them," he said, and buckled them tight.

He leaned in, hesitated as if shy, and then put a cool kiss

on the end of my nose. "Greta Stuart: See you on the other side."

And he left the room.

I was alone. My aloneness echoed around me. I took a deep breath, and counted it: One.

Two.

My implanted datastore sensed what I was doing and started scrolling milliseconds.

Three. Four. A tightness in my chest: pure fear.

Blessed and glorified, honored and extolled, adored and acclaimed—oh help me—

I choose this. Power in the choosing. I claim it. I claim it.

Five. Six.

Seven breaths and 25,172 milliseconds later, the beams switched on.

Is there any point in describing my death from induced currents in the brain? There were magnets; they induced currents; I died.

Does it hurt? I had asked the Abbot.

The word he'd chosen: "profoundly."

It hurt profoundly.

There is a threshold before which sensation is not painful. There is another, which few people know, past which pain becomes something besides sensation. There are no words for it, though some people call it light, the white light induced by the overload of the dying brain. Perhaps I should call it color, the thing that quarks are said to have. Quarks bind themselves into twos and threes so that their color adds up to white. Take one out of its pairing and hold it apart from the others, and the strain, the *wrongness*, will be so great that space itself will rip apart.

And create something new.

Dear God.

The magnetic fields reached inside me and pulled each color and held it alone in the universe:

The golden skin of Da-Xia's back, arching with joy.

The orange sparks of the funeral pyre rising against the ink-dark sky.

The fireweed, silver and white.

Grego's blood drying burgundy.

Ivory: the weathered ceramic of the Abbot's fingers.

Gray: the crushing stone of the apple press.

Black: the camera's eye.

Faster and faster they came: orange pumpkins, blue orbital weapons, Charlie's tawny coat, rose-red taffeta, the joyful multicolor of Christmas tree lights.

No, I said, looking into the camera, *of course I'm not afraid.*

Red: my mother's hair, ablaze with diamonds.

Blue: Talis's eyes.

Da-Xia blushing. Elián, his black hair tumbling over his face. His hands were bound.

My hands were bound. If they had not been bound, I would have ripped out my eyes.

A lightning strike. A feeling of charge building up, pulling and pulling and pulling. It was going to hit me. I was

THE SCORPION RULES 345

going to become lightning. I was going to die.

For one moment all the colors turned into white, a tunnel, a welcome. I looked over whatever it was that passed for my shoulder and saw the body on the table below me, convulsing against its straps.

It's a big one, the child Da-Xia shouted, singing to the lightning. *Are you afraid?*

Yes.

The grey room. The beams—gone. The collimators and emitters, no longer firing, are supercooled points, as blue as stars in my overlaid vision—and the lights are out. And I am floating alone in darkness, in stars.

Information.

The memory of making love with Da-Xia presents itself on the recently accessed list, below the origin of the term "cascade failure" and the theory of quantum chromodynamics.

Clock.

Twenty-nine minutes, fifty-four seconds.

Since when?

Since the command count received.

Recently accessed memory: counting breaths.

One, two, three, four, five, six, seven—partial list of digits/real numbers/positive integers. Someone counting breaths. Greta. Time to check on Greta.

She is not breathing.

Rectify: command breathe.

She takes a breath.

Inventory: datastore running hot; redirect lymph for cooling. Severe bruising, frontal boss of the skull. Residual currents in inductive webbing. Hormonal imbalance: adrenaline, cortisol, serotonin. Minor fracturing, metacarpal of left thumb; scaphoid carpal of left wrist.

That is—

(Hang on, Greta. Hang on fiercely.)

That is ironic, isn't it?

Why?

Recently accessed memory: struggling against the straps. Breaking. Compare. Twice broken.

Ironic, because—

I should breathe again, shouldn't I?

I take a breath.

And.

To claim that . . . I had been tortured. To be *I* was to claim that. Review the file apple press: terror, pain.

What advantage in that? Easier to close the file. Close the *I*.

The memory comes without me calling for it, this time, rising in the organic structures and overlaying itself on the webbing, so that I feel it twice: Talis's blue eyes, which are Rachel's eyes, and Talis the bird behind them, trapped.

Stubborn as a mule with a toothache. Reasonable tolerance for pain. All in all, Greta—

And another voice: *There is a fair chance that what's left of you won't be recognizable. That you won't, in any meaningful way, survive.*

Recognizable. I recognize this body, Greta's body, wrapped around me like a dress, constricting.

My ribs cannot move—I cannot breathe. I am only a painting, and yet I need to breathe. Then the artist—and it is Elián, of course, Elián—

Elián. And Xie, taking my hand. I know it by shape. Da-Xia.

I am not a painting. "Greta?" Her voice comes softly. I hear the tears move behind it. "Oh, please . . . Greta?"

I open Greta's eyes.

They are both there, Elián Palnik and Li Da-Xia, and each is fumbling with a buckle at my hands. Talis is leaning against the far wall with his foot tucked up, looking casual but with all his sensors on full: he is blazing like something falling to earth.

The buckle on Da-Xia's side comes free. She seizes that hand, lifts it toward her face.

That hand is broken.

"That hand is broken," I say.

"Oh!" Flushed, she puts the hand back. "I didn't—"

"I've overridden the pain," I say. "You can hold it if you want to."

"Oh," she says again. She does not pick the hand back up.

Elián frees my other hand but does not touch me. "Can we get these screws out?" he asks Talis.

"It's called a halo," Talis says, straightening up and stretching. "Isn't that right, angel?"

"I'm not an angel," I say.

Angels are pure souls without bodies. Demons are the ones who possess, and ghosts are the dead, still living. I might be either a demon or a ghost, but—but—

"What are you, then?" says Talis softly, privately, his sensors aglow.

I know it is important. I am as curious as he to discover the answer. We wait through 3,451 milliseconds of processing silence.

"I'm a monster," I say.

A smile comes onto his face, then, like bindweed growing across a grave. "Welcome to the club."

30
COCOONED

Unbolted, unbuckled, I sat up and made an inventory. The organic structures of the brain were of course disrupted by the mapping current, and presumably the damage there would be extensive, but it didn't matter. The datastore had captured both the memory and the sub-memory "instincts" that drove necessary functions—breathing and whatnot. From the datastore these moved through the inductive webbing. It was working flawlessly, pushing and pulling the brain exactly as it needed to.

Meanwhile the body. Its physiological death seemed to have been brief; the damage was minimal. The bruising to the skull could potentially have implications; I made a note to look into it. The rest was little more than aches and pains, and bothered me not at all.

I laced my fingers together and pushed my palms out, cracking the joints—a huge rush of data there. Fingertips reporting, tendons stretching, ears cataloging the cheerful pop of cartilage, the left thumb and left wrist flaring for attention like a child's sparkler.

"Don't hurt her." Da-Xia. A crack in her voice.

I turned to her, blinking. Another rush, a cascade, of data. The subtle intricacies of reading meaning from the expression on her face: it was the most challenging thing I'd yet been called upon to do. Oh, it was glorious, feeling my new intelligences flipping through the memory of every time I'd seen her face, building the database, gaining mastery. I *liked* mastery.

But I could not read her now. "What do you mean?"

"The hand?" She put her fingers on my forearm. "You said it was broken."

"No. What do you mean, '*her*'?"

She hesitated. "Greta."

"I am Greta."

And I was. I was a perfect duplicate of her memories, and at least for the moment wore her body. The only complication, in fact, was that the organic structures of memory did (at least in part) still exist. The datastore flipped through its catalog of Da-Xia's remembered face, looking for a fit for the current expression (immobility of the mouth, widening of the eyes). But meanwhile other memories rose from the squishy, murky depths of the mind—fragmented by the mapping, struggling like newly hatched butterflies. Da-Xia's face.

That image. It had come from, from—Greta. I am Greta.

"I am Greta," I said again.

Da-Xia put her hand flat on my cheek. "You're not." And then she turned and left the room.

Elián hesitated. "Are you— I mean, are you all right?"

"Certainly," I said.

Talis said, "She's in minimal danger at the moment. Go with Xie."

"Don't tell me what to do," snapped Elián. And then he went with Xie.

I blinked at Talis, who blinked at me. Was it semaphore? Code? I couldn't decipher it.

"You're bleeding." Talis pulled a one-sided smile and retrieved something from his pocket. It was a wipe in a small packet. He tore it out, reached up, and smudged away the blood from the compression wounds left by the halo screws. "Antiseptics, coagulants," he said. "Stuff to force the scars."

"It stings."

He made a shushing noise. "Yeah. I know."

"So I am in minimal danger?" I was not afraid. Though (my datastore was providing me with a complete catalog of the fates of AIs of the First Wave) perhaps I should have been.

"At the moment," Talis said again.

The datastore agreed: statistically, historically, any deterioration was likely to happen later. *Skinning*. I wondered what provoked it.

Talis frowned at me. "Don't worry about it now."

I obeyed, and easily. "Help me down," I said. "I want to see everything."

Outside the grey room, the world glittered with colors I was only beginning to see. Information overlays seemed infinite in their richness. It was—

Somewhat dazzling. Even the hallway, which I did not remember as interesting, was hung with information, gleaming virtual lights. It was like a Christmas tree.

The organic mind whispered about taffeta figured with flowers, champagne punch, and interview cameras. A nightmare.

My ribs felt oddly tight.

When I took the next step the complex dynamic equilibrium of keeping balance failed me. I staggered and fell to my knees.

Talis crouched beside me. "Dizzy?"

"No." Dizzy was not what I was. The patellae reported on the force of impact, substantial but not damaging. Silly to think that would once have been a message of pain. I tried to get back up but again balance eluded me.

Talis's voice was soft. "Close your eyes."

I obeyed. Greta obeyed. Something in me was glad to close that *I*.

"There," he said. "Reducing stimuli will always help. Remember that. Don't be afraid."

"I'm not afraid."

"Keep your eyes closed, and get up." I got up. "A few steps." I took a few steps. "Got it?"

"I'm a roadrunner."

"That's my girl."

I opened my eyes. We were at the door of the misericord (late Latin "misericors," meaning "compassionate"; noun, "a room in a monastery where the rules are relaxed," or "a small dagger for delivering a death blow to a wounded opponent"). Xie was standing there, folded against Elián. He had an arm wrapped around her. They were looking at us. And they were shielding the doorway.

Talis's eyes went wide. He strode over and shouldered past them. In the doorway he stopped.

The datastore, which had been mulling through the names of the AIs who had died, provided me with the human names of two who had lived.

Michael Telos.

And Ambrose Devalera.

Talis looked in at the supine wreck of the Abbot and said, "Oh."

I could see Talis's limbic response—his heart rate picking up, his skin conductivity rising. I wondered why he was allowing that, and I was not sure what it signified. "I wish someone had reminded me," he said, and he sounded purely petulant, as if he were discussing an overdue library book.

"He asked us not to," said Elián.

"Oh, and naturally you obeyed him," snapped the AI. "Just for the change."

"What will we do?" Da-Xia was ever practical. The Abbot had run the Precepture. Now he was dead. He had meant the running of the Precepture to be my job, but I was not ready to take it on. And in any case it sounded dull.

"Hmmm." Talis's limbic response was subsiding. "Well. I've got Swan Riders incoming, to take Greta and me to the Red Mountains. I can put one of them in charge."

I looked over at the Abbot. He lay like a discarded toy. He'd been such a finely made machine: it was sad to see such a finely made thing broken. The heat blush on Talis, his psychogalvanic response—could it be that? Could it be grief?

"Someone . . ." Xie hesitated. "Human?"

"Oh, you know," said Talis, tugging at an ear. "Roughly."

Da-Xia and Elián both looked at me.

"Greta," said Talis. "You should get some sleep."

I glanced upward, to the fading sky, and inward, for the clock. "Is it late?"

"It's been a big day," drawled Elián. My datastore compared that drawl to previous examples and tagged it as defensive hurt/anger, though I was not sure why he was hurt/angry. His friend (Greta) had been in pain and danger, but everything was fine, now.

"It's not particularly late," said Talis. "Nevertheless."

"All right." I turned to go to my cell.

"Go with her," said Talis, softly.

No one answered him.

"One of you," he said. "I don't care which. Keep her isolated, but one of you go with her. Call me if she screams."

I remembered that Greta had wondered if Talis could sleep, and later if Talis needed sleep. In the days that came after my death, I learned: a body needs sleep. Greta's, just then, needed vast stretches of sleep, to settle the uproar the grey room had made in the organic brain. A body's mechanism for that settling was, of course, dreams.

So it—she—I. I dreamt. Intense, disordered dreams. Near to dawn on that first night I dreamt a disjointed version of the business with the apple press, and woke up gasping, my hand (I had forgotten to have it knit) pierced with pain. "Xie—" I heard my rough voice rise, uncommanded. "Xie!"

She came scrambling to me. "Greta!"

"I dreamt—"

For a moment our eyes locked, and something happened that went beyond registration or recognition. Da-Xia drew air and leaned backward. The moment seemed to vibrate between us. Then she let the air out again as both breath and name: "Greta? Greta, come back to me . . ."

"Why would I come back to you?"

I was puzzled, because I hadn't gone anywhere.

At my words, Da-Xia's face shattered into a configuration Greta had never seen before. She ran from the room.

From then on Elián sat with me.

They wouldn't let me out of my cell, but that didn't trouble me. I was tired. I slept; I ate. Elián sat with me, or more often worked at pacing a groove into the floor.

We were waiting for the Swan Riders that Talis had mentioned. When they came, we—Talis and I—would go with them to the Red Mountains, the flooded bit of the Rockies that was home to master copies of the surviving AIs.

"Why do I need to go with you?" I asked Talis when he came to visit. "I hardly know you. I don't even like you."

Elián snorted, and Talis ignored him. "Ah, come on, I'm profoundly compelling. Everybody says so."

"Also, I've never been on a horse."

"Okay, that bit could be a problem." Talis shrugged his most profoundly compelling shrug. "We'll work it out. But you need to go, Greta. Think of it as . . . finding yourself."

"I'm right here."

Which made both Elián and Talis stare at me.

So. We waited.

There were three Riders coming. One would take over the Precepture. The other two would escort Talis and me.

"Strength in numbers," said Talis. "Just in case."

Elián, the son of a great line of strategists, turned sharply at that. "In case of what?"

"In case of anything. Discretion is my favorite part of valor."

"I'll bet," said Elián.

"As for you, Elián Palnik . . ." Talis grinned and I tagged it as a predatory grin, meant to disturb. "They're bringing you a horse and a map."

The word was ambiguous. "A smartmap?" I asked. A smartmap could find locations from positioning satellites, detect water and catalog plants, provide current information on settlements and cities, more.

"If it's not a smartmap," said Elián, "then you might as well shoot me in the head."

"Ooo, tempting!" Talis tilted an eyebrow twenty-three degrees. "Greta, dear. Does anyone in the Precepture have a gun?"

"I don't think so." I turned to Elián. "Do you know how to use a horse?"

That made him laugh roughly: a laugh with tears behind it. I was not sure why.

Two days, three.

In the day it was glorious. My body sat in its little cell, but inside me the data seemed infinite. I could close my eyes and picture a library like a forest, its columnar shelves going back and back, and no glimpse of an end to them. Whatever I needed, came—leaping, eager, easy. Someone left a pitcher of asters and coneflower outside the door, and I sat for three hours staring at them. Through my new eyes the homely flowers—the whole world—shone as if new.

The organic memories rose too, more often, now that the brain was not so acutely injured. I had lived thirteen-seventeenths of my life within the walls of the Fourth Precepture: there were memories soaked into the stone. The organic mind pushed at the inductive webbing; the webbing shoved the organics into correct positions, and both were me.

I dreamt and dreamt.

I was becoming something—twofold. When I leaned on the wall, I remembered that the stones were cooler at night, and remembered that the specific heat of granite was only 790 joules per kilogram. They were two different kinds of memory, and having both was not always easy. My skin was both my skin and a mesh of sensors. Sometimes I was sure it would not hold me, that I would come apart like sugar in water. Sometimes I simply knew I was larger than my own skin, and the thought did not bother me.

On the third night I dreamt that I went up among the graves. I walked in grass and tangled plants up to my waist. They brushed my arms. The sky was so open that if you made a sound there, it was tiny, swept away. I came to a crater and I climbed down into it, and stood in the open, blasted space. Scratching through the plants had left my bare arms and legs blistered. My limbs were thick with blisters the way a stem gets thick with frog's eggs, my body encased in translucent, gelatinous polyps. I sat down and waited for them to hatch.

Not once in the dream was I afraid.

But I woke sharply and felt swollen and—

I leapt up. I ran my fingers down my arms, my legs, turning my sensors up as high as they would go.

"What's wrong?" said Elián, rolling over in Xie's bed.

"Perhaps it is nothing," I said. "It is nothing. A dream."

I let my arms fall to my sides. There was nothing, nothing.

No, there was too much. Too much in me. Surely it would break me open.

I felt my body shivering—no, shaking.

Elián had staggered out of bed to stand in front of me. In the darkness he touched my hair, softly. "It's not nothing."

"The AIs—" I said. The *other* AIs. It would be factual to include myself in the grouping, but the phrasing did not come naturally. "There is a statistical cluster of anomalous neurological events on the third day after the upload. What was once called 'skinning.'"

"Yeah, I remember. The Abbot made Talis warn you." The cell was starlight-dim, and Elián was only a shape. I turned up my infrared vision to try to see him, but it made him look ghostly. I could see his eye sockets, as if he were a skull. He squinted and pushed his fists into those hollows. I looked away.

"So, skinning—what happens?" asked Elián. "What happened to the AIs?"

They had died. Mostly they had died. They'd gotten caught in a feedback loop, overloaded, died. I said nothing.

I felt Elián's hands settle on both my shoulders. "Greta? What did you dream about?"

"Hatching," I said. "I was . . . hatching."

"You're obviously not going to *hatch*."

No, I thought. I was not going to hatch. I had two skins, but there was nothing inside me, nothing to come out, because there was nothing in my heart.

Unless. Unless there was.

"I think . . . ," I said, slowly. "I think you should keep me away from Xie."

"But you—" Elián cut himself off, not quite able to say it. "Greta, don't you remember how you feel about Xie?"

I said nothing.

Elián stared at me in the darkness—almost four seconds of silence, which might have been his new record. But of course he couldn't hold it. "Come on," he murmured, and pulled me to him. "Come on. Talis said you should sleep. Sleep. It's late, or early, or something."

"It's four thirty-seven."

"See?"

But there were eggs in my sleep, eggs made of skin. My body stood there in the darkness, with Elián's hands holding my upper arms. My skin was rigid.

"Come on." I tagged his tone as coaxing: I had heard him speak thus to a skittish goat. "Lie down. I'll sit with you. I'll keep you safe. Just lie down."

There was really nothing else to do. Elián sat down at the head of Xie's cot, pushed the pillow down to rest beside one leg, and patted it as if I were a dog he were inviting up. And like a dog—like a machine, like a good hostage—I obeyed. I lay down with my head at his knee. I could smell Xie on the pillow; smell Elián, too. Smell is the first sense to develop in utero and retains powerful connections to the primitive mind—particularly to the amygdala, which processes emotion. More succinctly, it triggers memory. As I lay there, my limbic system struggled into life. Deformed memories crawled loose from my damaged brain. Landed all over me like moths. I was covered in them.

Then Elián put his hand in my unlocked hair. Not much weight, but some. He was holding me down, pushing me under. And that was enough. I was tired enough, damaged enough, that I did sink away.

When I woke up, Da-Xia was there.

I knew at once that she was going to kill me.

31
FLIGHT

Xie. I fluttered awake, and she was leaning over me.

I leapt from the cot and backed away from her.

"Greta?" She extended a hand toward me. A structure inside my parietal lobe lifted the sensation of her touch into my nervous system. My lips flushed; my stomach tightened. The sensation dropped down across my one, two, three skins, like water rolling down steps of ice.

Cascade.

The other AIs. They had died.

And this is what had happened to them. They had layers; they had two skins, two sets of memories, two ways of thinking. Some of them, a few of them, had found a way to live with that, to build a new self on that strange and shifting foundation. But most had not. Give one of these self-less creatures something that powerfully stimulates both sets of memories, the two memories rise, reinforce each other, feed back, overload.

I had backed all the way into the wall, and it was not nearly far enough. Our cell was small and thick with memories.

"Greta?" said Xie. "I only wanted—"

Strong light was coming through the glass ceiling, high morning, 9:53 a.m. The stones at my back were heating already. Their specific heat was 790 joules per kilogram. I grabbed them desperately.

"Greta?" said Elián.

"Get Talis," whispered Xie.

"He said, if she was screaming—"

"She is," said Xie, who knew me. "Go."

Elián bolted.

"I'm here, Greta," breathed Xie. "I'm here. I see you."

The light fell across her, her skin, the bright darkness of her hair—

The organics offered a memory as clear as anything from the datastore, and more brightly lit: Da-Xia stepping back to regard the haircut she'd just given me, her voice roughened with loss and desire. *There. There you are.* The datastore replied with the same memory. It echoed; looped; reinforced, it rose. Oh, I could see her, feel that moment: the shudder of anticipation and realization; fear and longing—the cord inside me pulled tight.

"Greta?" said Xie. "Is it you? Can you come back?"

She was turning me inside out.

"Stop," I begged her. "Stop, stop, stop."

Currents in the brain— I was overloading. Inside,

outside, again and again. How can one person be two things? How can two things be one person? I was turned inside out so many times that I had no outside— no protection, no defense. It was surely as deadly as losing one's skin.

I closed my eyes and held them closed, and held on. Colors—color. I began counting breaths. One. Two. Three. Four. Five.

Partial list of real numbers/positive integers. My knees gave way, and I sank down against the wall. Six. Seven. God. I remembered that the *Meditations* of Marcus Aurelius were important, so I read them all in four hundred milliseconds. Eight. Nine.

A crash of noise—someone coming in at a run. I ignored it, kept my eyes closed. I was standing on thin air, and it would hold me, so long as I didn't look down.

Hold on, Greta. Hold fiercely.

Ten. In front of me: Talis. Even with my eyes closed I was sure of it. I could smell the horse-scent that clung to his clothes; I could feel the current of his active sensors, sweeping into me. "Get her on the cot," he said. "She's going into seizure."

Someone—Elián—scooped me up. The pillow again. The smell.

"Greta." I could feel Talis's hands on mine, his thumbs rubbing over my knuckles.

"What's happening?" said Elián.

Talis didn't answer him. I wished he'd stop the movement of his fingers.

"What's happening?" said Elián again.

"She's skinning," Talis whispered. "Oh, I didn't think she would—"

My hands had been broken. Talis's hands moved over them, relentless, restless—*Reducing stimuli will always help.* Why didn't he know that? He ought to know that.

"Talis," I said. "Why don't you know that?"

Elián's voice cracked. "Well, help her!"

There was nothing to be done for me. Talis would know that. I knew that. I could feel our sensors meshing on the backs of my hands, like to like.

Da-Xia had still not spoken, but it was no good. I could sense her heat as if she were a sun; I could smell her, in the pillow and right in front of me, in memory and in real time—

"Greta," Talis said. "Greta, listen to me. The two memories are the same, yes?" he said. "It's only the thinker that's different—but what does it matter, if the thoughts are the same?"

"What does it matter!" I heard emotion in my voice: the organic mind had pushed the limbic system way up; the heart was beating fast, fast, fast. "It's only the whole construction of self, Talis!" The AIs of the First Wave—the overload. "They died, Michael! They all died!"

"What's the trigger?" he asked. "What did you remember? The last clear thing."

"Xie." I gasped at the sharp pierce of her name. "Xie, cutting my hair."

"Well, then," he said. "Look at her."

"Don't look down!" I shouted at him.

"Nah. You can fly—I know you can. Look at her."

And I heard the small voice again, no one's voice. Saying, *Greta.*

I opened my eyes. For a second the world was wild, flashing color. No different inside than out. No flying. Then I saw. Elián had taken a step back—Elián, always most frightened when he did not understand—but Da-Xia was standing there, holding firm.

The colors were gone. I saw her only. Her hand on the tangled blue quilt, inches from mine. Tears running down her face.

Rain on the mountains, said the organics, and the datastore listed the other times I'd seen her cry. She was a strong person who cried easily; my lover, weeping in our bed. *Rain on the mountains.* "Greta," she said.

There was a space inside me, cupped and still. It was small as cupped hands; it was large as the sky. It was untouched and it was touch itself. It was empty and it was full. I held love there, like a treasure. I held my own name.

"Greta?" said Xie.

I moved my broken hand two inches to the left. Opened it. Da-Xia laid her palm in mine, infinitely careful. I closed my fingers, one by one.

It hurt, yes. But it was me. I took a deep breath and let the pain of my broken bones and the feel of Xie's fingers be everything I was. In that way, and slowly, I became something. I held on to that something. I held on fiercely.

"Li Da-Xia," I said. I was not like the dying Abbot: I had only one voice.

She squeezed my broken hand in answer, and put her other hand against my face. "Greta. There you are."

And thus.

Thus, I did not die. I, Greta: I put aside my title and everything I had ever known. I put aside the self I had once had, and perhaps even my soul. But I did not die. I went into the grey room and I did not die.

Thus, love saved me.

The crisis point—I knew there would be others, but that first and critical crisis—passed away under Talis's cool voice, Da-Xia's brave hands.

All my life I had waited for the grey room. Very deliberately, I had never thought about the graves, with the wild morning glories growing over them. Very deliberately, I had never thought about what came after.

This, for me, is what came after. On the evening of the third day, that day on which I found a door into the stillness of my own heart—on that evening I went up to the ridgetop to watch the plume of dust.

Talis went with me, of course.

And all my friends.

Atta, who touched my hair and wished me blessings. Thandi, who touched my broken hand and wished me strength. And Han, who said without irony, "I hope you live."

Da-Xia whispered something to them, and they hung

back, letting the rest of us pass the rock pile, pass the ridge-top, and walk into the waving grasses.

Autumn was beginning on the tall-grass prairie, color coming into the stems and seeds of things. In the river bottom the noise of the cottonwood leaves was sharper, stranger. The monarchs swept through the coneflowers, getting ready for the journey from which they would never return. The spiral paths they traced were overlaid with mathematical patterns that were something close to music. Da-Xia took my hand, and Elián hesitated, and then took the other.

"So you're gonna ride off into the sunset?" he said.

"We'll need to go more south than west," I said. "But you could go west, if you wanted."

"I meant a kinda metaphorical sunset."

"I expect to make a hash of it," I said. "The datastore can't teach me how to use a horse."

This time I knew it was a joke. I knew it would make Elián laugh, and it did. Something else to cup inside the still place of my heart. Elián's laughter.

If you knew what to look for—and we did—you could see the crater from where we stood. You could see the graves.

"You're one of them now," said Elián. "An AI?"

Xie sighed. "Really, Elián? You're going to frame that as a question?"

"I only meant—they rule the world."

They did. I looked at Elián looking at the crater. At the graves.

Xie followed our gaze. "And they might rule it differently."

"So they might," I said.

"Uh-huh," said Talis. "We'll see about that."

"Live first," said Xie, softly. "Hang on to yourself. Live." Her hand tightened on mine. *Every callus and curve.*

To hold love in one's hands, and then let it go—that was the cruelest thing anyone had ever done to me, and I had done it to myself. I held Elián's hand. I held Xie's. I could see the three Riders now, at the base of the plume, their silhouettes bump-bumping in the golden light. It was a very long moment, watching the Riders, a very still one: so still that a bird might have nested on the surface of the sea. Halcyon.

When the Riders were close, when their hoofbeats sounded like drums under the vast sky, Elián's hand tightened and Xie turned to me. "Greta," she said. And nothing more.

I wanted to never let them go, but in a moment I would have to.

Elián's strength was at my back, and Xie's face was before me. Tears were making her eyes shine darkly. I looked at her, and looked at her, and looked at her, as the men with wings crashed in around us.

"I love you," I said.

And then I let go.